HIS ONE TRUE LOVE

"I guess I should have known you wouldn't have purposefully left me out."

Felty shook his head and smiled. "I never would have left you out. The only reason I go to anything, including church, is so I can see you."

Anna laughed. "You're such a tease, Felty Helmuth. It's a wonder I believe anything you say."

He suddenly grew serious, as if someone had blown out the candle behind his eyes. "I'm not teasing, Anna. *Ach*, how I want you to understand." He took off one glove and caressed her cheek. A thread of warm liquid trickled down her spine. "I have loved you ever since I was fourteen years old."

Her heart raced like a freight train. "That was a long time ago. Are you sure?"

"What kind of a question is that? Of course I'm sure."

"Are you sure you're sure?"

Felty chuckled. "You are going to drive me crazy, Anna Yoder. It was at that spelling bee. Some of the older boys were mad that you won, but I was amazed at your smarts. And you were pretty and feisty and so different from all the other girls. I fell in love at first sight. Of course, we were both too young, so I sat back and watched."

"You were wonderful quiet about it."

"I like to think I was patient . . ."

Books by Jennifer Beckstrand

The Matchmakers of Huckleberry Hill
HUCKLEBERRY HILL
HUCKLEBERRY SUMMER
HUCKLEBERRY CHRISTMAS
HUCKLEBERRY SPRING
HUCKLEBERRY HARVEST
HUCKLEBERRY HEARTS
RETURN TO HUCKLEBERRY HILL
A COURTSHIP ON HUCKLEBERRY HILL
HOME ON HUCKLEBERRY HILL
FIRST CHRISTMAS ON HUCKLEBERRY HILL

The Honeybee Sisters
SWEET AS HONEY
A BEE IN HER BONNET
LIKE A BEE TO HONEY

The Petersheim Brothers
ANDREW
ABRAHAM

Amish Quiltmakers
THE AMISH QUILTMAKER'S UNEXPECTED BABY
THE AMISH QUILTMAKER'S UNRULY IN-LAW

Anthologies
AN AMISH CHRISTMAS QUILT
THE AMISH CHRISTMAS KITCHEN
AMISH BRIDES
THE AMISH CHRISTMAS LETTERS

Published by Kensington Publishing Corp.

First Christmas on Huckleberry Hill

JENNIFER
BECKSTRAND

ZEBRA BOOKS
KENSINGTON PUBLISHING CORP.
www.kensingtonbooks.com

ZEBRA BOOKS are published by

Kensington Publishing Corp.
119 West 40th Street
New York, NY 10018

All Kensington titles, imprints, and distributed lines are available at special quantity discounts for bulk purchases for sales promotion, premiums, fund-raising, educational, or institutional use.

Special book excerpts or customized printings can also be created to fit specific needs. For details, write or phone the office of the Kensington Sales Manager: Attn.: Sales Department. Kensington Publishing Corp., 119 West 40th Street, New York, NY 10018. Phone: 1-800-221-2647.

Zebra and the Z logo Reg. U.S. Pat. & TM Off.
BOUQUET Reg. U.S. Pat. & TM Off.

First Printing: October 2021
ISBN-13: 978-1-4201-5205-0
ISBN-10: 1-4201-5205-X

ISBN-13: 978-1-4201-5206-7 (eBook)
ISBN-10: 1-4201-5206-8 (eBook)

10 9 8 7 6 5 4 3 2 1

Printed in the United States of America

Liz...
Its a great
read...
Relax and
enjoy...
Love,
Mom

Prologue

Martha Sue Helmuth stomped down the cellar stairs wondering just how she'd gotten herself into this mess.

Every smidgen of Christmas cheer had completely abandoned her. She didn't want to sing Christmas carols or hear her relatives wish one another "*Frehlicher Grischtdaag*." She did not want to decorate the house with pine boughs or light candles or go on a sleigh ride.

She wanted to put on her pajamas, sit next to Mammi's woodstove, and read a book—something depressing like *Martyrs Mirror* or *Tongue Screws and Testimonies*. But she couldn't even do that, because it was Christmas Eve and at least a dozen cousins and assorted aunts and uncles were congregated in Mammi and Dawdi's great room for the family's traditional Christmas Eve dinner and carol singing.

Martha Sue had volunteered to fetch Mammi Helmuth's famous—or infamous—huckleberry raisin jelly just so she could be alone with her unpleasant thoughts for two minutes instead of having to put on a *gute* face for her merry, filled-with-the-Christmas-spirit relatives. Huckleberry raisin jelly didn't sound half bad, but Mammi meant for the jelly to go on her famous—or infamous—cheesy jalapeño bread at tonight's Christmas Eve party. It didn't seem a very appetizing combination, but Mammi was famous—or infamous—for her out-of-the-ordinary recipes and stomach-churning food creations.

If she didn't want to starve, Martha Sue was going to have to take over the cooking while she stayed here with Mammi and Dawdi.

Martha Sue had arrived at Mammi and Dawdi's house three days ago, and she wasn't here just for the Christmas holiday. She'd be staying with Mammi and Dawdi all winter and into the spring. Martha Sue wasn't exactly sure whose idea it had been for her to come to stay with her grandparents. Mamm wanted her to get out and see the world—and by "get out and see the world," Mamm meant get out of Ohio and go to Wisconsin.

Dat said Martha Sue's visit was a *gute* way for someone in the family to keep a close eye on Mammi and Dawdi. They weren't getting any younger—Dawdi was eighty-seven—and Dat thought they might need some help. Mammi and Dawdi were old, but they seemed perfectly capable of taking care of themselves and their farm without anyone's help. Mammi was healthy enough to knit a dozen pot holders each week, cook three simply awful meals a day, and gather eggs every morning, rain or shine. Dawdi milked the cow and shoveled snow like a forty-year-old. They didn't need Martha Sue's help.

Martha Sue had been so eager to get out of Charm, Ohio, that she hadn't paused to consider why Dat or Mamm or Mammi really wanted her here in Bonduel, Wisconsin. And then, three days ago, when she'd stepped off the bus and had seen Mammi's beaming face, Martha

Sue suddenly knew why she was here. She'd been tricked into coming so Mammi and Dawdi could find her a husband.

Why hadn't she realized it before she made the long trip to Bonduel? Mammi and Dawdi were famous in the family for being persistent and successful matchmakers to many of their grandchildren, and Martha was the next victim on the list. She was thirty years old, and there were no prospects in Charm. *Ach*, *vell*, no prospects she hadn't already rejected, and she certainly wasn't going to give Yost Beiler a sideways glance ever again. Lord willing, her moving to Wisconsin would be the final nail in the coffin of that relationship.

Martha Sue wiped a foolish tear from her cheek. She didn't want to think about Yost Beiler or any other man from Charm—or any other man from anywhere else, for that matter. She didn't want Mammi and Dawdi to find her a husband, because at this point it would be some widower who was only interested in her as a *fraa* to care for his motherless children or an old bachelor who was sick of cooking for himself. It didn't matter that Mammi and Dawdi had found suitable matches for more than a dozen of their grandchildren. They wouldn't find anyone for Martha Sue, because she didn't want a husband.

And that was that.

Mammi was the dearest soul in the world, and she was going to be very disappointed that Martha Sue didn't want her help finding a husband. But it would be best to let Mammi down sooner than later, before she invited half the single men in Bonduel to dinner.

Martha Sue found a pint of deep purple huckleberry raisin jelly on the shelf next to a row of bottles labeled

"Pickled Kitchen Scraps." She didn't even want to know what that was. Huckleberry raisin jelly on cheesy jalapeño bread was bad enough.

Upstairs, someone knocked on the front door, and there were muted Christmas greetings and laughter when the door opened. The family was still gathering. Now would be the perfect time to mention to Mammi that she didn't want a husband and to please not try to set her up with anybody. Mammi would be too distracted to be upset, and then maybe Martha Sue could enjoy the party.

She hurried up the stairs and into the great room. At least another dozen relatives had arrived since she'd been downstairs. Cousin Titus and his wife, Katie Rose, knelt next to Dawdi's easy chair having a conversation with Dawdi while their two little girls ran around the great room with some cousins. Several of Martha Sue's cousins and aunts busied themselves in the kitchen with dinner preparations. Mammi didn't fix Christmas Eve dinner anymore. Her daughters had taken over the meal several years ago with the excuse of easing Mammi's burden, with the added benefit that the Christmas Eve dinner was actually something everyone enjoyed eating.

Mammi sat in her rocker holding the hand of little Isaac, Moses and Lia's youngest, listening intently as he told her something that looked to be very important to a three-year-old. Mary Anne and Jethro were there with their twins, as well as Martha Sue's sister Mandy and Mandy's husband, Noah, and their kids, Elsie, Sam, Beth, and Tyler. Even Cassie and Zach Reynolds had come. Cassie had jumped the fence a few years ago and married Zach, who was a very important doctor in Chicago. Cassie hadn't been baptized, so she hadn't been shunned, and everyone loved having them at get-togethers because Zach told the most interesting medical stories and didn't mind giving piggyback rides to all the great-grandchildren.

Martha Sue handed Mandy the jelly. Mandy grimaced when she read the label, then took it into the kitchen to add to the goodies piling up on the counter. Martha Sue sat on the sofa next to Mammi's rocker and waited for Isaac to finish his story about almost getting stepped on by a cow. Mammi listened and nodded at all the right moments and kissed Isaac's finger, which had been injured in a separate incident with a wringer washer.

Isaac skipped off to play with his cousins, and Martha Sue found her opportunity. She leaned closer to Mammi. "Mammi, *denki* for letting me stay here with you for a few months."

Mammi's eyes sparkled. "It's my pleasure." She patted Martha Sue's cheek. "You look so much like your mother. Just as pretty as a picture. I might just know some boys who will be very interested to meet you."

"Well, Mammi, I want to talk to you about that."

Mammi smiled. "Oh? About what?"

"Mammi," Martha Sue said, taking her *mammi*'s hand. "I love you very much."

"And I love you. I'm shocked that some nice boy hasn't snatched you up already."

Martha Sue cleared her throat. "That's what I want to talk to you about. I know that you invited me to Huckleberry Hill so you could find me a husband."

Mammi's eyes widened in surprise. "*Ach*, *vell*, I guess the cat is out of the bag. Who told you? Was it Felty? He's usually so *gute* at keeping secrets."

"*Nae*, Mammi. I figured it out on my own. But I'm not

here to meet boys. I'm here to spend time with you and Dawdi."

Mammi blew a puff of air from between her lips. "*Ach*, why would you want to spend time with us? We're old and boring. You need to be with people your own age."

Martha Sue was going to have to be more blunt. "I'm old too, Mammi. Nobody wants to marry me. It would be an awful chore for you to have to find me a husband."

Mammi patted Martha Sue's hand. "But, my dear, it's not a chore. I love helping my grandchildren find spouses." She gestured around the room. "Why, your *dawdi* and I have helped at least a dozen people in this very room to *gute* marriages. It would be our pleasure to do the same for you. No thanks necessary."

"But I don't want a husband."

She must have said that louder than she thought, because the adult chatter in the room went silent. *Die kinner* still made a commotion, but the noise level in the room dropped considerably. Twenty pairs of eyes stared at her. She felt her face get warm. This was definitely the worst Christmas ever.

"*Ach,*" Mammi said. "You don't mean that. Everybody wants to get married."

"Not everybody," Martha Sue said, because there really was nothing to do but stand her ground. "Besides, no one wants to marry me."

There were some murmurs of disagreement in the room, and Mandy shook her head. "That's not true, Martha Sue. How many boys in Charm wanted to marry you at one time or another?"

Dawdi patted the arm of his easy chair. "That's just what your *mammi* thought when she was a girl. She didn't believe anyone wanted to marry her, but every boy in Bonduel was secretly in love with her."

Mammi blushed from her neck to the top of her forehead. "*Ach*, Felty, no one was in love with me but you. And maybe not even you. Maybe you only married me for my cooking."

Dawdi laughed. "For sure and certain, I love your cooking, Annie-banannie, but I was so in love with you, I wouldn't have cared if you served cardboard every night for dinner. I would marry you all over again a thousand times."

Titus, who was kneeling at Dawdi's feet, leaned backward and sat down on the floor. "I ain't never heard the story of how you two fell in love, Dawdi."

Katie's face lit up like a flashlight. "Was it very romantic?"

Mammi nodded. "Very romantic. Your *dawdi* was persistent and determined. I still can't understand it. He could have married Rosie Herschberger or Lily Mishler or any other girl in Bonduel."

Dawdi waved his hand as if to dismiss any idea of another girl. "I couldn't have cared less about Rosie Herschberger."

"She made the best cinnamon rolls."

Dawdi gave Mammi a look that melted Martha's heart and made her squirm at the same time. It was the way Yost Beiler used to look at her. "You are the only girl I ever loved, Annie. Don't you forget it."

"Tell us," Cassie said. "I've never heard the story of how you met."

Dawdi stroked the beard on his chin. "I never talk

about it, because I don't especially like talking about the war."

Titus's eyes nearly popped out of his head. "You were in a war, Dawdi?"

Dawdi ran his finger over a line on his face. "It's how I got this scar."

Zach Reynolds, who was probably extra interested in scars, sat down on the sofa next to Martha Sue. "Now we *have* to hear the story."

Titus nodded eagerly. "We have time before dinner."

Mandy shook a wooden spoon in Titus's direction. "We do not have time before dinner. The chicken will get cold."

"Cold fried chicken is even better than warm fried chicken," Titus said.

Mandy folded her arms and huffed out a breath. "Oh, all right. The chicken can wait, I guess."

Dawdi rocked in his chair and grinned. "November 1952, fresh out of the army and fresh out of Korea, I stepped off the bus and caught sight of the prettiest girl to ever walk the face of the earth."

Chapter 1

"Uriah, don't kick your *bruder*," Anna said, not really believing Uriah would stop, but knowing it was her duty as the big sister to at least attempt to make her *bruderen* behave.

Ten-year-old Uriah stood in the threshold of the bakery, his gaze locked on Anna, his mouth puckered into a frown. Narrowing his eyes, he kicked Owen again without even looking at him, as if he was daring Anna to just go ahead and do something about it.

"Ouch!" Owen protested, as if he were the innocent victim of Uriah's foot, when he knew full well he had once again provoked Uriah beyond endurance.

It couldn't have been easy being the baby of the family, and Uriah seemed determined not to be picked on.

Anna gave Uriah the stink eye. "Uriah," she said, her voice as low and as threatening as she could make it. "Jesus said not to kick people."

Anna wasn't sure that was even true. She remembered the part about turning the other cheek and giving away your cloak and walking an extra mile, but she couldn't remember anything in Jesus's teachings about not kicking people. She resolved then and there to listen harder in church. She never knew when she'd need to knock some sense into her *bruderen* with a sermon or a verse of scripture.

Uriah stuck out his bottom lip. "He's copying me."

"He's copying me," Owen mimicked, pitching his already high twelve-year-old voice up another octave.

Uriah's face got two shades redder. He lifted his foot for another kick but must have thought better of it. He stomped on the ground instead. "Stop it," he screeched.

"Stop it," Owen taunted.

Anna sighed. It was useless to chastise Owen. He enjoyed the attention too much. She shrugged and loaded the bread into the back of the wagon. "*Ach*, Uriah, just ignore him and he'll stop." It seemed like the perfectly intelligent and reasonable thing to do, since Owen fed off goading Uriah into a tizzy.

"I can't," Uriah whined.

"I can't," echoed Owen.

This time Uriah hauled off and kicked Owen right in the gut. It was quite a feat, since he had to lift his leg high enough to meet his target. Owen clutched his stomach and doubled over, then scowled, rushed at Uriah, and tackled him right there in front of Zimmel's Bakery. Uriah hollered and managed to punch Owen squarely in the nose while flat on his back. Owen's nose started bleeding, and blood dripped all over Uriah's coat and smeared into Owen's as well. Anna growled under her breath. She'd just finished the laundry yesterday, and coats were wonderful hard to clean.

"Owen, Uriah, stop that this minute," she scolded, knowing they would ignore her completely, which they did. Anna sighed again and did the only sensible thing she could think to do. She turned her back and pretended she didn't know the two boys pounding each other to a pulp on the sidewalk. Her yelling at them would only attract unwanted attention. Tightening her cape around her shoulders, she pushed aside the tools in the back of the wagon so they wouldn't smash the four loaves of bread she'd just placed there. She did her best to ignore the stares of the people passing by while her *bruderen* made a spectacle of themselves.

Thank Derr Herr, the brawl didn't last very long. Her *bruderen* Elmer and Isaac came out of the grocery store next door, each with a fifty-pound sack of flour slung over his shoulder. Isaac was lanky, overconfident, and sort of handsome, though he thought himself much handsomer than he actually was. At fifteen, he was pretty much a waste of skin. Fortunately, Elmer was seventeen, more mature, and less likely to put up with his *bruderen*'s shenanigans.

With the flour securely resting on his shoulder and without missing a step, Elmer grabbed Owen by his coat collar, yanked him away from Uriah, and shoved him in the direction of the wagon. "Stop it, Owen. Get in and quit being a *dumkoff.*"

Owen swiped at the blood on his upper lip, looked at his hand, and grinned. In Anna's experience, boys liked it when they could draw blood, and a bloody nose was a sure sign of bravery. "I wasn't being a *dumkoff.*"

"*Jah*, you were. Next time, do what Anna tells you. She's the boss."

"She is not the boss," Owen insisted. "She's a girl."

Elmer set his flour in the wagon. "She's still the boss. And I don't want to hear another word about it."

"Look, Elmer," Uriah said, grabbing the front of his own coat with two hands. "I got Owen's nose. Look at all the blood." It looked more like three wet spots, since blood didn't show up well on black, but Uriah was still proud of it.

"*Gute* work," Isaac said, throwing his flour sack into the wagon.

Anna chided Isaac with her eyes. "Don't encourage him."

Owen climbed into the wagon and turned up his swollen nose. "It didn't even hurt."

Uriah stuck out his tongue at Owen. "I don't wonder but it hurt when I got you in the stomach."

"I'll probably get an ulcer," Owen said. "It will be your fault if I can't eat Thanksgiving dinner."

Anna rolled her eyes. "It's your own fault for teasing your *bruder*, and you don't know what an ulcer is."

"For sure and certain I do. It's when your stomach hurts and you drink Pepto-Bismol all day long. Maybe I'll die."

Owen wouldn't get any sympathy from Anna. "Then let this be a lesson not to tease your *bruder*."

Isaac chuckled, a little too loudly. "Who wants to eat Anna's Thanksgiving dinner anyway?"

Anna gave her brother a menacing look, as if she were going to smack him upside the head. The nasty look hid the pain she always felt when anyone disparaged her cooking. It was definitely a sore spot. Dat had taught her to cook after Mamm died, and he'd done his best, but Anna still took any comment about her lack of skill very personally. Her rolls weren't anywhere near as fluffy as Rosie Herschberger's, and she'd never been able to make gingersnaps that didn't come out of the oven looking like brown golf balls. She knew what her flaws were, but it still stung like a wasp whenever one of her *bruderen* or one of the girls in the *gmayna* pointed them out.

She wanted to be a *gute* cook. She really did. It was one of the only ways a girl could catch a husband. But could she help it that she enjoyed being a little adventurous with her cooking? Plain rolls were boring. Rolls with raisins and walnuts were something to write home about.

Thanksgiving was the perfect time to experiment with some new and delicious recipes. "If you don't want to eat my Thanksgiving dinner, Isaac, you can go ahead and starve. But you're not going to want to miss it. I'm making rolls—"

"They're always hard," said Isaac.

She ignored him. "And turkey—"

"It's always dry."

"And this year I'm making asparagus raisin casserole as a side dish. I got the recipe from Aendi Ruth."

Isaac raised his brows. "Aendi Ruth? The one who's been dead for six years?"

Anna nodded. "I inherited all her recipes."

Isaac wrinkled his nose in disgust. "You're making dead people's recipes for Thanksgiving? That sounds about right."

Elmer placed both palms on Isaac's chest and shoved him halfway down the sidewalk. Isaac stumbled backward but regained his footing and simply laughed. Elmer gave Anna a reassuring smile. "Don't listen to Isaac. He's joking, and it's mean." Elmer emphasized *mean*, glaring at Isaac while he measured his words. "You're a fine cook, Anna. If Isaac doesn't like it, he can just try making dinner for himself."

Anna loved Elmer for standing up for her, even though they all knew what a failure Anna was as a cook. But she still had hope for Thanksgiving. Maybe everyone would be pleasantly surprised. She turned her face away and pretended to rearrange the bread in the wagon so Isaac wouldn't know he'd upset her. "*Denki*, Elmer, but don't worry about me. I don't care what Isaac says." She sincerely hoped Gotte would forgive her for the lie. She just couldn't abide that smug smile stretched across Isaac's face. "He's a baby, and he wouldn't know what *gute* manners were if they jumped out and bit him."

"Who got bitten?"

Anna leaped out of her skin at the sound of a man's voice. She whirled around and came face-to-chest with a gray-green, perfectly pressed military uniform and what looked like an impressive collection of medals. She tilted her head back—way back—to get a look at the owner of the medals. He was tall, and she, unfortunately, was barely five feet, and that was only when she squared her shoulders and stood up perfectly straight.

Anna's heart skipped seven whole beats. Backing away from him as if he were a ghost, she caught her heel on the edge of the curb and fell ungracefully on her *hinnerdale* into the snow on the sidewalk.

The soldier's all-too-familiar and very attractive smile disappeared immediately, and he rushed to Anna's aid, holding out his hand and pulling her up before Elmer or Isaac even had a chance to react. Of course, Isaac wouldn't have helped Anna out of the deep well, but

Elmer was a little more thoughtful. "Are you all right?" the soldier said, his hand lingering in Anna's for a second too long.

While the soldier gazed at her in concern, Anna pulled her hand from his, brushed off her cape, then discreetly tapped the snow off her backside. "I'm fine," she said. "You just startled me, that's all. I sort of thought you were dead." She felt her face get warm. Felty Helmuth was obviously *not* dead, and it was impolite of her to mention it. She clamped her mouth shut. She most certainly wasn't going to mention the missing leg.

He didn't seem to take offense that she thought he had died. His smile came back full force and nearly knocked her down again with its brilliance. "You meet with the most unexpected surprises in Bonduel." His face seemed to glow with happiness. "Your eyes are still as blue as Shawano Lake on a clear fall morning."

Anna couldn't swallow. Was that normal when a boy looked at someone like he was looking at her?

"You've grown taller," he said, as if it were the most impressive accomplishment in the world.

Laughter escaped her lips in an unladylike explosion. "I've been this tall since sixth grade."

Felty grinned and shrugged, never taking his gaze from her face. "Then maybe you've just grown prettier, if that is possible."

She made a real effort to swallow. It wouldn't be seemly if she drooled all over herself in public. "I . . . I haven't grown taller, but you have."

He smiled wryly. "For sure and certain. I didn't mean to, but I put on three inches in Korea."

Anna glanced at Elmer. He and the other boys were

frozen where they stood, staring at Felty as if he were a two-headed goat. She couldn't blame them. Felty was probably the most magnificent sight she had seen in all her nineteen years, except for maybe the first time she saw her cousin's baby who was born with two thumbs on her right hand. Felty was dressed in a smart, dull green army uniform with not a wrinkle in sight. There were four pockets on the front of his jacket, with no shortage of shiny gold buttons. He wore a lighter green shirt with a darker green *Englisch* tie, and his hair was cut so short on the sides, she could see his scalp underneath it. He held his hat in one hand and an olive green duffel bag in the other. Anna couldn't see a gun anywhere. Didn't soldiers carry guns?

And then there was the scar, two full inches long down the left side of his face. Whatever had happened to him must have hurt, but the scar did nothing to mar his features. If anything, it made his face more interesting and mysterious, like Mr. Darcy in *Pride and Prejudice*.

Before she let her mind get carried away with Felty's magnificence, Anna took a deep breath and pulled her thoughts back to earth. Felty was tall, imposing, and very handsome. He was also the Helmuths' wayward son, who had left home more than two years ago to fight in the Korean War. He had shamed his parents and embarrassed the entire community. The Amish were against violence of any kind, even during wartime, when other men left home to fight for their country. It was better to let yourself be killed than to raise a hand or gun against anyone, even an enemy—even an enemy who would not hesitate to kill you.

Anna certainly couldn't forget the stain that Felty had put on the entire district with his decision. She would be wise not to have anything to do with him. Should she climb into the wagon and ride away as quickly as possible, putting needed space between her impressionable *bruderen* and someone as wicked as Felty Helmuth?

She willed herself to stop staring and cleared her throat. "*Ach*, *vell*, Felty. It is nice to see you again, but we have to be going."

His bright smile faded slightly, but he looked at her as if she was the kindest person in the world. "It is *wunderbarr* to see you too. You are more beautiful than I remember."

"Hey ho, soldier." A burly man with a bushy mustache strode toward the wagon and held out his hand. Felty's smile came back full force, and he shook the man's hand as if they were old friends.

"Hello, sir," Felty said.

"Back from Korea?" the man said.

Felty nodded.

"For good or just on leave?"

"For good," Felty said.

For good? He was here to stay? Would his parents be happy to see him? Did he want to join the Amish even after fighting in a war? Or was he firmly attached to his worldly ways? Anna was all the more suspicious. Felty was obviously of questionable character. He had fought in a war, his hair was unnaturally short, and those buttons were a sure sign of unfettered pride.

The man folded his arms and leaned against the wagon bed as if he was planning on staying awhile. "My name's Charles. Charles Patton, like the general, but you can call me Chuck. Who did you serve with?"

"Seventh Infantry Division, sir."

Charles scrubbed his hand down the side of his face. "I hear they took heavy casualties at the beginning there."

Felty drew his brows together and nodded. "They were brave men, sir."

Charles gave Felty's shoulder a stiff pat. "If you were in the Seventh, you're one of the brave ones too. Never forget that."

She saw Felty's Adam's apple bob up and down. He seemed unable to speak. They were talking about things Anna couldn't begin to understand, but she was intensely interested all the same.

"I was with the Eightieth during the Second World War," Charles said.

Felty stood up a little straighter. "I'm honored to meet you, sir."

Charles shook his head. "We all just did our duty."

"Yes, sir."

Charles frowned and looked into the distance. "And lost a lot of good men. That's what war is, a waste of good men." He seemed to pull his thoughts back as quickly as they had strayed. "They say the war can't last much longer. Everybody's tired of it."

"For sure and certain," Felty said.

Charles bloomed into a smile. "Hey, can I buy you a drink? The beer garden opens early."

Anna riveted her attention to Felty's face, curious to see how far Felty had waded into the waters of sin while he was in the army.

Felty gave Charles a kind, brotherly smile. "That is real nice of you, but I don't drink, and I need to get home. The bus dropped me off not twenty minutes ago, and I'm eager to see my parents."

Charles peered at Anna. "Are you with these folks? You Amish?"

Anna felt her face get warm. It was probably a sin to talk to a soldier. She didn't want a visit from the *Aumah Deanuh*, the head deacon. "He's not . . . with us," Anna stuttered. "We just came into town to buy bread." Neither Charles nor Felty needed to know that the reason they bought bread was because Anna had yet to make a loaf that wasn't as hard as a rock. Even Elmer complained when Anna made bread.

Felty stared at Anna for a second while she squirmed under his gaze. Did he think she was being rude? She was only nineteen. How was she supposed to know the proper and church-approved way to treat a wayward and wild member? She studied Felty out of the corner of her eye. He didn't seem particularly wild, although his haircut concerned her and his buttons were scandalous. But he was wayward, and Anna sensed that she should keep him at arm's length. Isn't that what the bishop would want her to do?

Felty finally stopped looking at her and smiled at Charles. "I am Amish." He inclined his head in Anna's direction. "She was in my district before I left. I happened to spot her wagon when I got off the bus. We're not together. I was just glad to see a friendly face." His last two words were directed at Anna, and they came out like a question.

"I thought the Amish didn't believe in fighting in wars," Charles said.

"We don't," Anna interjected, just in case Felty didn't know about that part of the Confession of Faith.

Felty's gaze once again rested on Anna's face. What

was he looking for? And why did his piercing look make her feel guilty? She hadn't done anything wrong.

"We don't," Felty repeated. "But I felt God calling me to fight. I had to go."

Anna pressed her lips together. Gotte would never do that, would He? Surely He didn't just come right out and communicate with normal people. It seemed like a disorderly way to run the world. Of course, Anna knew next to nothing about how Gotte ran things. She was still trying to figure out why men and women sat on opposite sides of the room at church. Gotte's ways were a mystery to her.

"God called you to fight?" Charles nodded. "I can respect that. I enlisted for freedom's sake. All people deserve to be free." He glanced at Anna as if he thought she might scold him for something. "It would be my honor to give you a lift home. My car's twenty years old, but it's always gotten me where I want to go."

Elmer put his arm around Anna. "Let us take you home, Felty." He tightened his grip. "He don't live but two miles from our house, and he's been all this time on a bus."

Elmer's tone made Anna feel ashamed. Where was her Christian charity? No matter how dangerous and unstable Felty might be, she should be nice. There was no harm in being nice. And Felty was Amish, or at least he used to be. That had to count for something. Besides, the poor boy had come home with a scar and one leg. How hard-hearted would she have to be to snub a one-legged man?

Despite her guilt and her confusion and the butterflies flitting about in her stomach, Anna managed a wide smile.

"We would love to drive you home, Felty." She could sort out her feelings and her sins later.

Felty's face exploded into a smile. *Ach*, his teeth were so bright, Anna was in some danger of going blind—and having a heart attack. "I would like that very much," he said. "You don't mind, do you, Charles? I've got a lot of catching up to do."

Charles waved off Felty's question. "I'd choose a pretty girl over an old soldier anytime, even on a cold day. Good luck, and I hope to see you again. I'm working on starting a VFW chapter. Maybe you could come."

"I'd like that," Felty said.

Charles pulled a piece of paper and a short pencil from his pocket and wrote something down. He handed the paper to Felty. "Here is my phone number and address. Write me a letter or give me a call when you're in town."

"We have a phone shack," Isaac said. "They installed it last year."

"But it's only for emergencies," Anna insisted. She didn't want Felty getting ideas about calling old soldier friends or other worldly people from the phone shack.

"Of course," Felty said, as if he wouldn't dream of calling anybody ever.

Charles and Felty shook hands again, and Charles headed across the street to the beer garden.

Felty hefted his duffel bag into the back of the wagon, and Anna was grateful that he was careful not to smash the bread. With the agility of a young child, he jumped into the wagon and sat next to Owen. Anna was impressed. He moved like someone who had two good legs, even when he only had one.

"*Nae*, Felty," Elmer said. "You ride up front. She's driving."

Felty smiled at Anna as if he liked that idea very much. "Do you mind?"

He was missing a leg and had a scar on his cheek. She couldn't very well say *nae*. Besides, her heart was now doing somersaults, and she couldn't think of one *gute* reason to refuse him. "I don't mind," she said breathlessly.

Felty stood up, jumped out of the wagon bed, and offered Anna his hand. The gesture so startled her that she took it, and he led her to the front of the wagon and helped her climb onto the seat. Then he went around to the other side and climbed up next to her. What would people think when they saw Anna sitting next to a soldier? What did she think about sitting next to a soldier? She couldn't even begin to understand her own thoughts.

It was cold out. Maybe all the neighbors would be in their houses staying warm and wouldn't think to look outside to see who was coming down the road.

Felty glanced back at the boys who were settling themselves into the wagon bed. "Remind me of your names," he said. "I've been away a long time."

Anna drew her brows together. Felty hadn't once said her name out loud since he'd been here. Had he forgotten it? She jiggled the reins, and Skipper and Sparky pulled the wagon forward. "I'm Anna Yoder. Mahlon's oldest and only daughter."

Anna flinched when Felty threw back his head and laughed. "*Ach*, Anna. I know who you are. You're the last person I would ever forget."

"It's because she's a terrible cook," Isaac said. "Everybody remembers her cooking."

Felty's eyes went soft at the corners. "As I recall, Anna's cinnamon rolls are so good, they could stop traffic. And her potato salad is better than anything I ate in the army. I love raisins."

Anna felt a blush slide up her neck. Felty liked her potato salad? Why had he never told her this before?

Anna looked back to see Elmer drape his arm over the lip of the wagon. "I'm Elmer. This is Isaac, Owen, and Uriah. He's the youngest. Ten."

Felty grinned. "I remember now. The five vowels. A, E, I, O, U. Anna, Elmer, Isaac, Owen, and Uriah."

Anna's mouth fell open. Surely Felty was the smartest boy she'd ever met.

"What's a vowel?" Uriah asked.

"What are they teaching you at that school?" Isaac growled. "You should know what a vowel is by now."

"If you're so smart, what's the capital of Wisconsin?" Uriah snapped back.

"You told Charles you're home for good," Anna said, changing the subject in hopes of avoiding the argument brewing between Isaac and Uriah. "Is the war over?"

"No, but my tour is over. The war won't last much longer. I heard they're in talks." He eyed Anna. "I was ready to come home. Ready for some peace."

"Did they give you a gun?" Owen asked.

Felty's lips curled into a half smile. "*Jah.* They gave me a gun. It was like the rifle I used to hunt with when I was younger."

Isaac knelt up and put his head between Anna and Felty. "Did you kill anybody?"

"Shut up, Isaac," Elmer said, yanking him back.

Felty stared off into the distance as if he hadn't heard the question. It was sort of an answer in itself.

"Was it fun? Shooting a gun and stuff?" Uriah wanted to know.

Felty glanced behind him. "It wasn't anything like fun. Nobody likes war, Uriah. Nobody." His words were stiff and cold, as if they tasted like sadness in his mouth.

Anna would rather not know anything about the truth of those words. And it was obvious that Felty would rather talk about anything else. "Were you long on the bus?" she asked.

"I got off the transport in San Francisco, and they put me on a bus for home. It sure feels good to be off that bus. It was so crowded, I had to stand for three hours."

Anna thought about standing on one leg for that long. "That must have been especially hard."

"Not too bad, but I couldn't sleep standing up."

She dared a peek at his legs, which were folded awkwardly beneath him, too long to fit properly in the wagon. She couldn't even guess which was his real leg and which was the fake one. "It looks so real. The doctors did a *gute* job."

"A good job with what?" Felty said.

"Your leg. You don't even walk with a limp."

Confusion lined Felty's forehead. "Why should I?"

"Because of the missing leg," Anna said.

"Can we see it?" Owen asked.

Anna heard a thud, and she imagined that Isaac or Elmer had pushed Owen over. "We can't see something if it's missing, you *dumkoff*," Isaac said.

Felty's mouth hung open like a dead fish. "Um. I've still got both my legs."

Anna studied his legs more carefully. "Are you sure? Sylvie Burkholder said your leg got shot off."

A low chuckle rumbled deep in Felty's throat. "I'm pretty sure."

"It's nothing to be embarrassed about," she said.

"How can I be embarrassed about a leg I'm not missing?"

Anna was dumbfounded. "But Sylvie was so sure . . . I felt so bad for you. Are you just trying to make me feel better?"

Not the least bit upset that he might or might not be missing a leg, Felty bent over and carefully rolled up one pant leg and then the other, revealing two identical limbs. They certainly looked like real legs. They were thin as fence posts, pasty white, and lightly furred with hair. Felty nodded. "Go ahead. Feel them."

Anna nearly swallowed her tongue. "What did you say?"

"Feel them. I don't want you to go on being concerned. Now is your chance to know for yourself."

Anna wasn't altogether sure it was proper to touch anybody's legs but her own, but she was curious enough to push her misgivings aside. She reached out and touched the leg closest to her. It felt soft and kind of hairy, and her heart raced for no good reason. She touched the other leg. It felt similar, if maybe a little colder. All noise and chatter from behind her ceased. She pulled her gaze from his legs and looked up at Felty. He seemed excessively amused.

"You're adorable," he said.

She snatched her hand off his leg. "What is that supposed to mean?"

If he had smiled any wider, his mouth would have

flown off his face. "I don't know. It's just . . . everything about you."

Anna eyed him suspiciously. He seemed to be giving her a compliment, but she couldn't quite make it out. It was also a possibility that he was laughing at her. You never could tell with boys. Anna grasped the reins and concentrated very hard on guiding the horse, deciding to ignore whatever it was he was trying to communicate. "I'm *froh* your leg didn't get shot off."

"I am too," Felty said, unrolling his pants back over his boots. "It will be easier to milk the cows and carry milk pails."

"You're going back to your *dat*'s dairy?"

"Of course."

Anna's heart lodged in her throat, but she was too curious not to ask. "It wonders me. Will you go back to *gmay*?"

"Church?" Felty grew more serious. He turned and studied her face with his intense, chocolaty gaze. The thought of fainting didn't cross her mind once. She must be getting immune to his appeal. "I want to come back, if they'll have me."

He looked so eager that she wanted to encourage him, but she stopped herself before she said something she couldn't be sure of. Felty had shamed the whole community, and while they were commanded to forgive, it didn't always go smoothly. Felty hadn't been baptized, so he wouldn't be officially shunned, but that didn't mean he'd be accepted with open arms. He'd hurt too many people. There had been a lot of shared bitterness and many tongues wagging while Felty had been away.

Anna herself worried about the repercussions of being seen with Felty—in his uniform, no less. What would people think? Would the gossips say she was rebellious or mocking *Gelassenheit*, submission to Gotte's will?

She kept her gaze focused on the road ahead. "Everyone is welcome at *gmay*." Again, she wasn't so sure about that, but it sounded like a nice thing to say. *Ach*, at times like these, Anna felt like a newborn *buplie*. She didn't know anything.

He seemed satisfied but not entirely secure with her answer. "Do you think they will let me go to the singings?"

"I'm sure there's always hope for you," she said, shifting uncomfortably in her seat. The feeling of guilt grew to the size of a large milk cow. She very much needed to be honest with him. "You shouldn't ask me these questions. Better to ask the bishop or the deacon. I don't know anything, and I'm not very smart."

"She doesn't even know all eighteen confessions of faith," Isaac interjected, with a bit of smug satisfaction in his voice. "Anna is as *dumm* as a fence post."

"Shut your mouth, Isaac," Elmer said.

Anna pressed her lips together in frustration and embarrassment. She was taking baptism classes, but the eighteen articles all sort of blended together in her head.

Felty's frown took over his whole face. "Well, that's a gross falsehood if ever I heard one."

"What's a 'gross falsehood'?" Uriah asked.

Felty turned around to look at Anna's *bruderen*. "It's not one bit true. Anna is the smartest girl I know."

Anna laughed awkwardly. "*That* is the gross falsehood."

Felty eyed Isaac. "What is half of one-eighth?"

Anna turned around in time to see Isaac scowl stubbornly. "Nobody knows that," he said.

Felty curled his lips and glanced at Anna. "Your *schwester* knows."

Anna laughed more easily this time. Felty was teasing them all. "One-sixteenth."

Owen piped up. "I knew that."

"Of course you did," Anna said, smiling at Felty for trying to make her feel better. "I'm not that smart. Everybody but Isaac can do fractions."

Felty cocked his eyebrow. "What's two-sevenths of three-fifths?"

"Six-thirty-fifths," Anna said.

"And four-elevenths of twenty-two-eighths?"

Anna grinned. "One. But like I said, everybody but Isaac can do fractions."

Slack-jawed and silent, Isaac stared at her for a full ten seconds. Then he waved his hand in the air as if swatting away a fly. "Now she's just showing off. And anyway, boys don't like smart girls."

"I do." Felty's smile was like hot cocoa on Christmas morning. Anna involuntarily shivered with pleasure. Felty turned to her *bruderen* again. "And do not—*do not*—challenge Anna to a spelling bee. She knows how to spell everything."

"Can you spell *religion*?" Owen said. "That's one of my words this week."

"R-E-L-I-G-I-O-N," Anna said. She smiled, then thought better of it and clamped her mouth shut. Isaac was right. Now she was just showing off.

Felty nodded. "When I was in eighth grade and she was in fifth, she won the school spelling bee. She beat me and all the other older kids."

Determined not to be touched by Felty's praise, Anna watched the road and fell silent. She had been so proud of winning the spelling bee, and Mammi Miller had come to the house, torn up Anna's certificate of achievement, and thrown it in the cookstove. "No *gute* will come of pride," Mammi had said. "You are a wicked little girl, Anna Yoder, showing up the boys like that and believing yourself better than anyone." Brokenhearted, Anna had cried for an hour without stopping. Dat had felt so sorry for her, he'd let her eat pie for dinner all by herself in her room. She loved that memory, even though the first part of it was sad.

"Don't puff her up," Isaac said. He sounded more and more like Mammi Miller every day. "She's supposed to be humble, and you're feeding her pride."

Felty didn't seem the least cowed by Isaac's admonition. He winked at Anna. "I'm not saying anything that isn't the absolute truth, Isaac. You said Anna was *dumm*. I'm just telling you that when you say it, you are spreading a lie, and you need to repent right quick."

Anna covered her mouth to stifle a giggle. How nice to see the tables turned on Isaac. Rarely was even Elmer able to put him in his place.

Felty turned back around and settled into his seat as if he was pretty much done talking to Isaac for the rest of his life. "You were saying something about singings. I want to come to the next one."

"I'm not the person you should ask for permission," Anna insisted. "I don't know anything."

Felty growled cheerfully. "We've already discovered that you know a lot of things. But I won't put you on the spot. I am hoping you'll be there. I want to see a friendly face."

Felty considered Anna a friendly face? A ribbon of warmth trickled down her spine. "I always go to singings. I suppose if I want to find a husband, I should go even if I can't carry a tune and the games are *dumm*. Do you like to play Pleased or Displeased?"

His eyes lit up. "I love Pleased or Displeased."

Anna shrugged. "I hate it, but Rosie Herschberger likes it, and all the boys want a chance with Rosie, so they like to play it too. If you want a chance with Rosie, you should definitely come."

"Why would I want a chance with Rosie Herschberber?"

"Because she's the prettiest girl in the *gmayna*, and her *dat*'s the bishop."

Felty pinned her with a look that made her a little dizzy. "She is not the prettiest girl in the *gmayna*, and I don't care who her *dat* is." He wilted like a plucked daisy. "Besides, he'd never agree to let his *dochter* associate with me. I'm a soldier, remember?"

"*Were* a soldier."

"*Jah,*" he said. "That's true. But I don't know if that will matter to anybody."

"It matters to me," Anna said, not really sure why she had said that, except Felty looked so sad and she wanted to encourage him.

Felty gave her a strange look, as if he were trying to open up her head and read her thoughts. "That's all I need to know."

Before Anna's heart burst out of her chest and galloped down the road, a fuss behind her made her turn around. "Uriah, do not stick your finger anywhere near your *bruder*'s eyeball."

With any luck, they'd be home before anyone went blind. Or had a heart attack.

Chapter 2

Isaac lugged one flour sack into the house, with Anna and the rest of her *bruderen* close behind, each carrying an armload of groceries. Dat looked up from the pot of soup he was stirring and smiled. "How was the trip into town? Did you remember the cranberries?"

Owen set his armload of bread on the table. "Anna touched a boy's bare legs."

Elmer lowered his flour sack to the floor and gave Owen a shove. "That is none of your business."

Owen made a face at Elmer. "I was sitting right there. If she didn't want anyone to see, she should have done it in private."

Anna narrowed her eyes. "I had to make sure it was real, didn't I?"

Owen shook his head. "He told you it was real. You didn't have to check."

Dat dipped his spoon into the soup and took a sip. "Sounds like a very interesting trip into town."

"It wasn't just a boy," Uriah said. "It was a soldier, and his name is Felty."

Dat turned his gaze to Anna. "Felty Helmuth? He's home?"

Anna busied herself putting groceries away so she didn't have to look Dat in the eye. Would he disapprove of her giving Felty a ride home? "*Jah.* He just got out of the war, and he says he's not going back. He wants to come to church."

"We gave him a ride home," Owen said. He'd always been a tattletale.

Dat set down his spoon. "A ride yet?"

Anna felt the need to defend herself. "The bus dropped him in town, and I thought it was the Christian thing to do."

"Of course it was," Dat said. "Especially since he got his arm shot off, though some people are saying that's his punishment for going to war in the first place."

Elmer dumped the flour from his sack into the bin. "He didn't get his arm shot off, Dat, or his leg. That's just a rumor."

"Anna touched his legs just to be sure, and I don't think it was right," Owen said.

Dat smirked. "*Ach*, *vell*, I suppose she had to be sure."

Anna made a face at Owen. "*Denki*, Dat." Should she have squeezed Felty's arms too? Maybe she'd misunderstood. Had he lost an arm instead of a leg? But *nae*, she'd seen him move all his fingers, hadn't she? You can't move all your fingers if you have a fake arm.

Dat tugged on one of Anna's *kapp* strings and chuckled. "You probably shouldn't make a habit of touching people's legs."

"For sure and certain, Dat."

"He has a scar on his face," Uriah said, "and I think he shot people."

Anna hissed at her *bruder.* "Hush, Uriah. We don't know that for sure."

"*Jah*, we do. I saw the scar."

Isaac laughed. "You should have touched it to make sure it was real, Anna."

Anna ignored her *dumm bruder.* "We don't know if he killed anybody, and we shouldn't go around spreading rumors." Although Anna was pretty certain Felty had killed someone. He'd acted so troubled about it when Isaac had asked. How would Anna feel if she'd killed someone? It made her sad to think about it, but then again, she hadn't volunteered to go to war. Had Felty wanted to kill people?

Elmer set the small bag of cranberries on the kitchen table. "How does Felty know so much about you, Anna? I didn't know you were *gute* at arithmetic."

Anna lowered her eyes in an attempt to show her humility, because it was hard not to be proud of her fraction skills. "I'm not anything special."

Isaac nodded. "We know. You're going to have a hard time finding a husband."

Elmer snapped the empty flour sack at Isaac, making the air crack and causing Isaac to hop backward. Flour dust billowed into the air like smoke.

"Our Anna is very special," Dat said. "We can be humble and still tell the truth."

Anna smiled to herself. Felty had mentioned that. It was a wonderful nice thing to say.

Elmer curled his lips upward. "I think he likes you."

"Likes me?" Anna had a hard time believing that.

"Our families know one another. We're in the same district, and we don't live that far from him. I don't know why he would like me in particular. He probably remembers the spelling bee because he lost to a fifth grader. He's been gone for two years. I'm surprised he remembered my name."

Elmer nodded. "It does seem strange, but I know what I saw. He couldn't stop looking at you."

"It's because she touched his legs. He was shocked and disgusted." That was Isaac's two cents, and it seemed just as believable as any other explanation.

Elmer folded his arms and grinned. "I wouldn't be shocked and disgusted if a girl touched my legs. I'd enjoy it."

Anna smacked Elmer on the arm. "You shouldn't say such things."

He backed away from her, still grinning like an idiot. "I'm only speaking the truth."

Dat took another sip of soup. "Of course he likes her. Every boy in the *gmayna* is smitten with our Anna."

Isaac chuckled under his breath. Anna sighed, lowered her head, and smiled to herself. Dat was blind when it came to his children, especially Anna. He loved her so very much and thought her so clever that he naturally assumed the boys were lined up to propose to her, or at least to take her on drives. Dat's regard warmed Anna's heart. Every daughter should be loved that way by her *dat*, even if he was greatly mistaken and couldn't see her as everyone else did.

She didn't want to hurt his feelings, but she needed to make him see the plain truth. Things would be easier for both of them if his expectations weren't so completely unrealistic. "*Ach*, Dat, no one is smitten with me. I expect to end up an old maid."

Isaac nodded. "I expect that too."

Anna gave Isaac the stink eye.

"I've never heard anything so silly," Dat said.

Anna decided to ignore Isaac altogether. "Rosie Herschberger's cinnamon rolls taste like you're eating a piece of heaven. I can't even make a *gute* loaf of bread. Mary Zook doesn't have a boyfriend, but she's already made her wedding dress and prayer covering. I can't sew a straight seam. Linda Schmucker is *gute* with children and babies, and the last four women who have given birth have asked Linda to be the mother's helper. I don't particularly like children. I don't even like half of my brothers."

"Which half?" Isaac asked.

Anna smirked at him. "*Ach*, I think you can figure it out."

Dat placed the lid on his pot. "I don't know what you're talking about, Anna. I like your bread. You just used the wrong yeast last time. You shouldn't give up just because your bread turned out a little crispy."

Crispy indeed. Elmer hadn't been able to saw through it with the bread knife. He'd been forced to use a meat cleaver.

Dat wiped his hands on a dish towel. "No girl in the *gmayna* can make asparagus raisin casserole taste like yours. Your chow-chow could win a prize, and your peanut butter spread disappears every time you take it to the fellowship supper."

Anna didn't want to mention that the last time she'd taken peanut butter spread to a fellowship supper, Linda Schmucker had hid it in the pantry so no one would have to eat it. That was why it had disappeared. Still, she loved Dat for trying to make her feel better.

"If there's a family out there that eats better than ours does, I'd like to meet them. And just because you don't like some of your *bruderen* doesn't mean you're not *gute* with children. When your *mater* died, you got the responsibility for caring for this house and everyone in it. I don't wonder but you find your *bruderen* tiresome. I can barely stand them myself some days." Dat wrapped his arm around Isaac's neck and scrubbed his knuckles back and forth along the top of Isaac's head. Isaac finally broke free, and they both laughed.

Neither Anna nor any of her *bruderen* believed that for a moment. Dat was devoted to his children, almost to the point of being overly prideful about them, but the deacon had never made a visit to censure him for it.

"And who cares if Mary Zook has a wedding dress already?" Dat said. "She thinks very highly of herself with those straight teeth and that little turned-up nose. I'd like to see her knit scarves and pot holders for her whole family."

Elmer scrubbed his hand down the side of his face. "I think she's pretty," he mumbled.

Dat always made her feel better *and* worse. Knitting was the one thing Anna could do well, but she wasn't supposed to acknowledge she was *gute* at it, because that would be prideful. Above all, the Amish must be humble, even about their knitting. It was hard to keep all the rules straight, especially about vanity. Anna could be good at knitting as long as no one praised her for it and as long as she didn't start to believe she was good. But it was probably too late for that. She'd already knitted well over a hundred mittens.

Knitting was the one thing Anna remembered Mamm teaching her to do before she died. She felt a special connection to her *mater* every time she picked up her knitting needles.

"I like to make scarves," Anna said. She was in the process of knitting each of her *bruderen* and her *dat* a new scarf for Christmas, each a different color. She couldn't wait to hand them out on Christmas morning. But she could only knit so many scarves before people got sick of them.

"That is why I think you should avoid Felty Helmuth." Dat set three loaves of bread in the icebox. "You did a nice thing driving him home, but he's gone against the *Ordnung*, and I don't wonder but he's picked up many worldly ways. He's not *gute* enough for you, but if he gets to know you, he'll fall in love for sure and certain. You'll break his heart, and then we'll all feel bad about it."

Anna laughed. "You might as well be a rabbit, jumping to so many conclusions like that."

Dat's eyes twinkled. "Rabbits have *gute* eyesight, but I don't need to be a rabbit to see what's coming."

Dat worried needlessly. He simply didn't know how much of a misfit Anna truly was. The boys thought she was odd, and the girls thought she was boring, like a sack of potatoes that had grown tentacle-like shoots. "I'm not likely to see much of Felty. He's going back to work at his *dat*'s dairy. He'll be wonderful busy. Besides, he won't give me a second look. Like as not, Rosie Herschberger will swoop in and snatch him up before his hair grows an inch."

"Why Rosie Herschberger?" Isaac said. "I don't remember her and Felty being sweethearts."

"They weren't, but Rosie is the prettiest, most popular girl in the *gmayna*, and Felty is tall and handsome. He's going to turn her head all the way around."

Elmer shrugged. "Maybe, but it's more likely she'll stay away from him. He's a soldier—"

"*Was* a soldier."

"Was a soldier," Elmer said, "and he embarrassed and hurt all of us when he joined the army. Rosie's *dat* is the bishop. She'll keep her distance from Felty."

Dat drew his brows together and peered at Anna. "Whatever you do, don't feel sorry for him. Remember how you felt sorry for that stray cat and fed her for three years? She ended up sleeping in my bed and shedding on my sofa."

Anna giggled. "But, Dat, you loved that cat."

"And what was the thanks I got? She disappeared one morning, and we never saw her again."

"And you were heartbroken," Anna said, shaking her finger at her *dat*.

Dat shook his finger right back. "That's exactly what I'm trying to warn you about."

"You don't have to worry, Dat. I'm sure I'm the last person Felty is thinking about, or will ever think about again. I've already nearly forgotten what he looks like." She'd very nearly forgotten how she felt when he smiled at her, and she had almost no memory of his warm eyes and infectious laughter.

Isaac cocked an eyebrow. "Stray cats only hang around

if you feed them, but that won't work for Anna. When she tries to feed boys, they run away."

Dat wrapped his arm around Isaac's neck once again and scrubbed his knuckles over the top of Isaac's head. "That's not true, and don't tease your sister."

Isaac laughed and begged for mercy before Dat released him. Dat and Elmer always defended Anna's cooking, and Isaac never had a *gute* word to say about it. At least he was honest. Honesty was his one *gute* quality.

Thank Derr Herr for Elmer. He was a *gute bruder*, sensitive, kind, and not cocky or sure of himself like Isaac. Lord willing, Isaac would grow out of being a pest and become a *gute* man like their *fater* instead of overbearing and resentful like Mammi Miller.

Owen came huffing and puffing from outside with the frozen turkey in his arms. "Where do you want me to put this, Anna?"

"In the icebox. There will be just enough time to thaw it before Thanksgiving. Six full days." She opened the icebox for Owen, and he hefted the turkey onto the bottom shelf. She smiled. She liked that no matter how badly she had failed with the turkey on previous years, there was always another Thanksgiving to get it right. "I'm going to make a brine for the turkey and soak it overnight. That's supposed to make it very tender."

Isaac opened his mouth, no doubt to make an unwelcome comment about the turkey disaster last year, but he promptly clamped it shut when Dat gave him the evil eye.

Anna did her best to ignore the snide looks coming from Isaac's side of the room. "And I'm going to make pumpkin and apple pies, and maybe a pecan if I have time."

"That sounds *appeditlich*, Anna." Dat clapped his hands

together and pasted a fake smile on his face. "And speaking of Thanksgiving, I have some exciting news. Mammi and Dawdi Miller are not going to Ohio this year. They are spending Wednesday and Thanksgiving Day with us."

Anna slumped her shoulders. Elmer's countenance fell. Isaac and Owen both groaned. Poor Mammi Miller would have been deeply offended by their reactions.

"*Ach*, the day before too?" Anna said, not even trying to hide her disappointment.

"*Jah.* She wants to help with all the food preparations." Dat smiled sheepishly. They all knew what Mammi was up to. "She very thoughtfully suggested that this would be a way to take some of the burden off your shoulders."

What Dat meant was that Mammi wanted to take over the cooking and the preparations because Anna was a complete disappointment to her. Thanksgiving dinner would *not* be a failure, if Mammi had anything to say about it. And she always seemed to have plenty to say about her oldest granddaughter and her lack of home-making skills. Mammi wasn't even impressed with Anna's knitting. To Mammi, knitting did nothing to make the world a better place or to glorify Gotte.

Mammi had been trying to "fix" Anna ever since Anna could remember, even before Mamm had died. Mamm had never seemed nearly as concerned as Mammi had about Anna's many shortcomings. Before Mamm went home to Gotte, Mammi had come over every week to try to turn Anna into a granddaughter she could be proud of. She'd attempted to teach Anna how to make soup, how to operate the treadle sewing machine, how to bake rolls, how to clean a toilet, how to butcher a pig. Pig-butchering day had been the worst day of Anna's eight-year-old life. But after Mamm died, Mammi's visits had decreased sharply, even though she lived not fifteen minutes away. Anna had been relieved when Mammi had stopped coming over so much.

Anna saw Mammi and Dawdi at *gmay*, and Dat took Anna and her *bruderen* over every Friday afternoon to help with chores at Mammi's house. Mammi never let Anna help her with the cooking, and Anna usually spent Fridays in the barn mucking out with Dawdi and the boys or in the house mopping Mammi's floor, which she never did to Mammi's liking.

Mammi and Dawdi Miller almost always spent Thanksgiving with Onkel Ben and Aendi Lisa. "Why aren't they going to Ohio?" Isaac asked, clearly indignant at this change of plans. "I'd rather eat Anna's cooking than listen to Mammi lecture me on my posture."

Anna gave Isaac a sour glare that could have peeled the paint off the outhouse.

Anna could always tell when Dat wasn't quite sure what to say. He hemmed and hawed like he had something stuck in his throat and wouldn't make eye contact with anybody. "She wants to help you with all the Thanksgiving cooking. She makes *appeditlich* yams. With marshmallows."

"What else?" Anna said, unwilling to let Dat get away with that answer.

He cleared his throat. "*Ach*, *vell*, okay then. She's concerned. Hannah Schrock got married last month, and she is younger than you are. I talked to Mammi at the wedding, and she is worried about your future." Dat gave Anna that funny little smile that meant he didn't agree with Mammi but wasn't going to say it out loud. "She doesn't approve of the job I've done rearing you, and she thinks she can fix it."

Isaac frowned. "If Mammi wants to fix Anna, why should the rest of us suffer? I could spend Thanksgiving with the Clays. They have two ovens and a TV."

Dat's ears perked up at that. "They have a TV? Do you ever watch it?"

Isaac widened his eyes, then narrowed them as if he was concentrating wonderful hard. "That doesn't really matter right now. What matters is that Mammi will ruin our holiday if we don't do something."

Anna exhaled a long breath. "She wants to make me a more suitable match for someone. Does she truly think she can teach me how to be a *gute fraa* in two days?"

Dat gave her a weak smile. "The Earth was created in six."

"It's not going to work, Dat, and you know it."

Dat put his hands on her shoulders. "Listen to me. You don't need fixing. You are talented and *wunderbarr*, and I like you just as you are."

"Dat's right," Elmer said. "You don't need to be fixed."

"*Denki* for saying that, but we both know it's not true. Mammi is afraid I'll end up an old maid if she doesn't step in and save me."

Dat shook his head. "Now, now, it's not as bad as all that. Your *mammi* only wants what's best for all of you, even though she doesn't always know what is best. I can't very well tell her to stay away. She hasn't spent Thanksgiving with us since your *mamm* died. She wants to spend time with her grandchildren. She loves you all, even if she sometimes has a funny way of showing it."

"She doesn't like me," Uriah said, swiping his sleeve across his runny nose. "I made Mamm die."

Dat practically leaped across the room to Uriah's side. Kneeling down in front of him, he pulled a hankie from his pocket and handed it to Uriah. "That's not true. Your *mamm* got childbed fever after you were born. It wasn't your fault. It was Gotte's will, and she's with the angels now."

Uriah nibbled on his fingernail. "Angels are just shiny people who look like birds. Why isn't she with us instead of the angels? We're her children. Doesn't she love us?"

Isaac tensed beside her, and the muscles of Elmer's jaw tightened. Even Anna clenched her fists involuntarily. Unanswered questions were the most painful ones, and none but the very young dared ask them. No doubt they had all asked the same questions in their hearts, and they all carried the burden of profound loss.

Anna loved that Dat never got mad at such unseemly questions. He was patient and kind and so sure of himself even in the midst of uncertainty. He placed his large hand on Uriah's head. "I believe Mamm would rather be with us, Uriah, but Gotte had another plan, and we have to obey Gotte's will no matter how hard it is."

"Why did Gotte want Mamm to die? He doesn't sound like a very nice person."

Dat didn't even flinch at Uriah's assessment of Gotte's character. "We don't know why Gotte took Mamm, and we probably won't know until we get up to heaven and can ask Gotte for ourselves."

Uriah seemed satisfied with that answer. "I want to hug Mamm first and then ask Gotte why He took her away."

"I want to ask Him why some people are blind," Isaac said.

Elmer furrowed his brow. "I'd ask Him why He allows war."

"I would ask why he made mosquitoes," Owen said.

Dat stood and eyed at Anna. "What about you, Anna? What would you ask Gotte?"

Anna thought about standing at Mamm's bedside listening to each labored breath, willing Mamm to live for just one more minute so Anna could keep hold of her hand. She thought about Mamm's smile in contrast to Mammi's stern frown. She thought about a little nine-year-old girl tasked with keeping the candle burning over the three days before Mamm's funeral. Anna thought about Dat's drawn, weary features as they lowered the box into the ground. She swallowed past the lump in her throat. "I'd ask Him if He loves me, or if it's all a big trick." She didn't mean for her words to come out sounding as bitter as they did.

The love in Dat's eyes was so intense, it took her breath away. "*Ach*, boys," he said, "Anna's question is the most important question of all, because if you know Gotte loves you, then you can do anything, because you know that everything He does is for your good. You know that He will make everything work out the right way and in the way that will make you the happiest in the end. You'll know it's not a trick."

Owen leaned against Dat's side. "There are a lot of bad things in the world. Wouldn't Gotte make them go away if He really loved us?"

Dat shrugged. "I *do* know that He will never give you a stone when you ask for bread, even though some of His gifts might seem like stones at the time." Dat put his arm around Owen. "What are some things that make you happy?"

"I like milkshakes," Owen said.

Anna thought about knitting first thing. "Pink, fuzzy yarn and raisins."

Uriah smirked. "I like it when Owen falls on his face."

"Hey!"

"I like French fries, puppies, and the sky right after a big rainstorm," Elmer said.

Isaac fingered the sparse whiskers on his chin. "Cute girls, doing doughnuts with the buggy, black licorice, birthday cake."

"I like the way Elmer can make me feel better just by smiling at me," Anna said.

Dat nodded. "All these things are gifts from Gotte to show us He loves us. That is why we are commanded to thank Derr Herr in all things. It helps us notice His love."

Isaac grimaced. "Does that mean we have to thank the Lord that Mammi and Dawdi are coming to spend Thanksgiving with us?"

"Yes, it does," Dat said. "Mammi's stuffing is famous, and maybe we can persuade Dawdi to read us a passage from *Martyrs Mirror*."

Anna sighed inwardly. Nothing like stories of torture and imprisonment to get you in the Thanksgiving spirit. Of course, with Mammi here, getting into the Thanksgiving spirit was going to be well nigh impossible. Anna pressed her lips together and repented of that thought right quick. They were commanded to thank Derr Herr in all circumstances, and she would do well to be grateful for her *mammi*. Who knew what blessings in disguise Mammi would bring with her when she came?

Gotte always gave bread, never a stone.

Chapter 3

Felty watched Anna Yoder, her *bruderen*, and their wagon until they disappeared over a rise in the road. He couldn't remember ever enjoying a wagon ride as much as he had that one. What were the chances that he would just happen to be in town in time to meet Anna and hitch a ride in her wagon? Gotte's hand had been in it, for sure and certain.

Anna was so delightfully sincere and guileless. She had been that way ever since Felty could remember, and he was completely captivated by her, or *real gone*, as his army buddies would say. Anna had no idea how much Felty had thought of her while he'd been in Korea. He had always feared that she barely knew he existed. She certainly never paid him any mind before he left for the war. And since he'd been a soldier, it was unlikely she'd be eager to have much to do with him now that he was back.

Anna was just another sacrifice he'd made when he'd turned his life over to Gotte and joined the army. The sacrifices had piled up, and Felty wondered how many more Gotte would ask of him. *Please, dear Heavenly Father, please. I've asked a lot of You over the past two years, but if You could see it in Your heart to give me a chance with Anna Yoder, I'll never ask for another thing in my whole life.*

He lifted his head and immediately bowed it again. *Okay, Heavenly Father. That was a lie, because I plan on asking for Your sustaining hand every day until I die. Please forgive me. But I'm still asking for a chance with Anna. She makes me so* ferhoodled, *I feel like I'm going to throw up.* But it was a *gute* kind of throw-up feeling, like happiness, terror, and anticipation all mixed into one. *Okay, Gotte. Disregard that comment about throw up. I'm not really explaining myself very well.*

Felty had learned how to pray, really pray, in Korea. When the bullets whizzed around your head, there was no time to leaf through a prayer book in hopes of finding something to keep you from dying. It was easier and more heartfelt to ask Gotte for protection and let Him tell you what your next step should be. You tended to live longer that way.

Felty's heart pounded against his chest as he strode across the yard, stepped onto his front porch, and knocked on the door. He'd cabled Mamm and Dat that he was coming, but he sincerely didn't know if they'd be happy to see him. He'd been gone a long time, and he'd effectively snubbed his nose at the Amish tenet of nonviolence. Would his parents even want him back? They'd written him letters, but no amount of reading between the lines could tell him how his parents had really felt.

He had broken their hearts. Was there any coming back from that?

The door opened, and an old man with a long white beard greeted him. It took Felty a split second to realize that the old man was his *dat*. A little bent over, he was still almost as tall as Felty, but he looked like he'd aged ten years while Felty had been gone.

Dat gasped, shouted "Hallelujah," threw his hands in the air, then wrapped his long arms tightly around Felty as if he were trying to squeeze all the air out of his lungs. Okay. Dat, at least, was happy to see him.

Felty was so relieved, the laughter burst from his lips like soda from a pop can that had been shaken too hard. He returned Dat's hug and laughed until tears rolled down his cheeks. He laughed and cried, and both kinds of tears mixed together on his face.

"Edna," Dat yelled, in his booming voice that always rattled the windows when he raised it. "Come and see the man at our door." He wrapped his fingers around Felty's upper arms and nudged him backward. "I think you've grown taller."

Felty nodded. "Three inches."

"Well, imagine that." Dat stroked his beard. "As you can see, I've grown older."

Felty laughed. "The white beard suits you. You look like the *Englisch* Santa Claus."

A shadow passed over Dat's features. "It started growing pure white the day you left us."

Felty's heart ached for the pain he'd caused his parents, but he couldn't apologize for joining the army. It was what Gotte had asked him to do. Felty looked past Dat when he heard the soft thud of footsteps on the wood floor. Mamm shuffled down the hall, her shoulders slumped, her gait slow and unsteady, her gaze glued to his face.

It felt as if someone had smacked Felty upside the head with a two-by-four. If he hadn't known Mamm's face so well, he wouldn't have recognized her. Mamm had always been a jolly, loud, happy woman with sparkly eyes and deep dimples on her round face. She loved to cook and she loved good food, and Dat called her "pleasingly plump," a description that made her giggle every time he said it.

Now she looked slight and frail, much older than her sixty years. She had lost at least fifty pounds and every hint of animation in her face. What had happened to her? Had this been Felty's doing? Of course it had. For sure and certain, she had worried herself sick.

But then she smiled, and Felty felt a little bit better. Mamm's smile had always been able to light up a room. Now it was dimmer than a flashlight, but at least Felty could see his *mamm* in there somewhere. "At last," she said, enfolding him in her embrace. "I feared I'd never get to hold my baby again."

Dat's gaze flicked from Felty back to Mamm. "But our faith sustained us, didn't it, Edna?"

A deep line appeared between Mamm's eyes. "Faith? Where was Gotte when I needed Him most? Where was He the night Felty decided to go to that terrible war?"

Dat's shoulders drooped ever so slightly. Felty was sure Mamm didn't notice, but it was obvious Dat had been carrying more than one burden while Felty had been away. "He has always been with us, Edna. Always. Look. He brought our Felty home again."

Mamm regained her smile and cupped Felty's cheek in her hand. "*Jah.* Felty is home. I think in spite of Gotte this time."

Felty's heart lurched. "*Ach*, *nae*, Mamm. Gotte never left me. He was faithful in every battle."

Mamm pressed her lips into a hard line. "So only atheists were killed in your war?"

Felty glanced past Mamm to look at Dat. Dat shook his head slightly, and Felty closed his mouth. He'd only been home five minutes. There would be plenty of time for the healing of war wounds—both the visible ones and those in the heart.

Mamm nudged his chin to the right and clicked her tongue. "You wrote that you got a scratch in one of your battles. This is not a scratch, young man. This is a deep cut, and I don't doubt they gave you stitches." She shook her finger at him. "'Thou shalt not bear false witness.'"

Felty's chest tightened, like it always did at the memory of that day in the field. He didn't want to remember. He didn't want to hear the sounds of explosions and gunfire and men screaming out their last breath on the battlefield. He tried to push it out of his mind, but no matter how prepared he thought he was for it, the memory always took his breath away.

Felty did what he had done every day of the war, especially on the darkest days. He reached toward Gotte in his thoughts and remembered the tender mercies Gotte had never failed to show him. In an instant, he felt stronger. He could show Mamm what she needed to see, and right now she needed to see a whole and healthy son who hadn't been deeply wounded by the war.

Felty grinned and playfully pulled away from Mamm's touch. "It's a scratch, Mamm. And it was twelve tiny stitches. Not worth writing home about. All the blood washed right out of my uniform."

Mamm rolled her eyes. "Oh, hush! Don't tease me." She studied his face. "The scar will fade. By the time you're my age, it will look like just another wrinkle on your face. But right now, I don't wonder but it makes you look even more handsome, if that is possible. But it is a permanent sign that you went away to war in spite of the community and your parents."

Felty didn't know what to say to that, so he simply took Mamm's hand and squeezed it.

"You are still handsome," Mamm said. "But you're too skinny, and you've grown taller, I think."

"*Jah*. Three inches."

Mamm smiled. "Well, just stop it. Soon you'll be too tall to fit in the buggy. Nobody will want to date you."

He most sincerely hoped that wasn't true. He hoped one girl in particular would want to date him. But would she avoid him like he feared all the other young people would?

Mamm seemed to grow more animated the longer they talked, almost like her old self. "*Ach*, *vell*, my son, I can't do anything about how tall you are, but I can do something about your width." She took his hand and pulled him forward. "*Cum*. I've been baking. We are going to fatten you up."

"I can't wait," Felty said, even though eating had always been no better than a chore. An accident as a little boy had left him with hardly any sense of smell or taste. But that was something he never reminded Mamm about, because she took such pleasure in feeding him.

Felty caught his breath as he walked into the kitchen. A basket of rolls and two kinds of jam sat on the table next to a tub of butter. Next to the rolls were a tall chocolate cake, a blueberry pie with a lattice top, and Mamm's homemade chocolate mint brownies. "*Ach, du lieva.* It looks like a Christmas bakery in here. I should leave home more often if this is the welcome I get when I come back."

Mamm's smile faded. "*Nae*, you shouldn't leave home ever again."

Wrong thing to say. He tried a different compliment. "All I know is that the queen of England doesn't eat this *gute*. You can be sure of that."

"Of course she doesn't," Mamm said.

Dat put his arm around her and gave her a squeeze. "She baked for two days straight."

"*Denki*, Mamm. All this baking, and you have to do it again for Thanksgiving in less than a week. How do you do it?"

Mamm blushed. "Oh, stop talking and sit down. You know baking is my pleasure."

"The thing I missed the most about home was the two of you and Mamm's cooking. I don't know how I survived. Army food is terrible."

Mamm turned her face away and folded her arms across her chest. *Hmm.* Obviously, she didn't like talk about the war. Okay then. He'd just stop talking about it. Nobody wanted or needed to hear about what had happened over there, and it apparently caused Mamm great distress when he mentioned it.

Dat pulled a chair out from under the table. "*Cum* sit. What do you want to eat first?"

Mamm wrung her hands together. "If you'd rather have a piece of chicken or a steak or something else, just say the word and I'll mix up whatever you want." She pulled a plate and drinking glass from the cupboard. "I'm that glad to have you home. *That glad.* My stomach's been tied in knots for two years. I finally feel like I can breathe. Your being home is a balm of Gilead to my soul."

Felty's heart brimmed with emotions too profound to even make sense of. There were relief, jubilation, and hope, but also pain, anxiety, and guilt. Guilt had been his constant companion for two years.

He hadn't needed to worry about the reception he would get from his parents, but he now had to come to terms with the destruction and pain he had left behind. Both parents had aged significantly, no doubt for worrying about him. Dat's workload at the dairy had increased because Felty hadn't been there to help him. What had that done to Dat's arthritis? Worst of all, Mamm, it seemed, had lost her faith—or it was wavering like a canoe in a hurricane. War and trials and heartache tested everyone's faith. Felty had simply never guessed that Mamm's would falter. She had always been his rock.

Felty knew where to place the blame. He took full responsibility for his parents' transformation. He had to fix it, had to make everything better, but he simply didn't know how. Could such deep scars ever be fully healed? Would Mamm want to pull Gotte close now when she had been pushing Him away? Or was her anger set like cement?

Felty sat down and motioned for his parents to join him. "There's plenty for all of us, and I want to hear about the family. I got your last letter more than a month ago."

Mamm pulled more plates and cups and silverware from the cupboards and set them on the table. Mamm poured Felty a tall glass of milk and sat down next to him. "The biggest news is that Sadie is in a family way. It's still a secret, so don't go telling anyone."

"That is *wunderbarr*," Felty said. Sadie was his brother Paul's wife, and they already had five children.

Dat scooted out the chair on the other side of Felty and sat. "Before we get carried away, let's pray."

Mamm acted as if such a thought was a great imposition, but she fell silent and bowed her head anyway. Felty did the same. *Dear Father*, he prayed silently, *You sent me to Korea. Help me make it right with my family*. He opened his eyes and promptly closed them again. *And please bless the food.* He looked up again before remembering one more thing. *And I would be more than grateful for that help with Anna, if that's all right.* He lingered for a few seconds with his eyes closed, just in case he had forgotten anything else. Nothing came to mind.

He opened his eyes and decided to tackle the pie sitting in front of him. Mamm's pies looked like works of art, so pretty that Felty almost hated cutting into them. "So Sadie is expecting," he said, cutting a large piece.

Dat picked up a roll and buttered it. "Paul wants to buy three new milking machines. We've got four new heifers, and we could use the equipment."

"That sounds like a *gute* idea. You already have plenty of work with a hundred head." Dat had started a small dairy when he and Mamm had moved to Wisconsin twenty years ago. Felty had worked at the dairy with his two *bruderen* ever since he'd been able to walk.

Felty's *bruder* Zeb was seventeen years older than Felty, with a wife and four children of his own. Zeb's three sons, Junior, Martin, and Wayne, also worked at the dairy. Paul was fifteen years older than Felty. Mamm called Felty her "delightful surprise" because he had been born years after Mamm and Dat had given up on having more than two children. Paul's oldest daughter, Mayne, and her *bruder* Paul Junior also worked at the dairy. It was a family operation, and Felty was eager to start pulling his weight.

They talked about the dairy, the nieces and nephews, repairs needed on the house, Thanksgiving. Felty avoided the war, and Mamm seemed blissfully happy.

"How was your trip home?" Dat asked, skirting dangerously close to the topic of the war. "Did you come by boat?"

"*Jah.* From Korea to Japan, then to San Francisco." He glanced at Mamm. "Then I took a bus the rest of the way. It wasn't pleasant, but after being on a transport ship, it felt like a vacation."

Mamm slipped another piece of pie onto Felty's plate. "Did you walk all the way from town yet? If we'd known when you were coming in, we would have been in town to fetch you."

Felty's heart beat double time at the memory of seeing Anna standing next to her wagon scolding her *bruderen* for fighting. Over the years, he'd often imagined jumping into her deep blue eyes and drowning. He would have died a happy man. "I ran into Anna Yoder and her four *bruderen*. They were kind enough to bring me home."

"Anna Yoder?" Mamm said, furrowing her brow. "She's very short."

Felty nodded, stifling a grin. Anna was little, over a foot shorter than Felty, but she was like a stick of dynamite—every ounce packed with explosive energy and lovability. He nearly told his parents about how Anna had touched both his legs to make sure they were real, but the story would have brought them closer to the war, so he kept it to himself. A smile tugged at his lips. Everything Anna did was a delightful surprise. "I like her," he couldn't help saying.

Mamm shrugged. "*Ach.* She's a very nice girl, and pretty too, but nice and pretty won't get her very far. Her cooking hasn't gotten any better, and she is the last person anyone wants at a quilting frolic. Her stitches are a quarter inch wide."

"*Ach*, *vell*, Mamm, she didn't have a *mater* to teach her all those things. Under the circumstances, she's done very well."

"That's what I'm saying. Lorene Miller is Anna's *mammi*, and she is beside herself. After poor Emma died, Anna's *dat* wouldn't let Lorene near Anna when Anna was young enough that it could have made a difference. Now I fear she's hopeless. She can't cook, can't sew, doesn't know how to clean, and seems more interested in reading books than in learning how to be a *fraa*."

Felty's ears perked up at this information. If Anna wasn't trying to find a husband, she probably wasn't attached to any particular boy. That thought sent Felty's hopes soaring.

Mamm reached out and patted Felty's hand. "She's a nice girl. Not *gute* enough for you, but nice enough for someone who isn't picky."

Dat nodded and gazed earnestly at Felty. "You're going to have a hard enough time fitting in. I would stay away from girls like Anna."

"What do you mean 'girls like Anna'?"

Dat cleared his throat. "I mean girls who don't fit in. Girls who wouldn't make *gute* wives. Girls who would embarrass you instead of raise you up. You want the community to open their arms to you, and you don't want to give them another reason to avoid you."

Felty was reluctant to remind them of his recent military history, but he had to ask the question. "Do you think they will avoid me? I went against the church when I enlisted in the army. I don't look Amish anymore. I look like a soldier." He was mostly thinking about Anna. He didn't really care what the other girls thought.

"That can be fixed," Dat said, glancing at Mamm as if to reassure her too. "All you have to do is change your clothes and wear a hat. Girls won't notice the hair, and it will grow back. The most important thing is that you haven't been baptized. You're still in *rumschpringe*. The *gmayna* wasn't happy about your military service, but you haven't made your promises to Gotte yet. There is still hope for you."

Felty grinned. "I'm glad you think so. Anna said something like that."

Mamm grunted softly. "Don't fuss about Anna. There are plenty of other girls in the *gmayna*. Two families moved in while you were away, the Beilers and the Kings."

Dat leaned closer and winked at Felty. "The Kings' oldest *dochter* is fifteen, and the Beilers' only daughter is thirty-seven."

Mamm reached across the table and swatted at Dat with her napkin. "I was trying to be encouraging, just so he knows there are options."

Felty chuckled. "A fifteen-year-old is not an option, Mamm."

Mamm pursed her lips as if she'd eaten a sour pickle. "I know. Don't tease me, or you'll be doing the dishes for a week."

Felty nodded. "Gladly. I've missed the chores around here."

Mamm cupped her fingers under his chin. "That's what I missed about you. You work hard and never complain about chores. You are truly my balm of Gilead."

No matter how he'd hurt her, she still loved him. It was a *gute* foundation. He could build on that, helping Mamm feel secure in his love and Gotte's faithfulness. Lord willing, Mamm would be back to her old self by Christmastime.

Chapter 4

"*Ach*, *du lieva*, Anna! You can't just throw sugar into the fruit without measuring it. For goodness' sake, use a measuring cup and read the recipe."

Anna held her breath and tamped down the emotions that threatened to overflow into a fit of temper or a flood of tears. Mammi had the unique ability to wound Anna's feelings and make her irrationally angry at the same time. Instead of stomping her foot or crying her eyes out, Anna pressed her lips together and thought about soft yarn and the sleeping hat she was making for herself. Was it selfish to be knitting something for herself instead of working on Christmas scarves for her *bruderen*? Maybe, but Anna ached to wear pink, and the only place she was allowed to wear such a fancy color was in the privacy of her own room. At night. When she was asleep and no one could see her.

She simply adored pink.

Ach. Her love of beauty would probably keep her out of heaven.

Mammi had swooped into the house this morning and immediately taken charge of the kitchen, the food preparations, and Anna's plans for Thanksgiving dinner. She had nixed all of Anna's menu ideas, including asparagus raisin casserole and green Jell-O with grated carrots. She had refused to let Anna shape the dinner rolls into little turkeys, and Mammi was completely against tomato cranberry sauce.

It didn't seem fair. This was Anna's kitchen. Mammi was just a guest. Why did she think she could be in charge and tell Anna what she could and could not make for her own Thanksgiving dinner?

Once Anna got her emotions in check, she tried to defend herself, which was probably a mistake. "All the *gute* cooks measure and add ingredients by feel, Mammi. I'm just following a tradition passed down for generations."

Mammi propped her hands on her hips. "Wherever did you hear such a *ferhoodled* notion?"

"I . . . I just heard it somewhere," Anna stuttered. She'd read it in a magazine at the library, but she wasn't about to tell Mammi that. For sure and certain Mammi would give her a lecture on reading worldly ideas that had no place in an Amish home.

Mammi raised an eyebrow. "Well, in *my* kitchen, we use a recipe and the measuring cups. We want the food to be *appeditlich*, not inedible."

Anna didn't know what *inedible* meant, but she got the idea. Mammi wasn't going to budge, and Anna would do well to do it Mammi's way, even though this wasn't Mammi's kitchen and Anna hadn't wanted her to come. Right now, she envied her *bruderen*, who were outside helping Dat with the milking and other chores. She'd rather be mucking out stalls than stuck inside with Mammi getting a lecture filled with words she didn't understand.

Anna unclenched her jaw and picked up the measuring cup. She shouldn't be so stubborn. It was wicked of her to think unkind things about her mother's mother. Mammi deserved respect, honor, and affection. Anna would try harder. There would be other Thanksgivings, other opportunities to make turkey-shaped rolls and five-layer Jell-O salads.

"Stop!" Mammi shouted, as Anna was about to pour a cup of sugar over the apples in the pie tin.

"But I measured it."

"Look at the pie, Anna. You've already poured at least a cup of sugar on it. You can't just start to follow the recipe when you're halfway in."

Anna tried valiantly to keep her voice from shaking, but it didn't work so well. "Then what do you want me to do?"

Mammi paused briefly, as if trying to work out a terribly hard math problem in her head. Huffing out a frustrated breath, she rummaged through the drawers. She pulled out a pencil and a piece of paper from the junk drawer and started writing furiously. "It would just be better . . . if you could occupy yourself . . . I'll have you . . ." She finished writing and handed the paper to Anna. "You can run an errand for me."

"An errand?"

"*Jah.* I want you to go see Edna Helmuth and ask if we can borrow the things on this list. Your kitchen is sadly equipped, and hopefully Edna will have some spare pans that she isn't using for her own Thanksgiving baking."

Anna looked at the list. *Cookie sheet. Large stockpot. Bundt cake pan.* "We have a cookie sheet, Mammi."

"I know, but we need two for the rolls. They need to breathe."

Anna felt her face get warm. Three weeks ago she'd ruined the stockpot. She had left some soup to boil on the cookstove and had gotten so absorbed in *Gone with the Wind* that she'd forgotten all about her soup until the smell of charred potatoes had reached her nose. The potatoes had been so badly melded to the pan, it couldn't be scrubbed out, and they'd been forced to throw the stockpot away. Dat had been very nice about it. He'd reassured her they could survive without a stockpot. "Are you planning to make a Bundt cake?" That sounded interesting. Anna had never tried a Bundt cake before, but she was enamored with the shape.

"*Nae.* I'm making a cranberry gelatin mold. It's going to be beautiful."

Anna longed to point out that layered green and orange Jell-O with carrots would be beautiful too, but she held her tongue.

"Run to Edna's and see if we can borrow these. If she can't spare anything, we'll make do."

Anna sighed. "I'll have Elmer hitch up the buggy."

"No need to bother Elmer. Just walk. It's not that far."

Anna drew her brows together so tightly, she was sure there was a line from the top of her forehead to the tip of her nose. "It's two miles, Mammi, and it's cold out there."

Mammi glanced out the window. "It's not even below freezing. The sun is out. It's a beautiful day for a walk." She stretched a smile across her face. "And, well, you'll be gone longer."

And that was the real point. Mammi wanted Anna out of the kitchen so she wouldn't ruin Thanksgiving. Anna's feelings weren't even bruised. She already knew exactly how Mammi felt about her. She didn't want to be here anyway. A brisk walk would do her good.

Or rather, a slow walk. Mammi wouldn't be put out if Anna was gone the rest of the day.

Anna took off her apron, went to the mudroom, and donned her black shawl and winter cape, her deep blue scarf and black bonnet. She decided against her boots. The snow wasn't so deep yet, and it would be easier to walk on the road without them. Of course, the boots would slow her down and give her more of an excuse to take her time.

She stepped into her boots and laced them up. Mammi was probably eager to make the pies by herself.

Anna tied her bonnet strings under her chin, stuffed Mammi's list into her pocket, and slipped on her mittens. She'd knitted them last year. She always felt a little guilty about wearing them, because they were a darling baby blue color and soft as a baby's cheek. She was never sure if there was sin in soft yarn and baby blue mittens. None of the other girls wore baby blue mittens, but Rosie Herschberger could occasionally be seen in cherry red ones.

Her heart skipped a beat at the prospect of possibly encountering Felty Helmuth on her errand. That irresistible smile of his just might cheer her up today, and if she was sneaky, she would be able to decide for herself if he had a fake arm or not.

Ten pounds heavier, Anna trundled to the back door, along the way passing Mammi, who was doing her best to rescue Anna's pie. Anna swallowed hard and mourned the loss. By the time Mammi was done with it, it would taste like a normal, everyday apple pie. Anna had been hoping to slip in some cheddar cheese or raisins to give it a little pep. Everything was better with raisins.

"If you see Felty Helmuth, stay far away from him. No good will come of having anything to do with a soldier."

Anna didn't respond to that. She couldn't very well find out about Felty's arm if she stayed away. The door squealed loudly when Anna opened it. Dat had asked Isaac to oil it a week ago. "Goodbye, Mammi." *If I freeze to death, at least your pie will turn out.*

"Have a *gute* walk," Mammi said, with a tinge of guilt in her tone, almost as if she felt bad for banishing Anna to the frozen outdoors. *Ach*, *vell*, maybe she felt bad, but not bad enough to call Anna back.

Anna strolled along the edge of the road, stomping what little snow there was on the ground with her boots and kicking at rocks that sometimes turned out to be embedded in the blacktop. She nearly broke her ankle on one of those.

She just couldn't imagine that Felty had a fake arm, but maybe he had a tattoo. Elmer said lots of soldiers and sailors had gotten tattoos in the last war. Sort of a souvenir, he had said. What kind of tattoo would Felty have been likely to get? She could see him getting a heart with his sweetheart's name written in the middle or a cute little puppy with sad eyes. Felty loved animals, or at least he had before he left for the war.

Did Felty have a sweetheart? Maybe a Korean girl or a nurse? Anna frowned. She didn't like the thought of Felty having a girlfriend.

There were three farms between Anna's house and the

Helmuths', but the Helmuths were their nearest Amish neighbors. Not a soul passed Anna on the road in either a car or a buggy. Everybody was at home, staying warm and getting ready for Thanksgiving. The stillness made Anna feel a little lonely.

The Helmuths owned a dairy that grew bigger every year. Along with a huge barn where they milked the cows, there were four other long, narrow buildings for the cattle to shelter in during the winter. Anna had been inside the barn once, and it was as clean and organized as her *mammi*'s kitchen. The white clapboard house stood on a little hill overlooking the road, and Anna loved the green shutters at every window. There was generous room on the porch, where two rocking chairs sat surveying the weather, and a cute little birdhouse was nailed to a post in the front yard. Everything about the house said, *Welcome. Come and sit awhile.*

Anna clomped up the stairs and knocked. Her heart jumped up and started running a race when Felty answered the door, looking more handsome and more like an Amish boy than he had last week. His short dark hair was wet, as if he'd just taken a bath, and he wore a traditional Amish-style cream-colored shirt with suspenders and black trousers.

Felty practically exploded into a smile, like one of those fireworks they set off on the Fourth of July. "Hey bean!" he said.

Anna hesitated before stuttering on her reply. "Um, I . . . uh, my name is Anna, remember? Not Bean."

Felty widened his eyes and laughed until he couldn't breathe. It got a little uncomfortable for Anna, standing on the porch while Felty tried to get control of himself.

He attempted to speak, but until he stopped laughing, she wasn't going to be able to understand him. Should she be offended that he was laughing at her or alarmed that he was laughing for no apparent reason at all? Had Korea made him crazy in the head?

He finally wound down. Sighing loudly, he wiped his eyes and smiled wider. "*Ach*, Anna, I'm sorry. I was just so happy to see you, and I said the first thing that popped into my head. 'Hey bean' means 'hello.' It's what the *Englisch* teenagers say to one another. I'm afraid I spent too much time with *Englischers* in the barracks."

Anna frowned and then decided it was okay to smile. He meant no offense, and he had said he was happy to see her. How could she be cross about that? In truth, she found it almost impossible to catch her breath. What was it about his smile that made her heart gallop like a runaway horse and her palms sweat even on a chilly day in November? She'd never experienced anything like it before.

Anna tried to gather her wits. She was here to get pans and to peek at Felty's arm. And maybe find out if he had a tattoo, but they might have to know each other better before she dared asked anything so private. "Did you learn a lot of strange phrases like that? It almost sounds like a different language."

His gaze was glued to her face, as if he feared she'd disappear if he looked away. "*Ach*, they say all sorts of things. They think bees have knees, and they say 'He's got it made in the shade' when they think someone has an easy life. My favorite is 'party pooper,' which means a person you don't want to invite to parties and such."

Anna scrunched her lips to one side of her face. "I

don't blame them. I wouldn't want someone pooping at my party."

Felty chuckled. "A lot of their phrases make sense, in a confusing sort of way." He stared at her for a few seconds before snapping out of his thoughts and opening the door wider. "What am I thinking, leaving you out on the cold porch? Please, *cum reu*. My *mamm* is making every food imaginable for Thanksgiving, and my *dat* is in the barn taking measurements. We just finished milking."

Anna stepped into the house and met with a wall of aromas that made her mouth water. "*Ach*," she said. "It smells *wunderbarr* in here, like rolls and gingerbread and chicken soup." This was what Anna wanted her house to smell like every day. How would she learn how to do it if Mammi wouldn't let her practice? Felty startled her when he slid his arm around her shoulders, until she realized he was helping her off with her cape. Why was she so jumpy? "You don't need to do that. I'm not going to be here long. I have a list I need to show your *mamm*."

"You have a list? We'd better get to it, then."

He led Anna into the kitchen, where Edna Helmuth was kneading dough. She wore a cheery yellow apron and had a spot of flour on her cheek. Edna's appearance always shocked Anna nowadays. Edna had changed dramatically in the last year or two. She used to be bright and merry, with more energy than most women half her age. Her laugh was an invitation to laugh with her, her smile a permanent fixture on her face. Now she was withdrawn and gloomy and too skinny for a woman who used to love to eat.

Edna looked up from her dough and gave Anna a half-hearted smile, the kind mothers of eligible boys often gave her, as if to say, *You're not who I'd choose for my son, but you're welcome in my house. Ach, vell*, it was better than nothing. "Anna Yoder. What brings you here today of all days? It wonders me if you shouldn't be home preparing Thanksgiving dinner."

"My *mammi* sent me for a few things. She's at our house helping with the food. But she says if you can't spare your pans, she can make do."

Edna nodded thoughtfully. "Your *mammi* is helping you today? I'm *froh* to hear it."

"She's going to let me do the turkey." That wasn't a lie. Anna hadn't even asked Mammi yet. Maybe Mammi would be grateful to let Anna take over the turkey. She had so many other things to do.

Edna sprinkled more flour on her counter. "It's best to leave the turkey to your *mammi*. There's no better cook in all of Wisconsin. You could learn many things from her."

Anna slumped her shoulders. "*Jah*, of course."

Felty folded his arms and leaned against the doorjamb. "How are you planning on doing the turkey this year? Four years ago the Porters set their shed on fire when they tried to fry a turkey in vegetable oil."

Anna giggled. "I remember. Mrs. Porter wouldn't speak to her husband for three months." She glanced at Edna and wiped the smile off her face. Was it a sin to laugh about someone's shed fire? She pulled Mammi's list out of her pocket and handed it to Edna. "I'm . . . I'm going to make a brine."

Felty suddenly seemed overly fascinated with the turkey-baking process. "How do you do that?"

"Well, you make a solution of salt and water and soak the turkey in it overnight. You can also put juniper berries, orange peels, or bay leaves in the salt water to give the turkey some flavor. I think I might try some rosemary and mint leaves I grew in our garden this summer."

"It sounds *appeditlich*," Felty said.

Edna drew her brows together. "Be sure to consult your *mammi* yet. Rosemary and juniper berries do not go together. And I can't see as a mint-flavored turkey would taste *gute* at all." She read Mammi's list. "I'm afraid I don't have a Bundt cake pan, but she is welcome to borrow my stockpot and a cookie sheet."

"*Denki* very much," Anna said. "I'm sure she can find something else to use for a cranberry mold."

"A cranberry mold?" Edna opened a cupboard next to her icebox. "I don't have a Bundt pan, but I have a cranberry mold." She pointed to the top shelf. "Felty, reach that for me, will you?"

Felty pulled the mold off the shelf and handed it to his *mamm*. Edna patted Felty on the cheek. "One of the many reasons I like having you around." She pulled a cookie sheet from a long, narrow cupboard and a stockpot from a shelf near the cookstove. "Tell your *mammi* to keep these as long as she needs them. I admire her for her patience." She stacked the mold and the stockpot on the cookie sheet and handed them to Anna. "There you go. And Happy Thanksgiving."

Felty practically tripped over his feet to take the cookie sheet from Anna. "I'll carry these to your buggy for you."

Anna was momentarily distracted by his smile. "That's very nice of you." *Ach, du lieva.* She didn't have a buggy. "But . . . you don't need to do that. I walked."

This news seemed to make Felty wildly happy. "*Wunderbarr.* I'll carry these home for you."

"No need. It's a long way."

Edna nodded. "You have plenty to do here at home."

Anna should have thought this through better. Walking here hadn't been a problem, but lugging all those pans home was going to be a chore. She should have brought a wagon. Or a *bruder*.

Felty smiled cheerfully at his *mamm* and kissed her on the forehead. "I will do every chore double-time when I get back."

"What is double-time?" Anna asked.

"It means twice as fast. In the army, if they thought we were being lazy, they'd make us march around the field double time." He looked at his *mamm*, and his smile faltered. "I can't let her carry these things by herself. I wouldn't be any kind of man."

Edna sighed. "Of course you can't." She pushed him away. "Go, then. And hurry back. I need you to go to Mary Zook's and fetch me some eggs."

Felty set the pans on the table and ran out of the kitchen. He was soon back with a coat, a straw hat, and some black mittens. What he needed was a scarf to keep his neck warm. He picked up the cookie sheet and gave Anna a bright smile. "Ready?"

Anna couldn't do anything but nod. He'd stolen her breath again.

She opened and closed the front door for him, and he followed her down the porch steps. "Mary Zook has eggs?" she said, because it seemed a little suspicious that Edna wanted Felty to go to Mary Zook's house when Mary didn't have chickens *or* a boyfriend.

Felty shrugged. "I suppose. It's the first I've heard of it."

"You really don't have to carry these for me. I'll manage."

"Of course I do. They're heavy. And think of all the things we can talk about for two whole miles."

Anna furrowed her brow. "Like what?"

He laughed. "I don't know. Anything you want to talk about."

"What do *you* want to talk about?"

"You," he said, grinning from ear to ear.

She tilted her head toward him. "What did you say?"

"I want to talk about you. I find you very interesting."

Anna rolled her eyes. "Now you're teasing me. I'm not interesting at all."

"Of course you are. You know how to brine a turkey, spell 'Mississippi,' and do fractions in your head."

Anna stopped walking and put her hands on her hips. He stopped too. "That's something that doesn't make sense. How do you know all that about me? We were three years apart in school."

For the first time since he'd been back, he seemed a little unsure of himself, maybe a little shy. "I . . . I notice things. It was hard not to notice how you beat me in the spelling bee. With 'mustache,' no less."

Anna raised her eyebrows. "You remember the word?"

"I'm strange that way, I guess."

She nodded. "I guess so." Since he claimed he was willing to talk about anything, she figured she should strike while the iron was hot. "There is something I want to know."

He winked at her. "Anything."

Boys should not wink at girls, especially when they were walking in the snow and likely to fall over from light-headedness. "You don't have any fake arms, do you? I know your legs are real, but then I got to thinking that maybe it was your arm that exploded. I mean, it doesn't look like your arms are fake, but I wasn't sure, because the doctors can do some amazing things these days."

One side of Felty's mouth curled upward. "My arms are as real as yours, and once I carry these pans to your house, I'll let you test them."

Hot embarrassment traveled up Anna's neck. She really shouldn't have touched Felty's legs. "That won't be necessary. If you had a fake arm, you wouldn't be able to carry those pans."

"That's probably true."

"I should have known better than to listen to the gossip."

He glanced at her. "Everybody gossips, especially the Amish. We like to stick our noses in everybody's business, and what else are we going to do for entertainment? We don't have televisions."

Anna smiled. "That makes me feel better. We heard a lot of things about you."

He nodded. "You heard I was dead."

"I guess that was just a rumor."

"I guess it was."

She glanced at him out of the corner of her eye. His smile was so wide, she could have counted all his teeth if she'd been looking at him straight on. "I mean, I don't *guess* it was a rumor. It was for sure and certain a rumor."

"What other rumors did you hear?"

Anna thought about that for a minute. "Well, I heard that you lost your leg. Dat heard that you lost your arm. We heard you shot a lot of people."

Felty slowed considerably, which in one way was nice, because Anna was having a hard time keeping up with his long legs, but in another way was not so nice, because his countenance fell and he wouldn't look at her. She'd hurt his feelings or made him angry or said something that shouldn't have been said.

Her stomach felt like a lump of coal. "I'm sorry. It's none of my business what you did in the war." Unexpected moisture pooled in her eyes, and a single tear slipped down her cheek. *Ach*, she'd stirred up a painful memory and ruined a perfectly *wunderbarr* afternoon. "I'm truly sorry, Felty." She was so ashamed, she couldn't even lift her gaze to his face.

To her surprise, Felty stopped and set the cookie sheet down in the snow. He stepped in front of her and placed his hands on her shoulders. "Anna, look at me."

"I can't right now."

A soft chuckle came from deep in his throat. "Okay. You don't have to look at me, but, Anna, there's no need to apologize. For anything. I went to war. I carried a gun, and I used it. I did what I had to do to protect my fellow soldiers. Some of the memories are very painful for me, but they are part of who I am. They are part of the story Gotte is writing of my life. I wouldn't erase those pages even if I could."

"You wouldn't?" she squeaked. It wasn't her normal voice, but at least she could speak.

"You can ask me anything you want about the war. I might not be able to talk about it just yet, but questions never hurt anybody. I'd rather you ask me hard questions instead of tiptoeing around the truth like Dat does or, worse, pretending it never happened, like Mamm." Pain traveled across his face. "It hurt Mamm even more than it hurt me."

"*Ach*, okay then. I'm sorry"—he held up his hand to stop her from apologizing again. She made a face at him and slapped his hand down. "I'm still sorry, but I'm *froh* the questions don't hurt you."

Felty winced. "*Ach*, they hurt plenty, but not because you ask them. They hurt because the memories are fresh and painful, but how does a wound heal unless you get it out into the sunlight and give it some air?" He brushed his mitten lightly down the side of her face. "I hate seeing you upset. You should always be smiling."

She froze with her eyes on his face. "I hate seeing you upset. You've had enough trouble to last a lifetime."

"I wish that were true. Troubles aren't measured out to each person equally. They're measured out by Gotte according to what we need to learn."

Anna grinned. "Gotte does it by feel! Like baking."

He laughed. "I suppose that's so."

"All *gute* bakers do it by feel."

"I didn't know that," he said.

Anna swallowed hard. Even though he'd told her she could ask him anything, her next question was sort of personal, but if she didn't ask it now, she may never get the chance. "It wonders me. Did you get a tattoo?"

He didn't seem offended by the question. "Is that one of the rumors?"

"*Nae*, but Elmer says that sometimes men get tattoos when they go fight in the war, sort of like when the Amish men grow beards. They all match."

He fingered the whiskers on his chin. "Do they?"

"That's what Elmer says."

"I'm not ready to tell you if I have a tattoo or not."

"Why?" Anna could understand his not wanting to talk about fighting in the war, but the tattoo thing didn't seem all that important.

His eyes danced. "I want you to think I'm a little bit mysterious."

"*Ach*, you're plenty mysterious. You let strange girls touch your legs, you have an exciting scar on your cheek, and you are the only boy I know who owns an olive green duffel bag with your name on it. Besides, you fought in a war but don't want to talk about it. That's so mysterious, I think I'm going to faint."

He smiled. "I guess I don't need to worry, then."

"Worry about what?"

"Impressing you."

Anna drew her brows together. "*Ach*, why would you want to impress me? Mostly nobody cares what I think."

"I don't know about anybody else, but I find you fascinating in every way."

Anna rolled her eyes. "You're teasing me again."

"I am not." He raised his hand to the air. "Honest truth."

She shook her finger at him, but it didn't really have much impact, because it was inside her mitten. "Swear not at all."

He drew an X across his lips. "I wouldn't dare." He bent and picked up the cookie sheet, the stockpot, and the cranberry mold. "So, your *mammi* is helping you fix Thanksgiving dinner?"

Anna sighed and started walking in the direction of her doom. "*Ach*, mostly I'm helping her."

"That's nice of you."

"I'm helping her by staying out of the way. Why do you think she sent me to your house on foot? She knew I'd be gone over an hour."

Anna felt her face get warm under his steady gaze. "Your *mammi* likes to do it her own way?"

"And she doesn't like the way I do it. And she's right. I'm a terrible cook."

Felty's mouth fell open. "A terrible cook? I've never eaten anything of yours at a fellowship supper that I haven't loved. Your cinnamon rolls are like candy. Your rice is cooked just the way I like it. I remember one time you made red Jell-O with little hot dog slices. It was a genius combination."

Anna grimaced. "That was the day they asked me not to bring anything to a fellowship supper again. They said it was because they always had too many leftovers, but it was really because they hated everything I made."

"Sounds like nobody has a sense of adventure when it comes to food."

Anna nodded vigorously, relieved that there was someone who felt the way she did. "I agree. Who cares about boring Jell-O with pineapple or whipped cream? Food should be more exciting than that. I know I should be grateful that Mammi is saving Thanksgiving, but I'm disappointed that I won't get to try out my new recipes. I just think cheesy asparagus casserole would be so beautiful next to the mashed potatoes and the cranberry mold. The colors would be breathtaking."

"They'd be very pretty on the table."

Anna kicked at some snow in her path. "I haven't even asked Mammi about the turkey. She'll make that face she always makes and tell me to go chop some wood or clean a toilet. But I really want to try a turkey soaked in brine. My mouth waters just thinking about it. The only time we have turkey is Thanksgiving. I won't get another chance to make it until next year, and that's only if Mammi decides to go to Ohio for the holiday."

"That's too bad, because turkey soaked in brine sounds like about the best food in the whole world, next to cheesy asparagus casserole."

Out of the corner of her eye, Anna focused on his expression. It didn't look like he was teasing. Had she finally found someone who shared her love of new and exciting food? Her heart raced at the possibilities. It probably didn't matter, because even though she loved trying out new recipes and experimenting with raisins and asparagus, nobody seemed to particularly like what she made, except her.

A canary yellow car whizzed past them, going much faster than was allowed on the backcountry road. "*Ach, du lieva,*" Felty shouted. "Did you see that?"

"*Jah.* He was going too fast."

"But did you see his license plate?" he said breathlessly.

"Um. *Nae.* Should I have?"

Again Felty set the cookie sheet down in the snow, took off his mittens, and pulled a small spiral-bound notebook and short pencil from his pants pocket. "That was Tennessee. I can't believe my luck."

"I don't believe in luck," Anna said. The Amish as a general rule didn't believe in luck. "But Dawdi Miller wishes me good luck whenever I leave his house, so I guess it's okay."

Felty's teeth were white and straight. She loved it when

he smiled. "You're right. Just another bad habit I picked up in the army. I know where my real blessings come from." He made a mark in his notebook. "Only three more to go."

"Three more what?"

"States. When I got on the bus in San Francisco, I started the license plate game."

"What's the license plate game?"

Felty showed Anna his notebook. The names of the states were written in tidy, slanted handwriting. "I wrote down all the states, and when I see one on a license plate, I cross it off my list. I've found forty-five of the forty-eight states so far."

"How do you even know the names of all the states?" Anna said. "That's a long list. I always remember Wisconsin because we live here, and Ohio and Pennsylvania because I have some cousins. And Michigan is the next state over, though I've never been there."

"A woman on the bus helped me—or I should say, her daughter helped me. She had just memorized all the states for a school assignment."

"*Ach*, *du lieva*, and you found forty-five between San Francisco and here?"

Felty peered at his list. "Well, forty-four. I just saw Tennessee." He stuffed the notepad back into his pocket. "I'm trying to find all forty-eight before Christmas, but I don't know that I will. This isn't exactly a place people come for a visit, especially in the winter, and the three I have left are quite rare."

"What are they?" Anna asked.

"West Virginia, Mississippi, and New Hampshire."

"Like as not you'll find more in a big town like Shawano."

Felty shook his head. "Anna, some of the big cities I've seen would make your head spin. San Francisco has buildings so tall, you can't even see the sky."

"Did you like San Francisco?"

"*Nae*, I felt hemmed in, like being in a room with no door. I prefer the sky and the fresh air and friendly faces. In San Francisco, everybody is a stranger. People don't even smile when you pass them on the street." The lines around his eyes etched themselves deeper into his face. "Bonduel has always been home for me, but there are people in the *gmayna* who will have trouble forgiving me."

"You should have heard the sermons. For weeks after you left, the ministers preached the evils of violence and warned us of the snares of Satan. It wonders me if they didn't want other boys following your example, though there were only three in the district who were even the right age to join." She winced. Not a week ago, she'd been determined to stay away from Felty Helmuth, and now here she was, feeling sorry for his predicament. Felty had gotten himself into this mess, but how many times had she gotten herself into trouble or nearly burned down the house or added too much sugar to the pie? If she wanted mercy from Gotte, then she should extend mercy to everyone else. *Blessed are the merciful, for they shall obtain mercy.*

But what about her chances of finding a husband if she was Felty's friend? Would people avoid her if she was nice to him? She snorted out loud. She was fooling herself. People avoided her already.

Felty eyed her as if he wasn't quite certain what sound had come out of her mouth. Anna frowned. "I'm sorry. I shouldn't have said that."

He curled one side of his mouth. "You mean the snorting?"

She cuffed him on the shoulder and almost made him drop the cookie sheet. "Not the snorting. I just wanted to be honest with you about what people are saying."

Felty smiled sadly. "I expected it. The deacon came to visit me right before I left. He gave me a stern warning that the church might not welcome me back."

She lowered her eyes. "My *dat* and *mammi* both told me to stay away from you."

He pressed his lips together and stared into the distance. "Oh. I see."

She felt horrible saying it, but there was no use pretending people didn't think otherwise. "My *mammi* doesn't like that you went to war."

"And your *dat*?"

Anna huffed out a breath to hide her embarrassment. "*Ach*, he doesn't . . . it doesn't matter."

"Was it that bad, what he said about me?"

"*Nae,*" Anna protested. "Of course not." Her face got warmer and warmer. She must be red as a beet by now. "*Ach*, *vell*, maybe it was bad. He thinks too highly of me."

"I don't think it's possible for anyone to think too highly of you."

Anna ignored the compliment, even though her face would surely burst into flames any minute. "My *dat* thinks you're not *gute* enough for me."

"Because I was a soldier?"

"Because he doesn't think anyone is *gute* enough for me, and because you were a soldier."

Felty slumped his shoulders in mock dejection. "Your *dat* is right, but I was hoping you wouldn't figure that out."

Anna grunted. He was just trying to make her feel better. "The whole district knows I'm not *gute* enough for anybody. I've told Dat time and time again, I'm going to be an old maid. My *dat* has never been able to see clearly where I am concerned."

"*Ach*, Anna, your *dat* sees well enough. You are the prettiest, smartest, kindest girl in the whole district. In the whole state of Wisconsin—and that includes all the *Englisch* girls too."

Anna nudged his arm as hard as she dared without making him drop the pans. "I am not."

"You are too," he said, in that whiny voice children use on the playground when they argue with one another.

She tried not to take pleasure in what he said. He'd been gone for two years. He didn't know anything. "*Die youngie* call me a bookworm behind my back. They laugh about my cooking and quilting in front of my back, and Mark Hostetler once stole my copy of *The Three Musketeers* and made paper airplanes out of half the pages."

Felty narrowed his eyes. "That's a lot of paper airplanes. He should be ashamed of himself."

"*Jah*, especially since planes are against the *Ordnung*," Anna said.

Felty fell silent for a few minutes. Had she talked him into thinking about her the way everyone else thought? The crunch of the snow beneath their boots was deafening.

"Mark Hostetler always did *dumm* things to try to impress the girls."

Anna sighed. "I don't think he was trying to impress me. For sure and certain I wasn't impressed."

Felty's lips twitched with the hint of a grin. "I suppose you have to honor your *fater*."

An unexpected twinge of disappointment twisted in Anna's stomach. She didn't know why she would feel that way. What was Felty Helmuth to her but a nice neighbor who helped her carry pans and let her touch his legs? She certainly wasn't interested in any sort of relationship with him, friendship or otherwise. Besides, Dat disapproved, and like Felty said, she should honor her *fater*'s wishes.

Felty suddenly veered to the right and walked down the center of the road. "How far away do you think is *gute*?"

"*Gute* for what?"

He seemed on the verge of bursting into laughter. "Your *dat* told you to stay away from me. How far away do you think you have to stay and still be obedient? Six feet? Seven feet? Is two feet *gute* enough?" He slid closer and put an arm's length between them. "Personally, I like five or six inches."

Anna giggled. "He didn't say, but putting a measurement to it seems more like the letter than the spirit of the law."

"It depends on the law you're talking about. 'Honor your *fater* and *mater*' has more wiggle room than the commandment to not eat bacon."

Anna frowned down to her toes. "We're not supposed to eat bacon?"

He chuckled. "That is an ancient Old Testament law. I'm just saying it's easier to define and keep some commandments than others."

Anna caught her breath and burst into a smile. "Not to change the subject, but cheesy asparagus casserole with bacon sounds like just about the most heavenly dish in the whole world."

"*Jah*, it does."

She frowned and eyed him suspiciously. "You distracted me with talk of bacon."

"Everything is better with bacon."

"And raisins." She shot another stink eye his way. "Maybe I should ask Dat to clarify how many feet. Or maybe I should use my own best judgment. Dat is worried that you're not *gute* enough and I'll break your heart and then we'll all feel bad about it. But since no one will ever fall in love with me, I won't break anybody's heart. It seems a needless rule." Felty gazed at her with an unreadable expression. Did he think she was trying to sidestep the Ten Commandments? *Ach*, she always said the wrong thing. "Just to be clear, I don't believe in breaking any commandments."

This time, the silence lasted for about three years. What was he thinking? Did he disapprove of her love of bacon? Was he wondering how many commandments she had broken? Was he measuring the inches between them? They were not an eighth of a mile from her house, and they hadn't yet decided how far away to stay from each other. "Anna," he finally said, "I don't want to make anything harder for you, especially between you and your *dat*."

"*Ach*, things between Dat and me aren't hard. Dat doesn't always see straight when it comes to me, but I never doubt his love. And Elmer watches out for me. He's always making sure Isaac doesn't get too big for his britches."

Felty's smile was warm and genuine. "Elmer is a *gute* sort. I'm wonderful glad and grateful he watches out for you."

Something about the way he looked at her made Anna feel like she was made of bubbles. She wouldn't have been surprised if she floated off the ground. Unfortunately, all the bubbles popped when they approached the house and she saw Mammi standing on the front porch with her hands propped on her hips. Had Anna taken too long or not long enough? Or maybe it was the sight of Felty that Mammi found irritating.

Anna held out her hands. "*Denki* for walking me home. I will carry everything from here."

Felty glanced at Mammi. "If you think it's best."

Anna nodded. Mammi was already in a sour mood, and the sight of a soldier less than six feet away from her granddaughter couldn't have been a happy one. Felty handed her the pans, and his coat sleeve brushed against her exposed wrist. The touch sent a zing of electricity up Anna's arm. *Ach, du lieva.* Maybe six feet was a *gute* rule from now on. She'd be walking around in a daze for the rest of the day.

He turned so his back was to Mammi and winked at Anna. "I hope you get to brine your turkey," he whispered.

She managed to breathe almost normally, even though that wink hit her right between the eyes. "I hope you get your six inches."

His eyes lit up with surprise. "You do?"

Her heart pounded against her chest. "It's a lot easier than bringing a six-foot pole to singings."

He laughed. "That's what I like about you, Anna. Always so practical."

Chapter 5

Anna stood up and sighed, glad to be rid of that uncomfortable bench. They spent almost three hours in church every other week. Would it be so hard to set up chairs instead of benches, especially for the old ladies? It was just another question Anna would never ask and nobody would ever answer. Uncomfortable seating at church wasn't in the *Ordnung* anywhere, but it was one of those traditions that used to have some meaning but now just kept going because nobody ever thought of changing it. Probably the benches had less to do with austerity and religious devotion and more to do with the fact that the *mamms* in the *gmayna* wanted their children to have *gute* posture. No slouching for three hours was a *gute* way to strengthen your back muscles.

Anna glanced at Felty for about the thousandth time this morning. He had that same pleasant, serene look on his face he'd worn all through the sermons and songs and prayers, which couldn't have been easy. Every sermon was obviously meant for Felty and any other boy in the *gmayna* who might have gotten the wicked notion to fight in a war. Anna didn't know how Felty stood it. David

Hostetler's sermon was nearly an hour long, and he must have read every scripture in the Bible with the word *kill* in it—as in *Thou shalt not*. There was even mention of killing the fatted calf, which to Anna didn't seem to have anything to do with his topic.

By the time the service was over, Anna had stopped listening and started feeling quite indignant for Felty. He knew what he'd done was wrong. Why did they have to keep hitting him over the head with it? Their badgering gave new meaning to the phrase *beating a dead horse*. She should respect her elders, for sure and certain, but maybe it was possible to respect someone and still feel irritated by their actions.

Jah. That was the answer. She felt respectfully irritated and sorrier than ever for Felty. After the last prayer, the men and boys rearranged and stacked the benches in preparation for fellowship supper. Felty attempted to help, but no one would lift a bench if Felty had hold of the other end. The boys near Felty's age completely ignored him, and the men weren't much better. Were they all following the six-feet rule? And here Anna had thought Felty had made that up as a joke.

Felty ended up leaning against the wall with his arms folded, watching the others set up tables, still with that pleasant look on his face, as if he hadn't a care in the world. As if everybody weren't ignoring him or casting hostile glances his way.

Anna's heart hurt like a bruise. Felty had made a wrong choice. Weren't they supposed to love the sinner, like the father of the prodigal son? But what if Felty had killed people? Was he beyond Gotte's forgiveness? Was Anna risking Gotte's displeasure by feeling sorry for Felty?

Sorry, indignant, and irritated.

Anna took a shaky breath as Elmer strolled up to Felty and held out his hand. Felty's eyes flashed with surprise before he reached out and shook Elmer's hand. Anna couldn't hear what they said, but Elmer motioned for Felty to help him with one of the benches. Felty jumped into action as if Elmer had offered him a whole pie for dessert. Anna couldn't contain a smile. How could Gotte be displeased with Elmer's kindness?

Anna's heart melted into a puddle on the floor before she remembered that she should be helping with the food. She hurried into the kitchen to retrieve her asparagus casserole. Someone was bound to be annoyed with her for bringing food, but Mammi had taken over Thanksgiving, and Anna hadn't gotten a chance to make cheesy asparagus casserole with bacon. She couldn't wait to see the looks on people's faces at the taste combination of raisins, bacon, and asparagus. It was going to be *appeditlich*. She especially wanted Felty to taste it. The bacon had sort of been his idea, and she wanted to give him proper credit.

The kitchen was crowded with women slicing bread, stirring church spread, and putting food on serving platters. Anna slid an oven mitt onto her hand and opened the cookstove's warming oven. Her casserole had been sitting in there for almost three hours, and a crusty brown layer of cheese had formed over the top of the casserole. Lord willing, it wouldn't be dry or crunchy. Maybe she should have put a lid on it.

Anna pulled out the casserole and followed Rosie Herschberger into the great room. Rosie passed her platter of bread down the first table filled with boys.

Anna's heart pounded an uneven rhythm. Felty sat at the very end of the row across from Elmer. Would there be any asparagus casserole left by the time her casserole got to him?

Isaac was on the end closest to her. He smiled and blushed as he took a piece of bread from Rosie Herschberger's platter. Anna rolled her eyes. Rosie was four years older than Isaac, but that didn't matter to him. Rosie was pretty and sweet, and every boy over twelve years old in the *gmayna* had a crush on her.

Without taking his gaze from Rosie, Isaac passed the platter on down the row. Anna stepped up next to Isaac and held out her casserole. "It has bacon in it," she said, maybe a little too sure of herself.

She shouldn't have let her pride get the better of her. Isaac sniffed at the casserole, made a face, and shook his head. "It looks like a cow pie."

Anna frowned. "Just try it. You're going to love it."

"Not likely," Isaac said. "I'm not *that* hungry."

Mark Hostetler, sitting next to him, snickered. "Another one of your kitchen creations, Anna? No thank you."

Anna wasn't discouraged. Isaac thought he was so clever, but he was really just a *dumm* teenage boy, and everybody knew Mark didn't have a lick of sense. She looked down her nose at Isaac and Mark. "You'll wish you'd tried it when everybody raves about how *gute* it is."

Rosie stood staring at Anna as if she felt sorry for her, or as if she just couldn't understand her. Rosie was pretty, tall, and quite concerned about being the most righteous girl in the *gmayna*. She was nice enough, but she certainly wasn't interested in being friends with Anna. Anna was a short, clunky bookworm who liked to knit. Rosie had the prettiest friends, the smallest quilting stitches, and the best homemade bread in the district.

Warmth spread up her face clear to the top of her head. She didn't know why it mattered, but she craved Rosie's approval. She craved everyone's approval. She just wasn't quite sure how to get it. Surely the bacon would help. "Rosie, would you like a taste of my cheesy asparagus casserole with bacon?"

Rosie's serene expression faltered, as if she'd just accidentally swallowed a gnat. "Um, why don't you serve the boys, and if there's any left over, I'll try some."

Anna nodded, hoping against hope that there wouldn't be any left over for Rosie to try. If it all got eaten, Rosie and Isaac and Mark would have to admit that they should have taken some before it got gobbled up. Anna moved down the row to Eli and Andy Mast. "Would you like to try my bacon, cheese, and asparagus casserole?" Mentioning the bacon first might get them to try it.

Eli shook his head. "*Nae*, *denki*, Anna. I'm going to be full after I eat Rosie's bread."

Anna glanced over her shoulder. Rosie smiled and giggled. "*Denki*, Eli. You know I like making sure the boys have enough to eat."

Andy cleared his throat. "I don't like bacon, Anna. But *denki* anyway."

He didn't like bacon? What kind of a monster was he? *Ach*, *vell*, at least the two *bruderen* had been polite in their refusals. She moved on. "Joseph, what about you?"

Joseph looked into her dish and grimaced. "I don't want a stomachache like the last time."

Crist also shook his head as Anna passed. She walked slower and slower as a ten-pound boulder settled in her stomach. She couldn't swallow for the lump in her throat. She had been so excited about the bacon and cheese, but no one even wanted a taste. Not even bacon could tempt them to try a little. No one would ever think of her as anything but a bad cook and a strange girl who just didn't and couldn't fit in.

"I want to try some. It looks *appeditlich*."

Anna looked up. Felty gave her an open smile, as if he'd been waiting patiently for his turn at the end of the table.

Joseph partially covered his mouth with his hand. "Look at the soldier trying to be nice," he mumbled to Andy.

"Don't be mean, Joseph," Rosie said, though she glanced at Felty, clasped her hands together, and sniffed into the air as if she really didn't even want to look at him.

Anna wouldn't have cared if Felty had been wearing his uniform and carrying a gun. He wanted a taste of her casserole, and her embarrassment crumbled like bleu cheese. Anna blinked away the threatening tears and smiled, hoping Felty hadn't noticed her distress. Mammi would say she was being proud, but Anna so desperately wanted someone to enjoy her cooking. She took so much pleasure in it, and she loved the thought of bringing pleasure to others.

She held out the dish to Felty, and his smile could have melted all the snow in the county. He didn't have another thing on his plate, not even a slice of Rosie's delectable homemade bread. Had he been waiting for Anna's casserole? He grabbed the serving spoon and chipped away at the brown crust on top. "How much am I allowed to have?" he asked. "It would be selfish to take it all."

Anna glanced down the table. "Have as much as you want. The other boys don't seem to be interested." That was a delicate way of saying that nobody would eat it even if she paid them.

Felty craned his neck to look down the row. "You are all missing out. Anna is the best cook in Bonduel."

Behind her, Anna heard Rosie sniff, louder this time. She was getting huffy, but it wasn't Anna's fault that Felty preferred her cooking over Rosie's.

Isaac and Mark laughed out loud. Joseph smirked in Felty's direction, then turned his body so neither Felty nor Anna was in his peripheral vision. The other boys pretended they hadn't heard Felty, which was what they had been doing all day—completely ignoring him.

Felty finally broke through the casserole crust and scooped a large helping of casserole onto his plate. The cheese was a little gloppy, and the asparagus looked slightly limp, but steam rose from the dish, and the smell was heavenly. Everybody would be able to smell the bacon. Surely they were starting to regret not taking any casserole for themselves.

Felty took three big scoops, which turned out to be about half of Anna's casserole. He set the spoon back in the dish, picked up his fork, and skewered a piece of asparagus with a bit of bacon. Anna held her breath as he slid it into his mouth. He sighed, closed his eyes, and chewed slowly. "*Ach*, Anna. This is heavenly. I haven't tasted anything this *appeditlich* for a very long time." He picked up his spoon and scooped up some of the cheesy sauce that had taken over his plate. It was a little runnier than Anna had wanted, but the consistency didn't seem to matter to Felty. He popped the end of the spoon into his mouth. "*Ach*, this is so *gute*. Even better than my *mamm*'s rolls." He winked at her. "But don't tell my *mamm*. I wouldn't want to hurt her feelings."

"Of course not," Anna said, breathlessly giddy. Surely her face was glowing like a lantern. She peered down the row of boys. None of them was looking at her or Felty. Hadn't they just heard his praise of her casserole? Wouldn't they at least want to try some?

Apparently not. Isaac and Mark were taking turns shoving each other, and most of the other boys were intently studying the food on their plates. Anna turned around to offer some casserole to Rosie, but Rosie had moved to another table with her platter of bread. Or escaped, as the case may have been.

Anna tried not to let *die youngie* ruin her happiness. Felty liked her casserole. She would be greedy to wish for more. Besides, Felty had been all over the world and eaten many different kinds of foods. If he liked her casserole, she must not be that bad of a cook.

She looked across the room at the other tables. No one else was likely to want any of her casserole, and she decided not to embarrass herself in the effort to get them to taste it. It was enough that Felty enjoyed her asparagus casserole.

Someone cleared his throat. "Anna, you forgot me."

She turned and grinned. She'd completely overlooked Elmer sitting across from Felty. Elmer was thoughtful and kind and ate everything she cooked. He held out his plate, and Anna gave him a scoop of casserole. It wasn't a very big scoop, because, at the rate Felty was eating, she'd need to save the rest for him. Her heart beat a little faster. It was clear that Felty genuinely liked it. She'd never been so grateful for bacon.

Elmer picked up his spoon. "*Denki*, Anna." He tore off a chunk of Rosie's bread and used it to soak up the cheese sauce from his plate, then popped the bread into his mouth. "Mmm. You can taste the bacon. And the raisins."

Anna smiled hesitantly. "I thought the raisins would add a little tangy sweetness."

Felty took another bite and nodded. "Most cooks don't really understand how important tangy sweetness is."

Anna nudged Crist, who was sitting next to Felty. "Are you sure you don't want to try some?"

Crist winced, glanced at Felty, and turned his face away. Was he opposed to asparagus bacon casserole or Felty Helmuth or both? Well, Anna refused to volunteer for any more humiliation, and she refused to put Felty through more blatant rejection. Why were people so mean? Turning down Anna's casserole was insensitive, but excluding and ignoring Felty was downright hurtful and unchristian.

Their treatment didn't seem to bother Felty, who wore a perfectly contented and blissful look on his face as he ate Anna's casserole. But Anna knew better. As someone who got a lot of ridicule and many cold shoulders, she knew how *gute* someone could get at hiding their hurt feelings.

And she wasn't going to stand for it.

She set the casserole dish on the table in front of Felty. "I need to talk to someone. I'll be right back."

Felty raised his eyebrows. "Is it okay if I eat the rest?"

She nodded, unable to keep a smile from creeping onto her lips. How nice that he really liked it.

Felty didn't waste any time. He scooped half of what was left onto his plate. "These boys had their chance."

Anna found Dat, who was sitting at the far table with the bishop and Jakob King. She didn't want to interrupt his supper, but this was an emergency. "Dat, can I talk to you?"

The bishop looked a little put out that she had interrupted their conversation, but Jakob smiled and patted Dat on the shoulder. "We'll save your spot so the women won't clear your plate."

At a fellowship supper, the women served the men first. The *fraaen* tended to shoo the men off quickly so the women and children could eat. Anna pulled Dat into the mudroom, which seemed to be the only place that wasn't crawling with people. "Dat, I have always tried to honor you in all I do."

Dat eyed her curiously. "*Jah.* I know. You are a *gute dochter.*"

"So I need you to change one of your rules."

His eyebrows inched up his forehead. "Which rule do you want changed? Because I can tell you right now that I'm not kicking Isaac out of the family."

Anna grinned and waved her hand in the air. "*Ach*, Dat, don't tease me." She pursed her lips. "Unless that's really truly a possibility?"

Dat chuckled. "Don't even think about it."

"Okay then. Do you remember how you told me to stay away from Felty Helmuth?"

"*Jah.* He's a soldier."

"*Was* a soldier," Anna insisted.

"Was a soldier. What's to keep him from packing up and leaving home again to see the world? He's not steady. He's unpredictable. Besides, you have a heart for the downtrodden, and it's too risky that he'll fall in love with you. You'll break his heart, and he's had enough hardship in his life."

"I don't care about any of that, Dat. Felty is not going to fall in love with me."

"Of course he isn't, because you are going to leave well enough alone."

Anna huffed out a breath. "Dat, Felty is not going to fall in love with me because I'm short and odd and a wonderful unsuitable *fraa*. And that doesn't matter, because right now, Felty needs friends, and I should be his friend."

Dat's eyes softened at the corners. "You think he needs friends?"

Anna wrapped her fingers around Dat's wrist and pulled him down the hall to peek into the great room. Felty was working on the rest of the casserole in the dish while Elmer visited with him. To the other boys, including Isaac, he might as well have been invisible. "Look, Dat. No one but Elmer will talk to him."

"Elmer is a *gute* boy."

"*Jah*, he is, but Felty is five years older. Dat, I need to be his friend."

Dat fingered his beard. "Everyone needs friends."

"For sure and certain. I want to honor my *fater* and my *mater*, but I need your permission to be his friend. It's not the Christian thing to do to keep my distance, no matter what the bishop or the *Ordnung* says. And six feet is a silly rule. I think six inches is just as silly, though a ruler is easier to carry around than two yardsticks."

Dat squinted with one eye closed like he always did when he was thinking hard. "What do you mean about six feet?"

"*Ach*, it's just something Felty and I talked about."

He sighed. "My first responsibility is to protect you, Anna."

"I'm not in any danger. Felty is nice, but like every other boy in the district, he wants to have a *fraa* who will do him credit." Anna did her best to keep her voice from cracking. Might as well face the truth. "Can I have your permission to be his friend?"

Dat smiled at Anna the way he often did when they talked about boys and getting married, as if he knew better but he would go along with her version of things to avoid an argument. "Okay. You can be friends with Felty. It's very thoughtful of you to think of his feelings."

"I can't stand the way they treat him."

Dat peered in Felty's direction. "Don't worry, *heartzley*. It will get better with time. If he shows a commitment to the church and nonviolence, people will be less suspicious."

"But how will he gain a commitment to the church when the members are unkind? If they were that rude to me, I might never come back."

Dat's gaze seemed to pierce right through her. "But, *heartzley*, they *are* that rude to you."

Anna's mouth went dry. "I didn't think you noticed."

"*Ach*, I notice. What I like about you is that you won't let them drive you away. You forgive them and keep trying."

Anna shook her head and smiled sadly. "I don't know why I keep trying. It's a waste of time to try to win anybody's approval."

"That's just one of the many things I admire about you, Anna. You don't feel sorry for yourself."

Anna's smile stiffened on her face. "You'd be surprised."

Dat chuckled. "Okay, then, you don't wallow in self-pity. And there's no reason to. It is very proud of me to say, Anna, so don't repeat this to anyone, but you are extraordinary."

Anna knew how to spell *extraordinary*, but it certainly didn't describe her. She grunted her disagreement. "That's not true."

Dat was still gazing into the great room, his eyes darting from Felty to Rosie to Mark Hostetler, of all people. "You are smarter and kinder and more talented—and, of course, prettier—than anyone in this room. Elmer knows it. So do your two youngest *bruderen*. Rosie Herschberger suspects it, though she is too wrapped up in herself to see it. I fear that Felty has noticed it too."

"*Ach*, Dat, now you're talking nonsense."

He laughed when she nudged his shoulder. "I am not." He took both her hands. "You have my permission to be friends with Felty. It is what Jesus would do. But don't get carried away. Felty is still a soldier at heart, and I don't want you to settle for just anybody. You can have your choice of any boy in the *gmayna*, plus any boy in the next district over. So be picky. You'll be stuck for the rest of your life."

Anna smiled. "You make it sound so terrible."

He cocked his eyebrow and made her laugh. "Only if you make the wrong choice."

A ribbon of warm memories traveled up Anna's spine as she asked the question she always loved hearing the answer to. "Did you make a *gute* choice when you married Mamm?"

Dat stared into the distance, beyond the walls of the

Zooks' house. "I couldn't have made a better choice. Gotte smiled down on me that day and every day after I married your *mamm.*" He rubbed his knuckle down her cheek. "I want the same happiness for you. You deserve it." He clapped his hands. "Now, did you save me a bite of your famous asparagus casserole?"

Anna drew her brows together. "Oh, dear. I think Felty ate it all. He and Elmer were the only ones who wanted any."

Dat's eyes flashed with some sort of unreadable emotion. "Felty ate it all?" He turned and gazed at Felty's side of the room. "I'm *froh* he enjoyed it."

"I think it was the bacon."

"I think it was the cook," Dat said.

"I don't think so, but it's nice of you to say." Anna leaned over and kissed Dat's cheek. "*Denki.*"

He hadn't convinced her of anything, but she'd gotten his permission to get closer than six feet to Felty. It was hard to be a *gute* friend from six feet away.

Her heart skipped a beat, even though she wasn't exactly sure why.

Chapter 6

Felty stopped the buggy abruptly, and his mare whinnied her disapproval. Bundled in winter clothing, Mark Hostetler and Rosie Herschberger ran in front of his horse and into the house where the singing was taking place. They didn't acknowledge him, didn't wave, didn't glance his way, even though his horse almost ran over them.

He gritted his teeth in dread. He could do this.

Couldn't he?

Only the thought of spending time with Anna Yoder kept him from turning the buggy around and going home. No one wanted him there. No one welcomed him. To them, he was an outsider, someone to be avoided, certainly not anyone they'd want to be friends with. Mark Hostetler and Yost Neuenschwander had been Felty's best friends before he had joined the army. Yost had since married and moved to Ohio. Mark had made it very clear that he didn't even want Felty sneezing in his direction.

He hadn't expected rejoining the community would be so hard. Even though he was Amish, it had been easier to make friends in the army. The soldiers in his unit had come from many different places, but they watched out for one another, had one anothers' backs. Here, it felt like he was completely on his own.

Except for maybe Elmer and Anna Yoder. His lips twitched into a smile. Anna had been nice to him, but he tried not to read too much into it, because Anna was nice to everybody. Elmer was a lot like her. They watched out for people, even the ones nobody else liked.

Felty climbed out of the buggy. The cold air stung his nose and chilled his throat. He blew into his gloved hands and unhitched the horse as quickly as possible. On the way to the barn, three young people passed him going the other way, but none of them said a word to him, even though they had to sidestep his horse to get to the house. Felty stalled the horse in the barn, gave her some water, and headed for the house. Would they give him dirty looks if he tried to eat a cookie? Would they let him play the games? Would they make faces at his singing?

Die youngie always used to laugh when he messed up the words to songs. After two years away, would they scowl at him instead?

Felty pasted a wide smile on his face and strolled into the house, shutting the door quickly behind him to keep in the warm air. For a split second, the room fell silent, and every eye turned in his direction. But then, as if he were a bad smell they all wanted to ignore, everyone turned back to what they had been doing or the people they had been talking to. With a gut full of rocks, Felty pulled harder on his smile, took off his coat, gloves, and hat, and moved to an inconspicuous corner where he wouldn't be in anybody's way.

Eva Zook, a round, severe-looking woman with graying

hair and thick eyebrows, approached Felty as if he were a spider and held out her hands. "Felty Helmuth, let me take your coat. Welcome to our home. We are *froh* to see you." She didn't seem glad, but since it was the most hospitality anyone but Anna had shown Felty since he'd arrived, he was sincerely grateful.

"*Denki* for letting me come," he said. "I know I'm not the most welcome sight."

Eva shrugged, and her mouth hinted at a smile. "It will take some time, young man. I don't have to remind you that you left us."

"I suppose I did."

Eva slung his coat over her arm. "No one wants to experience the consequences, but there are always consequences. Don't resist the consequences. As I remember, you're likable enough, and obviously handsome enough, even with that haircut. You'll be fine. And be sure to get a pretzel. It turned out to be a *gute* batch."

Eva disappeared into the kitchen, leaving Felty with no one to talk to but the calendar on the wall. It almost made him long for the camaraderie of the army.

But then the sun broke through the clouds as Anna and Elmer came through the door. They took off their coats and scarves. Elmer's scarf was hunter green. Anna's scarf was a deep purple. Felty's lips curled upward. For sure and certain she had knitted both of them. Anna wore a navy blue dress that made her eyes look as blue as the sky. Felty found it impossible to look away. She was beautiful, and apparently, none of the boys knew it but him. Lord willing, no one else would realize it until it was too late for any of them to do anything about it.

Two girls called Anna's name and waved to her from across the room. Anna smiled and waved back, but she seemed distracted, as if she was looking for something.

Or someone.

Felty held his breath as her gaze traveled around the room and stopped on him. She burst into a smile. Had she been looking out for him? Was she happy to see him? Did she care about him even just a little? His pulse coursed through his veins like a river during a flood. That smile was worth all the embarrassment he would ever have to endure. Hope grabbed him by the shirt and pulled him in for a stiff hug. If Anna liked him, nothing else mattered.

Elmer found some friends on the other side of the room, but Anna made a beeline for Felty, causing his already fast pulse to break some sort of speed record. "You're brave to come tonight."

"Brave?" He didn't know if it was bravery or just being smitten with Anna Yoder that had induced him to come. "I'm not brave."

"*Ach*, you're brave. I saw how they treated you at *gmay* this morning."

Felty shrugged and grinned. "They were mad at me for eating all the asparagus bacon casserole."

Anna laughed, then startled herself with a snort. She clapped her hand over her mouth. "Oh, dear. Mammi says I'll never get a husband if I snort." Her giggling got louder, then subsided. "They were grateful to you for eating all the casserole."

"They didn't look very grateful."

Anna nodded smugly. "I told you. They weren't nice, and I think you're wonderful brave to put up with that again."

"The only reason I came was to see you."

"Lying is a sin, Felty Helmuth," Anna said, shaking her finger at him.

Should he tell her he wasn't lying—not one little bit? If he were that honest, would he scare her off? "Eva says the pretzels are *gute*, but I can't imagine they're better than your cinnamon rolls."

An attractive blush spread over her cheeks. "Eva's pretzels are *gute*, and I don't make cinnamon rolls anymore. Not after Mark Hostetler got sick that one time." Bright red embarrassment replaced her blush.

"That's a pity. That you don't make cinnamon rolls, I mean. Mark always had a sensitive stomach." Maybe he shouldn't say any more about that. He cleared his throat. "I didn't get a chance to ask you earlier—how did your Thanksgiving turkey turn out?"

Anna wilted like a plucked daisy. "*Ach.* It was delicious."

"That's *wunderbarr*." He studied her face and frowned. "Isn't it?"

"Mammi let me cube the bread for the stuffing, but she wouldn't let me touch the turkey. She rubbed all sorts of spices on it and let it sit out on the porch overnight. Then she roasted it for four hours in the cookstove oven. The house smelled so *gute*, and the turkey was as tender as could be." She scrunched her lips together. "I really wanted to try the brine, but Mammi wanted to do the turkey the way she'd always done it. 'Why meddle with a *gute* thing?' she said."

"Where's the fun in that?" Felty said.

She nodded vigorously. "That's what I think."

He sighed and winked at her. "You can do it next year. Lord willing, your *mammi* will want to spend her Thanksgiving in Ohio."

"That would be wonderful *gute*." She lowered her eyes. "*Oy*, anyhow. I'm sorry. It is very wicked to want my mammi to go to another state. I love her and am so grateful she wanted to help with Thanksgiving dinner. I try not to have wicked thoughts, but sometimes they just pop into my head."

"It's not wicked at all. Some relatives are better in small doses, but that doesn't mean we don't love them."

She seemed to perk up a bit. "That's what I think too. I'm *froh* to know it's not a wicked thought."

He shook his head. "Just a perfectly reasonable one."

Junior Zook tapped a spoon on the table until he got everyone's attention. "Okay, everybody. Be sure to eat as many pretzels as you want, or my *mamm* will get cross." Some of *die youngie* snickered. Eva Zook had a well-earned reputation for being a grump. "Since I am leading the games tonight, I got to pick all of them. First we are going to play Please and Displease."

Anna let out a soft groan that only Felty could hear. He felt sorry for both her and himself. Please and Displease was one of those games that almost everyone thought they wanted to play, but someone's feelings always got hurt, and more than one person often left embarrassed or downright humiliated. Anna had mentioned that Rosie Herschberger liked to play, which didn't surprise Felty at all. Girls like Rosie loved the attention and never felt the sting of rejection like so many others. Felty clenched his teeth tighter and hoped that nothing would happen to hurt Anna's feelings. Right now, his own feelings didn't matter.

"Mary Zook," Junior called out to his sister, eyes sparkling with mischief. "Go downstairs and sit in the basement holding hands with Mark Hostetler for five minutes."

Mark stretched a smile across his face while the perspiration beaded on his forehead. No one wanted the embarrassment of being rejected by Junior's choice of victims.

Mary covered her mouth with her hand and giggled. "Pleased," she said.

Mark's smile relaxed into something more natural. He grabbed Mary's hand and led her down the stairs.

Junior pulled out a pocket watch. "I'm timing you," he called.

The pleasant hum of voices was soon drowned out by Junior's voice. "Now for the next couple." He peered around the room dramatically, as if the fate of everybody's future was in his hands. The younger girls and boys tittered in excitement. For those who had just started *rumschpringe*, these games were like a ticket into a forbidden world where kissing was allowed and holding hands was expected.

Junior pointed to the boy standing directly in front of him. Felty didn't know how old the boy was, but he didn't look a day over fourteen years old. He had to be at least sixteen, though, because that was the minimum age for someone to attend a *singeon*. Felty smiled to himself. The teenagers looked younger all the time.

In his deep, booming voice, Junior announced, "Jonathan, get down on one knee and sing three verses of 'The Puppy Parable' to Dinah King."

A petite girl in the corner started laughing. She was definitely one of the younger ones here. "Pleased," she said, in a voice that probably sounded loud to her but was barely audible to the rest of them.

Jonathan made a great show of pulling Dinah forward so everyone in the room could see her. When she was front and center, Jonathan knelt down and sang a very energetic, very flat rendition of "The Puppy Parable." Everyone, including Dinah and Jonathan themselves, got a big laugh out of it before Jonathan led Dinah back to her corner, where, Lord willing, her breathing would go back to normal.

Junior pounded on the floor with his boot. "Mark and Mary, your time's up. Stop whatever you're doing before I have to send someone down to get you."

More howling laughter from the group. Felty was glad they were having fun, but he couldn't join them. Anna had turned to stone beside him, and her shallow breathing made it plain that she was increasingly uncomfortable.

Mark and Mary emerged from the basement, looking a bit disheveled and a little bit sheepish. Most people didn't even notice their return, focused on Junior's next pairing.

Jonathan pointed to Joseph Lambright, who had been in the same grade as Anna in school. Felty wasn't inclined to like Joseph very much, not after he'd flatly refused to try Anna's cheesy asparagus bacon casserole earlier today. Joseph fancied himself to be deliriously handsome and irresistible to the girls. Felty wasn't too keen on a boy who was so full of his own importance that there wasn't room in his heart for anyone else.

"Joseph Lambright," Junior said. "Give Anna Yoder a kiss."

Felty didn't know about Anna, but his heart flipped

over itself, as if it had missed a step and tumbled down a long set of stairs. Anna's face went pale, and she slowly backed into the wall behind her. Was she more afraid that Joseph would kiss her or that he would flatly refuse?

Joseph didn't even wait half a second. "Displeased," he moaned, as if Junior had messed up the whole singing for him.

Many of *die youngie* laughed, but it was more subdued than before. Some of them probably recognized that this wasn't a very nice game and that Joseph wasn't a very nice boy.

Felty wanted to put his arm around Anna and pull her close, but he sensed that anything he did would bring Anna unwanted attention. Like as not, she longed to fade into the furniture and never be noticed again.

Junior tapped his finger to his lips. "Oooh, so Joseph isn't brave enough to kiss Anna."

Joseph's face turned red, but he folded his arms and stood his ground.

"Let's see who *is* brave enough to kiss." Junior planted his feet and looked to his left. "Rosie Herschberger, give Felty Helmuth a kiss."

Felty withered in complete mortification. What in the world was Junior thinking? Felty had just come to the singing to see Anna and try to break the ice with some of his old friends. He most certainly didn't want to kiss Rosie Herschberger.

Rosie grimaced before squaring her shoulders, giving Felty a charming smile, and saying, "Displeased."

The laughter was scattered sparsely around the room. Even the mere thought of Felty seemed to make the whole group uncomfortable. He made a feeble attempt to laugh, though he wasn't sure why. Felty didn't know which feeling was stronger—the embarrassment of Rosie's complete rejection or the utter relief that she didn't want to kiss him. But the others would follow Rosie's lead when it came to Felty. It was clear no one wanted anything to do with him.

Junior was undeterred. "All right, then. Lily, go in the other room and hug Felty for five minutes."

"Displeased," Lily said, as if spitting something bitter out of her mouth.

Without even a glance in his direction, Anna wrapped her fingers around Felty's elbow, obviously trying to comfort him. And the touch *was* oddly comforting, even though Felty had never felt more awkward in his life—had never wanted more to be anywhere else but where he was, and that included the battlefield.

Junior exhaled a deep breath. "A bunch of scaredy-cats." He made a face and peered around the room again. "Miriam, go sit in the hall closet with Felty for five minutes."

Sometimes Junior didn't know when to leave well enough alone.

Miriam glanced at Rosie and frowned before giving her answer. "Displeased," she said, though she acted nicer and more deliberate about it than Lily.

Felty flinched when Anna let out a loud and indelicate growl. "*Ach!* You're all a bunch of party poopers." Grabbing Felty's hand, she pulled him so forcefully she almost dislocated his shoulder. She tugged him down the hall to the closet, where she opened the door, shoved him inside, and sidled up next to him.

"I think that's against the rules," someone remarked

as Anna slammed the door, leaving them in complete darkness like two sardines in a can of oil.

All he could hear was his own hammering heartbeat and her indignant breathing.

The closet was barely big enough for one person and an assortment of coats. Crammed against the coats, he and Anna faced each other, her hands tightly pressed against his chest, her breath caressing the folds of his shirt. He didn't smell well, but he imagined she smelled like cheese or bacon, and the warmth of her hands radiated through his shirt into his chest. His heart leaped into his throat. Despite the humiliation of mere moments before, this was exactly where he wanted to be, with exactly the person he wanted to be with.

Unable to believe his good fortune, he wrapped his arms around Anna to create a little more space—not that they needed more space, but he was happy to create it. "I'm sorry if Joseph hurt your feelings."

"I wouldn't kiss Joseph if his lips were made of bacon."

"He wouldn't be so handsome with a pair of bacon lips," Felty said, half in jest, half in bitterness. Joseph had hurt Anna's feelings twice today. Felty could barely stand it.

"Did I use it right?" Anna said, her words clipped with irritation.

"What?"

"'Party pooper.' Did I use it correctly in a sentence?"

"Perfectly," he said. She whimpered softly. "*Ach*, Anna. I'm so sorry. That was horrible. I'm so sorry."

In an attempt to comfort her, he rubbed his hand up and down her back until he realized she wasn't crying.

She was stifling a giggle. The soft, hissing sound turned into an uncontrolled spasm of mirth. Her whole body shook against him as she attempted to laugh without making a sound. It didn't work out so well. Laughter finally exploded from her mouth, so that not only *die youngie* in the next room would be able to hear it but anyone outside passing by in a buggy.

Her laughter wound down, and she took a deep, exasperated breath. "I shouldn't have said anything about poop, but sometimes I can't bear all my pent-up righteous indignation."

Felty chuckled. "No need to worry. They had no idea they were being chastised."

"*Ach*, for sure and certain they knew." She sighed, a tone of resignation in her voice. "Everyone is trying their best, I suppose, but it's not *gute* enough. They should be ashamed of themselves for not showing more kindness. No one should treat you like that, Felty."

"It will take time for them to accept me. I made a choice. I will bear the consequences." Felty couldn't resist reaching out and running the backs of his fingers down her cheek. "But they should never treat you like that, Anna. You are one of them."

She grunted. "It's obvious I'm not."

"Well, I don't know what they're thinking, but I wouldn't change one thing about you. Not one."

"Even that I use words like 'pooper'?"

He chuckled. "Even that. Besides, you make the best cheesy asparagus and bacon casserole in the world. Why would I want you to change?"

She fell silent for a few seconds. "They don't understand

it now," she murmured, "but Lily and Miriam and Rosie are going to be kicking themselves for their shortsightedness."

Felty smiled, though Anna couldn't see it. "Rosie has no idea what a *gute* kisser I am."

Anna stiffened. "You are?"

He felt his face get warm. Would she think he was childish? "*Ach, vell.* I've never kissed a girl before. I'm saving it up for someone special."

"You've never even kissed at a *singeon*? Or a taffy pull? Or a wedding?"

"*Nae.* Not even once." Even though Tooley had tried real hard to find him a girl in Korea. "It doesn't seem right to kiss a girl I don't want for my *fraa*."

A long pause. He wished he could see her face. "*Ach.* That's a lovely thought." Another long pause. "I kissed Mark Hostetler at a *singeon* two years ago. I didn't think it would be nice to say 'displeased,' even though Mark is wonderful rude sometimes. And I kissed my second cousin once when I was twelve. We were playing Love in the Dark."

Jealousy against Mark Hostetler seized Felty by the throat. It shouldn't have mattered who Anna kissed, especially in a silly game, but it mattered a great deal, though he'd never tell her that. Instead he pulled her a tiny bit closer, which felt so *gute*, it was probably a sin. "It's sort of crowded in here," he whispered. "What would your *dat* say? We're breaking the six-feet rule, not to mention the six-inches rule."

Anna patted his chest, sending Felty's heartbeat through the roof. "*Ach*, I've worked it out with Dat. I told him I can't very well be your friend if I have to measure the distance between us every time I see you."

"Does this mean you don't have to stay away from me anymore?"

"That's what it means, which is a *gute* thing, because we couldn't be six inches apart in this closet if we wanted to."

Felty most definitely didn't want to. It felt *wunderbarr* to hold Anna in his arms, like coming home after a long absence. How long could they stay in the closet before Eva or Junior made them get out?

They both jumped when somebody rapped on the door. "One more minute for kissing," Junior said.

Anna sighed. "Time to get back to the fun." He could just imagine her rolling her eyes when she said *fun*.

"*Denki* for helping me," he said. "That was wonderful embarrassing out there."

She stiffened. "They shouldn't treat you that way, like you don't matter. Like you don't have feelings. I couldn't let them do it, not even if they never speak to me again."

A knot tightened at the base of Felty's throat as the realization of his own selfishness nearly choked him. No one was particularly mean to Anna, even if some of the boys were rude. Some of the girls even went out of their way to be nice. But mostly, Anna was treated as an afterthought, someone they only considered or cared about because she was in the district and a fellow believer. Felty didn't understand how it was possible that they had overlooked Anna all these years, when he had been captivated by her from the first word of the spelling bee.

But if Anna's name became attached to his in the minds of church members, would they ostracize her or try to shut her out they way they had with him? Would being friends with a former soldier hurt Anna in the eyes of the community? Would people avoid her because of him? How could he hope to win her love if he drove a wedge between her and the *gmayna*?

He squeezed the words past the guilt on his tongue. "*Denki*, Anna. You are a *gute* friend. I don't deserve you."

"Everybody deserves a friend. You most of all." She pulled away from him and opened the door, blinking against the light on the other side. "Mammi says we should be nice to soldiers, because they're going to hell, and this life is the only happiness they'll have." Her countenance fell. "I shouldn't have said that. I want you to know, I don't believe it for a second."

He shook his head, unable to keep a grin from curving his lips. Anna was so sincere and real and honest. He wouldn't want her any other way. "I'm not offended when people are nice to me, no matter why they're being nice."

Her face turned red. "Just so you know, I don't believe you'll go to hell. Why would Gotte make such a nice heaven if He planned on sending most of His children to hell? If it were me, I'd want them all together in one place, like a giant happy family."

Felty chuckled. "A very *gute* question."

She clasped her hands together and lowered her eyes. "I don't mean to question Gotte. I hope you don't think I'm wicked for having an opinion on how Gotte will sort the sinners. His ways are higher than our ways."

"Not at all. If you can't form your own opinions about religion, what can you ponder over? I think you're wonderful smart. And a deep thinker."

He loved seeing her blush. "Not that smart. Not smarter than you. And not as interesting."

"Interesting?"

Her blush got deeper. "Once they get to know how interesting you are, every girl in the district will be happy to kiss you right on the mouth."

He laughed. "I hope not."

There was only one girl he ever wanted to kiss, and she might not want his affection if the cost was too high. How could he win Anna's love without inviting the disapproval of the community on her head?

Facing his drill sergeant every morning seemed like an easier task.

Chapter 7

Watching for the cars that never seemed to be watching for her, Anna pulled her buggy onto the road and prodded Skipper into a brisk trot. She didn't have to give her *bruderen* a ride to school, but when the trees turned lacy with ice crystals and her breath hung in the air like curls of smoke from a chimney, she felt sorry that they had to walk. Elmer felt sorry for them too. On frosty mornings, he hitched up the buggy for her, and all she had to do was climb in, wrap a quilt around her legs, and go.

It was the first day of December in what promised to be a wonderful chilly winter. Anna smiled to herself. She didn't mind the cold, and she loved the thought of Christmas just around the corner. There would be caroling to the shut-ins, Christmas *singeons* and parties, pine boughs hung above every door, and lots of baking. She always made several loaves of Mamm's famous stollen to give to neighbors, and this year she was going to have another try at making Bienenstich cake for Second Christmas. Bienenstich cake, or Bee Sting cake, was so delicious that the bees would sting you for a piece, but it was also the hardest thing Anna had ever tried to make. There were about five hundred steps to it, and if you got the almond topping wrong, it looked more like a chunk of asphalt than an actual dessert. But that was last year's bad memory. Anna had set her sights on a more successful cake this Christmas. And if it didn't turn out, she could always whip up a batch of gingersnaps. She had that recipe down by heart.

Anna felt her face get warm. Felty seemed to have fond memories of her cinnamon rolls. Maybe she'd dust off her recipe and bake some for Felty as a Christmas gift. Of course, if they turned out as bad as everyone said they were, maybe Felty would decide he didn't want to be her friend anymore. She straightened in her seat. Even if they tasted terrible, it was the thought that counted. That's what Dat always said.

Felty would like them. He liked everything she baked.

Anna sighed loudly and allowed herself a secret smile, even though any smile alone in her buggy was a secret. Felty had liked her cheesy asparagus bacon casserole. He had praised her cinnamon rolls to the sky. He was unusually handsome, even with shorn hair, and he was so tall and good-looking, he attracted openmouthed attention whenever he walked into a room. He always stood up straight, as if he wasn't ashamed of being tall. Some of the girls in the *gmayna* slouched to hide their height, afraid the shorter boys wouldn't be interested. Anna didn't understand it. If she were tall, she'd square her shoulders like Felty and walk around gracefully with her head held high. Anna approved of *gute* posture. Of course, maybe standing up straight and looking down on everyone would be considered proud. Maybe that was why Gotte had made her short, so she wouldn't be tempted.

Felty hadn't seemed to mind that she'd dragged him into the closet last night. After the third girl had rejected him, Anna hadn't been able to stand it anymore. They had been purposefully trying to humiliate him, and it was the most unchristian thing she'd ever seen. *Ach*, *vell*, maybe not the *most* unchristian thing, but certainly the most unchristian thing she'd seen since some *Englisch* boys in town had beaten up Benjamin Kiem for being Amish.

Anna had been *froh* she'd gotten permission earlier from Dat to be Felty's friend. She had been able to cram into the closet without feeling guilty about not honoring her *fater*. And she wanted to think that Felty had been grateful, though she couldn't be sure. Maybe her actions had drawn more attention to him than he had wanted. Still, she wasn't sorry for what she'd done. No one should treat anyone the way Rosie and the others treated Felty. Those girls' noses were so high in the air, they'd drown in a rainstorm.

When they'd emerged from the closet last night, Rosie had given Anna a small smile, as if she felt sorry for Anna and her misguided sense of indignation. Most of the other young people had ignored both Anna and Felty the rest of the night, except for Elmer, who had pulled Anna and Felty into his circle of young teenagers and tried to make them feel comfortable. Anna sent up a silent prayer of thanks for Elmer. He was the only person keeping her from being a complete outcast.

Anna's heart did three cartwheels when the buggy approached someone walking down the road and she realized it was Felty himself. He was bundled up tightly against the cold and carrying a long walking stick. She pulled back on the reins and stopped alongside him. "Do you want a ride?" she said, wondering if the bishop would consider it a date.

He turned and bloomed into a smile. The smile made her heart beat even faster. "You run into the nicest surprises on the back roads."

Anna nodded. "Like license plates and such."

"License plates and Anna Yoders," he said, apparently quite happy to see her, though she wasn't sure why. He glanced down the road ahead. "I would love a ride, but you can't take a buggy where I'm going."

"You can't?"

"One of our cows is missing. Dat sent me to look for her. She busted right through a fence in the middle of the night. She was long gone by this morning."

Anna drew her brows together. "*Ach*, that's too bad. Can I help? I have wonderful *gute* eyesight, and I know how to herd a cow. My legs are short, but I'm a sturdy walker."

His eyes sparkled merrily. "I don't want to impose, but I would love your company."

"No imposition. I've got chores waiting at home, but they aren't going anywhere." She pointed to his walking stick. "You should get one of those real cattle prods with electricity. My *onkel* Gary has one for his cows."

Felty's smile faded to nothing. "I wouldn't ever use one of those. They hurt the cattle. It doesn't seem very nice to use it on an animal that never meant any harm to anyone."

Anna pressed her lips together. "I never thought of that. Do animals have feelings?"

Felty shrugged. "I'm not smart enough to know the answer to that."

"You're plenty smart," Anna said. "I heard you use the

word 'miscellaneous' last night. I didn't even know that word existed. I had to go home and look it up, and it wasn't easy to find, because I didn't know how to spell it."

He curled one side of his mouth. "I thought you knew how to spell everything."

"I don't hardly know how to spell anything."

He pointed to Skipper. "Horses seem to have fun running around the pasture. I've heard animals moan in pain or squeal when they're caught in a trap. Only Gotte knows for sure, but I think animals feel as much as we humans do. They just don't have the words to say anything about it. Gotte created the animals just like he did man and woman, and I don't doubt He would want us to treat them kindly—for sure and certain never purposefully hurt them. It feels wrong." He gave her a warm smile. "That's why I won't use one of those fancy cattle prods. I wouldn't want one used on me."

Anna lifted her eyebrows. "I wouldn't either. Isaac says it stings something wonderful."

Felty chuckled. "I'd like to hear that story sometime."

Anna rolled her eyes. "Someday Isaac is going to find some common sense, but I'm afraid it will come from a lot of hard lessons taught by his foolishness." She eyed Felty with new understanding. "I never considered that animals might have feelings. You think deep thoughts, Felty. I'm going to ask Onkel Gary to throw his cattle prod away."

His look was like soft butter. "I'd be wonderful grateful."

Yet again, Anna found herself struggling to breathe normally. Onkel Gary was going to get a phone call *and* a letter. "Do you mind if I go home and put on boots?

Then I could put Skipper in the barn and tell Dat I'm going out to help you find a cow. I don't want him to wonder where I've gone."

Felty jogged around to the other side and jumped into the buggy. "I don't mind. It's more time I get to spend with you."

Anna jiggled the reins, and Skipper moved forward. The heat of her blush warmed the air around her. Felty Helmuth was turning out to be quite a disturbance to her emotional state. What should she do about that?

Anna rushed into the house to change while Felty unhitched the buggy. After she'd put on her long johns and an extra pair of wool stockings, she pulled on her snow boots and clomped outside. Felty was waiting for her with a bright smile and a second walking stick. He handed it to her. "I hope you don't mind. I found it in the wood pile, and I thought you might want one."

She handed him the bright red scarf she wore on special occasions. "Wear this. You're more likely to get a cold if your throat gets chilled."

He turned it over in his gloved hand and gazed at it as if she'd given him a gold coin. "This is beautiful, Anna. Did you knit it?"

The awe in his voice made her feel shy all of a sudden. "*Jah.* It's the one thing I'm *gute* at."

"Not the *one* thing. I can't think of anything you're *not gute* at."

Anna laughed. "*Ach*, *vell*, don't think too hard about it."

Felty wrapped the scarf around his neck, and Anna tried not to be overwhelmed with the excitement of seeing him wearing one of her creations. She refused to faint when she realized their scarves were made from the same knitting pattern. Even though they were different colors, the scarves were almost like twins. *Ach*, her heart was likely to pound out of her chest.

Felty pointed them in the direction of the gentle sloping hill covered with trees behind Anna's pasture. "From our house, the hoofprints led up the other side of Sugg Hill." He frowned. "I'm a little worried. We've seen coyotes stalking the perimeter of the dairy."

Anna pressed her lips together. "Could they have gotten your cow?"

"Lord willing, they didn't." They hiked across Anna's backyard through the ankle-deep snow, then went gradually up the hill into the woods, where the trees were thick and the going was slower. Felty glanced in her direction and smiled. "I owe you a great debt of gratitude for saving me last night."

"Saving you?" Anna laughed. "I don't know if it was as dire as all that."

"Three girls flat out refused to be alone with me." He tapped his finger to his lips and looked skyward. "Though I was honestly glad for it. I did not want to kiss Rosie Herschberger. And being in the closet with Miriam wouldn't have been anywhere near as fun as being in the closet with you."

Why did her face always seem to heat up like a stove when Felty looked at her that way? "I hope I didn't embarrass you even more when I pulled you into the closet."

"Not at all. Like I said, I enjoyed it."

Her face felt as if it *had* burst into flames. They'd gotten pretty close in that closet. She gave him a wry smile. "Now you're just teasing."

He grinned. "I've never been more serious in my life."

They walked halfway up the hill and into the heart of the woods, where a little stream of water ran alongside straggly sumac and barren huckleberry bushes.

"We pick huckleberries here every summer," Anna said. "Dat got permission from the man who owns the hill, but I don't know who that is. Mamm would make us a huckleberry pie every day during huckleberry season. She'd send Elmer and me up the hill to gather them. Sometimes she made us take Isaac." Anna stepped around a thick pine tree. "Some days, when Mamm could see that my *bruderen* were trying my patience, she would say, 'Anna, I need you to go pick more huckleberries,' even if it was June or September when there weren't any huckleberries to pick."

Felty smiled. "Where would you go?"

"I would take a bucket to make it look real, climb up this hill, and find a *gute* reading tree."

"A reading tree?"

"*Jah,*" Anna said. "I would find a tree I could sit in and read. When the trees were full of leaves, my *bruderen* couldn't see me, and I could read for hours without being disturbed. My *mamm* knew I would come back much happier than when I left." It was a *gute* memory. Mamm had always watched out for her like that. "When Mamm died, I came to the hill more often. I did more crying than reading in those days."

"I can't imagine what it must have felt like to lose your *mamm*."

Anna winced. "It hurt. I don't understand why Gotte would do that to our family. We need her so badly, especially Isaac."

"I don't know the answer to that, but I know that all

things work together for good to them that love God, even the bad things."

"I hope that's true," Anna said. "I do know that being sad about it won't bring my *mater* back. She would want me to be happy."

Felty cupped his hand around her elbow and helped her over a rock in the path. "For sure and certain."

"I still come up here and climb a tree and read sometimes—when the weather's warm. Being here makes me feel closer to Mamm and helps me keep my patience with Isaac the rest of the time."

There was still no sign of the cow, no hoofprints or cow pies. They turned uphill and followed the stream, even though it was hard to follow because it mostly ran under the snow. Anna stepped right into the water twice, and Felty yanked her back before her boots got saturated.

"Do they have winter in Korea?"

"*Jah,*" Felty said, positioning himself between Anna and the stream, probably so she wouldn't keep stepping in it. "I shiver just thinking about it. That first winter came early, and we didn't have proper winter gear. At thirty below zero, we had to adjust our big guns to the cold, or they would miss their targets. I wrapped a towel around my head to keep my ears warm, but some men lost ears and fingers to frostbite." He glanced at her, grinned, and slid the straw hat and wooly hat underneath off his head. He leaned in Anna's direction. "Take a look. I still have both my ears."

Anna sheepishly peeled off her mittens, reached out, and lightly pinched each of his ears between her thumb and index finger. He had freely offered his ears to her, and she would have been *deerich*, foolish, not to take advantage of the opportunity. She certainly couldn't resist being close enough to catch the smell of cedarwood and strong soap that always hung about him. "I'm *froh* you still have both your ears," she said. "What about fingers and toes?"

His eyes flashed with amusement and something more earnest. He put his hats back on and pulled off one of his gloves. He held up his hand and wiggled his fingers. "I've still got all of them. But I want you to be sure." He took her hand in his and laced his fingers through hers. His touch sent a zing of pure energy up Anna's arm, stealing her breath and making her knees wobbly. "How does that feel?" he said.

How does that feel? Anna didn't have the vocabulary to describe what she was feeling, and even if she did, she wouldn't just come right out and say it. "It feels real," she stammered.

They walked uphill hand in hand for a hundred feet or so, but then Felty gave her back her mitten and put his own glove on. "I'm afraid it's too cold out here to be without mittens."

Anna nodded. "We don't want to end up like your friends in Korea."

"We took to pouring gasoline on the ground and setting it on fire for warmth. They wouldn't let us light campfires, though some of the men did anyway. Our rations froze, and I carried extra batteries in my pockets because the cold killed them. When it was extra cold, our machine guns just froze over."

"That's terrible."

He sighed. "I'll never forget it. I hope I'm never that cold ever again."

Something leaped from the ground and snapped at Anna's walking stick. Anna squeaked in alarm. Felty's arm shot around her from behind and pulled her back against his chest. "What was that?" Anna gasped, feeling his racing heartbeat keeping time with hers.

He pointed to the end of Anna's walking stick. "Look."

Anna lifted her stick and gasped. A steel-jawed trap was stuck to the end of it, like a dog with its teeth held fast to a bone. "*Ach, du lieva*. I almost stepped into that."

Felty took Anna's walking stick, lifted the trap closer to his face, and examined it carefully. It was attached to a chain that looked to be staked into the ground. "Barbaric," he hissed.

"It could have cut my foot off," Anna said, breathless at the possibility of having to learn to cook on one foot.

Felty shook his head. "Your boots would have protected you. For sure and certain, it would have stung something wonderful if you'd been barefoot."

Anna looked at the trap. "I've seen traps like this at my cousin's house. They use them to catch coyotes so they don't kill their goats."

Felty threw Anna's stick to the ground. A fire flared to life behind his eyes. "Steel-jawed traps are one of the cruelest ways to catch an animal. They snap onto an animal's leg, causing horrible pain. Sometimes they die of starvation before the trapper can come by to finish them off. Sometimes animals try to chew off their own foot to escape. It's horrible."

"*Ach,*" Anna said. "I don't think my *onkel* knows that."

"We Amish talk about nonviolence but don't see anything wrong with doing violence to Gotte's creatures like this." His voice got louder. "It's all upside down."

Anna had never seen Felty so upset, even on that day when she'd asked him if he'd killed anybody. "I'm sorry, Felty. I didn't know until you told me. I think people just don't understand."

All the strength seemed to drain out of him like water from a leaky bucket. He leaned his back against the nearest tree and wrapped his arms around his waist. "I know, Anna. But they need to understand. Animals are suffering and dying, and people need to understand." He bowed his head, but not before she saw the tears in his eyes. "I don't have anything against hunting for food. Gotte provides so His children don't go hungry. But I can't stand the thought of people killing animals for their fur, making them suffer so they can take a profit. It's not right. And it's too easy for pets to be caught in these things. These traps are made for pain."

His anguish called tears to Anna's eyes. More than anything, she wanted to fix it, to make it so no animal ever suffered, so Felty would never have cause to be sad again. She placed her hand on his arm. "How can we make them understand?" she said softly. "What can I do?"

He lifted his gaze to her face. "*Ach*, Anna. There is so much suffering in the world. I don't know what any of us can do."

It was an utterly hopeless speech, but Anna refused to agree with him. "There is always hope," she said, slipping beside him and leaning against the tree. She pointed to her walking stick, still imprisoned by the trap. "We saved one animal today that won't get caught in that trap."

Felty studied her face, inhaled a deep breath, and gave her a promising smile. "As always, Anna, you are right. I can't save everybody. I will never be wise enough to do

Gotte's job for Him, no matter how smart I think I am." He bent over and yanked the chain out of the ground. It had been secured into the dirt with a stake. "Trappers don't usually set just one trap. That means there are more along the water here." His face glowed with indignation and purpose. "Do you want to help me find them?"

"What do we do with them once we find them? Is it stealing to throw them in the trash?"

He frowned. "I suppose it is. But we can trip as many as we find and maybe think of a way to keep critters from wandering into them."

Anna's heart raced. "It sounds dangerous and exciting and maybe a little rebellious."

Doubt traveled across his features. "You don't have to do it if you're not comfortable."

Anna grunted. "Comfortable? Who wants to be comfortable? I want adventure. The last time I had anything close to exciting happen to me was when I found a potato that looked like Harry Truman, and there was nobody to share my discovery with, because nobody at my house even knows who Harry Truman is."

Felty's lips twitched upward. "I think we can do better than Harry Truman. I mean, you could conceivably lose a finger with these steel traps."

Anna clapped her hands. "Danger *and* excitement. I'm going to faint, and I mean that in a good way."

Felty laughed, and Anna's heart swelled bigger than the sky. She never again wanted to see Felty cry. "Okay," he said. "Let's look for traps while we search for the cow. We still need to find the cow."

Anna furrowed her brow. "Do you think she got caught in one of the traps?"

"I don't think so. Cows' hooves are too big for a small animal trap."

"There's something to be glad about."

Felty handed Anna her stick. "Hold this while I remove the trap." He bent over and pressed a lever on the side of the trap, and its jaws came apart. Anna pulled her stick away, and Felty picked up some snow and packed it on top of the now-useless trap. He stood up straight and shrugged. "Maybe it will make it harder to find." He folded his arms and let his gaze travel along the ground to the east. "Now we need to figure out what to look for."

"Aren't we looking for traps?"

"*Jah*, but they're partially buried under the snow. We need to look for footprints or mounds or signs that someone has disturbed the snow."

Anna pointed a hundred feet ahead. "Do you see that little hill of snow up against that bush? That doesn't look natural."

Felty raised his eyebrows. "You have *gute* eyes, Anna."

"I've been eating my carrots—usually mixed in green Jell-O."

They hiked to the bouquet of bare branches that used to be a bush. "Is this a huckleberry?" Felty asked.

"*Jah.* You can find them all over the hill."

Felty poked his walking stick into the snow, and a trap snapped around it. Anna had been expecting it, but it still made her jump. Felty laughed with delight, yanked the anchor chain from the ground, and released the trap from his stick. "We're doing a great service to the animals of Sugg Hill," he said. "Thanks to you, Anna, there will be at least two coyotes or foxes or beavers that will be able to go home to their families tonight."

When he said it like that, it made Anna feel proud and teary at the same time. "Let's find more," she said. "I've always had a special place in my heart for beavers."

In another half an hour, they had found three more traps, and it was worth the cold toes and runny nose to see Felty so happy. His brilliant smile was better than ten potatoes shaped like Harry Truman. After he yanked the fifth chain from the ground, he eyed Anna, and his smile faded. "Your cheeks are bright red. I've kept you out here too long."

Anna pressed her mittens to her cheeks. "I don't mind. I've had enough excitement to last me clear to Ascension Day."

"Your *dat* would never forgive me if you caught a cold looking for traps. We should get you home."

"But what about the cow? We really need to find that cow."

As if the animal had been waiting to be summoned, a low, mournful moan rose up through the trees. Felty guided Anna in the direction of the sound, and they soon came upon Felty's lost cow standing in a clearing crying up to the sky, swaying as if she were rooted to the ground. She was a beautiful Jersey cow with a silky, tan hide and large brown eyes. Felty jogged through the snow to his cow and clucked his tongue in sympathy. The cow's leg was tangled in some baling wire, and she had a nasty cut on her front right fetlock.

"*Ach*, poor Daisy, poor girl," Felty said, patting the cow's neck. "Look at your leg. Poor girl."

"Her name is Daisy? That's sweet."

Felty pulled a short rope from his pocket and looped

it over Daisy's head. "*Ach*, *vell*, we have over a hundred cows. I call all of them Daisy."

Anna giggled. "I guess you never get their names wrong."

"I guess not." Felty pulled some wire cutters from his pocket and smirked at Anna. "I came prepared. Could you hold her steady?"

Anna gripped the rope while Felty cut the wire wrapped around Daisy's pastern. Daisy didn't even flinch and didn't try to run away when Felty finally freed her. She'd probably had a long and tiring day.

Felty took the rope from Anna. "*Cum*, Daisy. Let's go home, and I'll get your leg fixed up real *gute* for you." He tossed his walking stick away and grabbed Anna's hand as if it was the most natural, normal thing in the world. "*Cum* to my house, Anna. You can get warm, then I'll drive you home in the buggy. We've walked far enough for one day."

She was barely able to pay attention to what he was saying while her head was spinning like a child's top. Even with his gloves and her mittens between them, the feel of her hand in his was more exciting than almost anything she'd ever experienced. More exciting than hunting for animal traps. More exciting than finding lost cows. And much more exciting than Harry Truman.

She'd never be able to go back to normal life again.

Chapter 8

The snow fell in chunks, as if someone had torn open all the feather ticks in heaven and sent the feathers floating to Earth. It was a terrible day to be out running errands, but Mamm needed molasses and brown sugar for the shoofly pie she was making. The snow on the road was too deep for a buggy but not quite deep enough for a sleigh. The buggy would have to do one more time before Felty started using the sleigh for the heavy winter travel.

A baby blue Studebaker roared past Felty's buggy, missing him by inches and leaving Felty gasping for air. Georgie, his horse, whinnied and veered sharply to the right before arcing back onto the road. The buggy dovetailed and righted itself, but Felty's knuckles were white around the reins, and his heart felt as if it were lodged in his throat, pumping a violent rhythm. It would be so easy for a car to lose control on the ice and slam into him. Cars were seldom careful when they passed a buggy. Sometimes Felty wondered if *Englisch* drivers were purposefully reckless to scare the Plain folk, just to let the Amish know they weren't welcome on their roads or in their country. It wasn't like that with all *Englisch*, but there were a few who didn't look kindly on the Amish or their stance on the war. Some *Englischers* thought the Amish were shirking their duty to their country when they refused to fight. People could be wonderful ugly sometimes.

Felty knew that as well as anybody.

When his heart returned to a normal rhythm, he tried to put the Studebaker and the war out of his mind. He would rather think about Anna. He should have gone shopping yesterday before the snows, but on Monday, Anna had mentioned that she was going to be in town *today*, so Felty had put off his shopping trip. His need to see Anna was a physical ache at the bottom of his gut. It was either a chance meeting in town or seeing her at the *singeon* on Sunday night, and if he never went to another *singeon* again, it would be too soon. The only *gute* thing about any singing was that Anna might be there, and seeing her was almost worth the risk of being coupled up with Rosie Herschberger for Love in the Dark.

Felty's plan was to be at the market the moment it opened and hang around until Anna showed up. Mamm wouldn't like it if he was away for several hours, but he'd wait all day if it meant he got to see Anna.

The buggy lurched and skidded on the icy road as Felty turned the horse into the parking lot behind the market. He smiled when he saw another buggy already parked there. Wouldn't that be the bee's knees if Anna was there already?

He tethered Georgie under a wide lean-to type of shelter next to the other buggy. Georgie would be out of the worst of the snow, now coming down harder than ever.

Felty could barely see the market through the blizzard, and he wasn't more than a hundred feet away.

He ran for the door, stepped inside, and brushed the snowflakes off his coat, savoring the warmth of the indoors while keeping a sharp eye out for Anna. A few *Englisch* customers strolled up and down the aisles, as well as an Amish couple Felty didn't know. *Ach*, was that their buggy parked outside? He turned down one aisle to see Rosie Herschberger with her older *schwester* Lizzy and Lizzy's two small children. Rosie looked up at Felty, gave him a polite smile, and promptly turned her back on him. She obviously had no interest in being even slightly friendly. He was a soldier and an outcast, after all. Felty didn't mind. He truly didn't care what Rosie thought of him. He was more concerned over whether her *fater* the bishop would agree to let Felty take baptism classes.

Felty peeked down two more aisles and finally found what he was looking for. He couldn't keep from smiling. Anna and her *bruder* Elmer stood looking at the shelf dedicated to tubs of colorful Christmas candy. "You run into the nicest surprises in the grocery store," he said, trying to stroll slowly down the aisle when he really wanted to run to Anna and wrap her in his arms.

Anna knocked the wind out of him when she looked up and burst into a smile, as if she was overjoyed to see him. As if maybe she liked him. A lot. That smile was worth braving a hundred blizzards for. "Felty, you're just in time to settle a question for us. If you were baking Christmas cookies for the shut-ins, would you add"—she held up a plastic tub of assorted licorice candies—"these licorice candies with interesting shapes and colors, or these"—she held up a tub of small red candies—"cinnamon candies that are spicy and Christmassy red?"

Felty laughed. He loved that Anna enjoyed experimenting with food. Who wanted a boring snickerdoodle when they could have an oatmeal cookie laced with Red Hots? Strong cinnamon was something Felty could actually taste.

Elmer grabbed the licorice candies from Anna. "Nobody likes licorice. And these will melt in the oven for sure and certain. Your cookies will be a mess."

Anna frowned. "How do you know? Besides, even if they melt, they'll make interesting shapes on the cookies. What do you think, Felty?"

Felty had been momentarily distracted by Anna's cute, upturned nose and didn't hear what came before the question. "Umm. I think both candies would be *appeditlich* in cookies."

Elmer made a face. "You can't say that, Felty. You have to choose."

"I do?"

Elmer nodded. "Or we'll be standing here all day."

Felty rubbed his hand down his face. "I can't choose between two of Anna's wonderful *gute* ideas. Maybe you should get them both and make two batches."

Anna grinned. "That is the best idea yet. There are lots of shut-ins, and we'll be caroling several times before Christmas."

Three *Englisch* teenagers casually strolled past Elmer, and before Felty had time to be suspicious, one of the boys reached out and knocked the hat off Elmer's head. Felty flinched. Surprise and alarm popped all over Elmer's face. He hesitated, then bent over to pick up his hat.

One of the boys kicked it underneath the row of shelves. "Lose something, Amish boy?" he taunted.

"You don't have to be so rude," Anna said.

Felty's throat tightened into a knot, and he stepped in front of Elmer and Anna. "Just move along and quit bothering people."

One boy laughed, his laughter sounding more like mockery than amusement. The other two sneered so hard it looked as if their lips would break. The laugher reached up and knocked Felty's hat off his head. Felty knew better than to pick it up. He held up a hand when Elmer moved to pick it up for him.

Two of the boys had that strange hairstyle that Felty's friend Tooley had called a "D.A.," with a curl neatly fashioned right in the middle of the forehead. It looked ridiculous. "We don't want any trouble," Felty said, and he meant it. He'd witnessed enough violence and hatred to last a hundred lifetimes. But he wouldn't stand by and let these germs bother Anna or Elmer. "Just go away before I do something you'll regret."

The tallest boy got right in Felty's face, obviously trying to scare him or make him back down. What the *Englischer* didn't know was that Felty wasn't scared of anything anymore. "Is that a threat, Amish boy?"

Felty didn't even blink. "That's a promise."

Something like doubt flickered in the boy's eyes before he stretched a stony smile across his face and laughed again. "You don't get to say anything to me, Amish boy."

"You tell him, Ronnie," one of the other boys said.

Felty resisted the urge to roll his eyes. He didn't want to provoke Ronnie-boy, but Ronnie wasn't very smart if the only insult he could think of was "Amish boy." Felty wasn't intimidated. He had at least three inches on Ronnie, and he'd stared down the barrel of a rifle and lived to tell the tale. When a man had faced death, everything else felt sort of trivial. But that didn't mean Felty wasn't on edge. Even though he wasn't touching her, he could feel Anna's apprehension behind him. It was one thing to harass Felty. It was quite another to scare Anna.

Ronnie held a crinkled paper in his fist. He raised it and shook it in Felty's face. "Do you know what this is?"

Ronnie held the paper still long enough for Felty to catch a glimpse. *Jah.* He knew what that was. His heart sank, and he suddenly felt wonderful sorry for Ronnie, even though Ronnie was a *dumkoff* who needed to grow up. *Ach*, *vell*, he'd grow up in Korea all right. Felty nodded. "You got drafted."

Ronnie growled and let out a string of curses. Felty could only hope that Anna didn't know what any of them meant. "I have to go to war because you're too much of a coward to go yourself. All you Amish are cowards, and I have to take your place. You hide in our country and take advantage of our freedom while us real Americans fight to protect you."

Elmer tried to help, even though his interference would make more trouble for both of them. "We aren't cowards. We don't believe in violence."

One of the other boys pressed his hand against Elmer's chest and backed him into the shelf. "You wanna take it outside? We'll show you what violence feels like."

Anna gasped. Felty clenched his teeth. This had gone on long enough.

Felty grabbed the coat collar of the boy threatening Elmer and yanked him back so forcefully, his feet left the ground for a split second. When Ronnie tried to intervene,

Felty took a fistful of Ronnie's shirt and pulled him forward. The other kid froze where he stood, not sure how to react to an Amish boy who knew how to fight back. Firmly grasping the one boy's collar and Ronnie's shirt, Felty pulled them down the aisle away from Anna and Elmer, who watched him in stunned silence and probably a fair bit of alarm. The third boy followed, shuffling his feet as if he didn't want to get in a fight but felt obligated to stick by his friends.

When Felty was far enough away from Anna not to be heard, he leaned in close and spoke softly, menacingly, hoping to strike fear and respect into their juvenile delinquent hearts. "You think you scare me? You and your Mickey Mouse friends coming in here trying to frighten innocent people who ain't never done you any harm? Well, I've been to Korea. I've seen things that would make you wet your pants and cry like a baby. My best friend died right next to me. I got the scar on my face from a grenade that killed my sergeant. And then there was the knife fight with the North Korean who was either going to kill me or I was going to kill him."

He let go of both of them, unbuttoned the first four buttons of his shirt, and pulled it back to show them the nasty five-inch scar right above his heart. This was one he would never, ever show Mamm. Ronnie's eyes nearly popped out of his head. The other two boys looked sufficiently impressed. "Another soldier saved me before I bled to death." He glared at Ronnie. "Don't you dare call me a coward. You don't know what bravery is until you've seen one man give his life for another. You better learn how to make friends, true friends, because if nobody has your back in a war, you'll die the minute you get off the boat."

Beads of sweat formed on Ronnie's upper lip. "I didn't know . . ." he mumbled, his eyes locked on Felty's jagged scar.

Felty swallowed the righteous indignation lodged in his throat, took a deep breath, and buttoned his shirt. Even though Ronnie was a foolish, stupid teenager, Felty shouldn't be so hard on him. He was about to learn first-hand what war and terror and pain felt like. "You'd do well to zip your lip and try to show people a little more kindness. You never know what the man in the bunk next to you has been through. You can't guess at the pain in someone else's life. And don't take your anger out on poor Amish folks who are just trying to live their lives the way they think God wants them to."

Felty couldn't hope that Ronnie was the humble type who would admit to a mistake, but he did seem a little less sure of himself. He smoothed his hand down his shirt where Felty had grabbed it. "You don't have to flip your lid, man. I get it. If I'd known you were a soldier, I never would have knocked off your hat."

"That shouldn't have mattered," Felty said. "You need to treat everyone kindly, whether you agree with their politics or not. Lots of people are mad at the Amish for not fighting, but how many of the angry ones live their religion twenty-four hours a day, seven days a week? If you're not willing to die for what you believe in, don't attack the people who are." He folded his arms across his chest. "And you should know better than to do anything like that around women or girls. We're supposed to protect them, not frighten them."

A store clerk with white hair and a white apron appeared at the end of the aisle and frowned at Felty. "Are these boys bothering you?"

"No," Felty said. "We were just having a discussion."

The clerk pursed his lips and raised an eyebrow. "Maybe, but these boys were just leaving, weren't you, Ronnie?"

"No I wasn't," Ronnie said. "I came to get a Pepsi-Cola."

"Not anymore," the clerk said. "You come in and cause a ruckus and scare my paying customers away. Go to Rexall's and get a Pepsi-Cola. I want you out." He grabbed Ronnie's coat sleeve and yanked him toward the front of the store. "Out. You and your two musketeers."

Ronnie's voice rose with his agitation. "You can't throw me out. I just got drafted."

The clerk was unmoved. "I'm sorry to hear that, but maybe the army will make a man out of you." A little bell above the door rang when he opened it, and the snow blew in.

Felty followed the three boys outside, and the clerk slammed the door behind them. "One more thing," Felty said.

Ronnie growled and turned around. "What, Amish soldier boy?"

"If you let it, hate will eat you up in Korea. Remember the greatest of all gifts from God is love. Don't let the hate destroy you."

Ronnie regained some of his original swagger. "Go take a long walk off a short pier." He and his friends laughed and ran down the sidewalk in the direction of Rexall Drugs—or rather, they jogged gingerly. The sidewalks were wonderful slick.

Ach, *vell*, Felty had tried to help. It wasn't his fault if Ronnie didn't really care. Maybe he would someday.

Anna and Elmer were right inside the door waiting for him when Felty went back into the store. Anna brushed the snow off his coat. Elmer handed him his hat. "*Denki,*" Felty said. "It's wonderful cold out there without a hat."

"We're the ones who should be thanking you. Those boys were very naughty." Anna rested her hand on the door handle and peered out at the retreating figures of Ronnie and his friends.

Felty eyed her with concern. "I'm sorry they scared you."

"I wasn't especially scared. But Benjamin Kiem got beat up once by some boys in town. I didn't want them to hurt Elmer."

"I remember," Felty said. He pressed his lips together and gazed solemnly at Anna and Elmer. "It's one of the reasons I joined the army."

Anna gave him a puzzled look. "It is? Were you afraid you'd get beat up if you didn't join?"

"*Nae*, but it made me start to wonder why our neighbors were so mad at us, what would cause *gute* people to hurt other human beings like that. I did a lot of soul-searching." He stood at the door with Anna and looked out into the storm. "Ronnie is frightened. Going to war is terrifying, and he doesn't even realize how scared he should be. I feel sorry for him."

Anna blew a puff of air from between her lips. "I suppose this means I'll have to knit Ronnie a scarf or something, just so he knows I forgive him and that love is more powerful than hatred."

Felty smiled. "That would be nice. He'll need it in Korea in the winter."

"What did you say to them?" Elmer asked. "They seemed very interested in whatever you showed them under your shirt."

Anna's face glowed with curiosity. "Did you show them your tattoo?"

Felty chuckled. "Nice try, Anna, but I refuse to reveal whether I have a tattoo or not."

Elmer's ears perked up. "What kind of tattoo is it?"

Felty made a show of putting a pretend key to his lips and turning it. "My lips are locked." It was a *gute* way to deflect questions about what he had really shown those pesky juveniles. Sometime he'd tell Anna about that scar, but he wasn't ready to relive it twice in one day.

Elmer groaned, obviously disappointed, but he didn't push it further. "We left the candy on the shelf. Do you want me to go get it, Anna?"

"*Jah*, please." Anna didn't take her gaze from the street outside. "Then we should finish our shopping and go home before the snow gets worse."

Elmer nodded and walked away. Felty loved the thought of being alone with Anna, even though they weren't really alone. There were shoppers scattered all around the store. But standing here staring out at the snow together made him feel connected to her. He was relieved she hadn't been hurt and relieved he hadn't been forced to punch somebody. Anna wouldn't have liked it, and he wouldn't have either.

She glanced at him. "I'm *froh* it's snowing. Maybe the trapper won't be able to find his traps buried in the snow. Maybe he won't want to leave his warm house to check."

"I went back there last night," Felty said, sliding his hand along the door handle until it touched hers.

"You did?" she squeaked, as if his hand had taken her by surprise.

He hoped it wasn't an unwanted surprise. "I wanted to see what had happened with the traps, and I wanted to try something that might keep the little critters away."

"What did you find?"

"All the traps had been moved a few feet farther from the stream and reset." He grinned at her. "I tripped them all again, and then I thought it might be *gute* to . . ." He stopped himself before he told Anna something that might shock her to the core.

"Good for you," Anna said, moving her hand so her little finger sat directly on top of his. His heart did a little jig. "Then you thought it might be *gute* to what?"

He caught his bottom lip between his teeth. "*Ach*, Anna, it's too disgusting to tell."

She curled one side of her mouth. "I'm well acquainted with disgusting. Have you ever cleaned an outhouse regularly used by four boys?"

"Funny you should mention that." He looked at her face and laughed softly. "I heard that animals avoid things that smell like humans." He cleared his throat and lowered his voice. "So I urinated on each trap."

Anna's eyes grew as round as dinner plates. "Felty, you didn't!"

"I thought it was a clever idea."

She giggled. "It was a clever idea—indecent, but clever. And probably wonderful cold."

He nodded, not about to mention how cold it *really* felt to certain parts of his body. "I told you that in Korea, it got so cold our machine guns froze. That is how we thawed them out."

"By . . . urinating on them?"

Felty nodded.

Anna gasped and clapped her hand over her mouth. "*Ach*, *du lieva*, Felty. Don't tell Isaac that story. I don't know what kinds of ideas it will give him."

"I won't tell anyone but you." And he wouldn't. Mamm and Dat had no desire to hear about the war, and stories like that just reminded everyone else that he had been a soldier.

"Anything for the animals, I guess," Anna said.

Felty nodded. "Just about anything."

Anna caught her breath. "*Ach.* With all the excitement, I almost forgot." She shoved her hand into her coat pocket and pulled out a piece of paper.

"What's this?"

Anna's smile warmed the air around them. "I thought about what you said, how there is so much suffering in the world and there is nothing we can do about it. I thought of something to do. I went to see our veterinarian on Tuesday, and he mailed in the paperwork." She unfolded the paper. "You and I are now members of the American Society for the Prevention of Cruelty to Animals. They call it the ASPCA for short, and they try to get laws passed that will help animals. We should get our membership cards in a few weeks."

Awestruck, Felty took the paper and fingered it as if it were made of spun glass. "*Jah*, I know who they are."

"I didn't get it approved with the bishop, but I don't think he will object to us trying to help Gotte's creatures." She studied his face and frowned. "Do you think it's okay I didn't get permission from the bishop? I'm always forging ahead without considering the consequences. That's what Dat says."

"*Ach*, Anna. It's more than okay. This is *wunderbarr*."

She smiled and looked down at her hands. "I hoped you'd like it."

His insides felt like melted chocolate, and his eyes stung as if tears were only seconds away. He blinked them back. "No one has ever given me a more thoughtful gift. *Denki*." If they hadn't been standing in the grocery store, Felty would have taken her into his arms and given her the biggest kiss a man had ever given a woman—if she had been willing, of course. Anna was absolute perfection. Was there anyone else who would have thought to give him such a present?

Someone cleared her throat. Felty and Anna turned at the same time. Rosie Herschberger and her sister Lizzy stood behind them, patiently—or not—waiting for Anna and Felty to move so they could leave the store. Lizzy smiled thinly at Felty. "We parked across the street."

"*Ach*, of course," Felty said, stepping aside so they could pass.

"*Denki*." Lizzy opened the door, inviting a flurry of snow and an icy wind inside, and stepped out into the storm with a bag of groceries in her arm, pulling her *dochter* along with her.

Rosie had hold of her little nephew's hand. "Hold tight, Marvin," she said. She took one step out the door and turned back to Felty, pinning him with a stern eye. "We work hard to be seen as peaceful and God-fearing people. *Englischers* hate us more when people like you return anger for anger. You may have thought you were doing a *gute* thing, scolding those boys like that, but really you didn't help any of us. It would have been better to turn the other cheek."

Felty gave Rosie a polite smile and shrugged. "I'm not especially concerned about winning your approval, but you are free to your own opinion."

Apparently deeply offended, Rosie's nostrils flared, and her lips formed into a tight pucker. Marvin let go of her hand and followed his *mamm* outside. The door shut behind him. Rosie was so caught up in her indignation, she didn't even seem to notice. "I'm sorry you don't care what I think," Rosie said. "It was kindly meant. If you truly want to be welcomed back into the community, you've got to start behaving like an Amish man instead of a soldier."

"He was protecting Elmer," Anna said.

Felty appreciated that Anna was trying to help, but he didn't have the time or the inclination to care about Rosie Herschberger's opinion. He hadn't done anything wrong, and he wasn't about to apologize for teaching those boys a lesson—and a peaceful, measured, significant lesson at that.

Rosie glanced at Anna as if she were a piece of lint on her shoulder. "I'm sure Elmer would have been just fine. It is an honor to suffer shame for Christ's name."

Felty folded his arms. "Isn't it even better to stop violence before it happens? Help the sinner see the error of his ways before he sins?"

Rosie lifted her pretty little nose into the air. "I'm not going to split hairs with you, Felty Helmuth. You know Gotte's word well enough."

Why in the world was he standing in the store debating with Rosie Herschberger? It was a complete waste of time. He opened the door for her. "Goodbye, Rosie. See you at *gmay*."

Before Rosie could walk through the door, a movement outside drew Felty's attention. Marvin, who couldn't have been more than three, started across the street in an attempt to catch up with his *mater*. Felty's breath stuck in his throat. Little Marvin didn't see the car, and the car certainly wouldn't be able to see him in this blizzard. And with the icy roads, the car wouldn't be able to stop in time.

Marvin stared into the oncoming headlights and tried to get out of the way, but he slipped and fell on the ice.

Everything seemed to happen in slow motion as Felty shot out the door and slid into the road, yelling his guts out as the car barreled toward Marvin. The driver might have hit his brakes, but the road was so slick, the car kept coming. Felty slipped and hit his knee hard on the pavement, got up again, and scooped up Rosie's nephew.

With his arms tightly around the boy, Felty dove out of the way of the oncoming car. A blinding flash of pain knocked him forward as someone screamed his name. The last thing he remembered was seeing the license plate of the car that hit him. It was a New Hampshire. If it hadn't hit him, he never would have seen it. Lucky and unlucky, Tooley would have said.

The world spun before dropping him into darkness.

Chapter 9

The pies and cakes and casseroles started coming not six hours after the accident. Mamm was beside herself, partly because Felty had sort of been run over by a car, but mostly because they would never be able to eat all the goodies accumulating on the kitchen table.

Felty wasn't completely comfortable with all the attention, but his shoulder and knee hurt too much to worry about it. The man who had been driving the car had called him a hero. Rosie Herschberger had bawled like a baby and thanked him seven times for saving her nephew's life.

Felty limped into the kitchen, clutching the blanket draped over his shoulders. Even the light pressure of the blanket on his aching shoulder was too much, but the house was cold, and after a winter in Korea, Felty had learned that he'd rather be acutely uncomfortable than freezing cold.

Mamm turned and propped her hands on her hips. "What do you think you are doing?"

"I need a drink."

"You were just run over by a car. Go sit in the living

room, and I'll bring you a drink. For goodness' sake, Felty, that's why I had Dat bring in the cowbell."

Felty curled up one side of his mouth. "I refuse to summon my *mamm* with a cowbell. You're not my servant or a cow."

Mamm laughed softly. "It won't hurt me to wait on you for a change. You do more than your fair share around here."

Felty shrugged and immediately regretted it. Pain tore through his shoulder and down his back. "You gave birth to me. I'll never be able to repay you for that."

Mamm nodded. "Twenty hours of labor, and don't you forget it. So be obedient and go sit down. I don't want you aggravating your injuries. If it gets worse, I'm taking you to a doctor."

A nasty reddish-purple bruise was already forming, covering his entire left shoulder and a *gute* portion of his upper arm. Felty didn't even want to guess what his left upper back looked like. He'd be black and blue by morning, and he wasn't sure how he would be able to keep Mamm from wanting a look. But if she looked, she'd see the scar near his heart, and he didn't want her to know. At least he could protect her from that.

Mamm handed Felty a glass of water, and he drank the whole thing. "Now go sit," she said. "We need to change the bandage on your knee."

Someone knocked on the door, and Mamm sighed even as her eyes lit up. She didn't want more goodies in the house, but this was the *gute* kind of attention, the positive kind of attention from the community that Mamm had missed for two years. It warmed Felty's heart to see Mamm less worried and more her old self.

Felty turned to answer the door, but Mamm clucked her tongue in a scold. "Go sit. There have been people in and out of here for an hour. You can't answer the door every time someone knocks. You'll wear yourself out."

Mamm was right. They'd already had about a dozen visitors today, and Felty was tired. He *had* been hit by a car this morning. It felt like a pretty *gute* excuse to do nothing. What Mamm didn't know was that Felty was hoping for one specific visitor and his excitement at answering the door had everything to do with her.

Felty hobbled into the living room and sat down on the easy chair usually reserved for Dat. It was the most comfortable chair in the house, and Mamm had insisted Felty use it.

He heard Mamm open the door. The person at the door said a few words Felty couldn't make out, but Mamm's voice was clear enough. "It was wonderful nice of you to come over, but Felty is too worn out for visitors right now."

Felty frowned. Every person who'd come over today had been ushered into the living room to see Felty. Mamm had gushed about Felty and soaked in the praise that members of the *gmay* had heaped on him. Ach*, Edna, Felty almost died saving one of our own. Isn't that just what Jesus would have done? Felty certainly is a* gute *boy. We're sorry we were suspicious before.*

Had Mamm suddenly decided he'd reached his visitor limit?

"*Denki* for the cinnamon rolls," Mamm said. "What did you say you put in them? Spicy cinnamon candy? I'm sure he'll enjoy them."

Felty leaped from his chair as if he'd been zapped with a cattle prod. The pain knocked the wind out of him, but he wasn't going to let Mamm shoo Anna away like a mosquito. "Anna," he called as he ran into the entryway, the pain making his head spin. Mamm had already halfway closed the door. She opened it wide and pressed her lips together as if she was quite annoyed with her son. Anna and her four *bruderen* stood on the porch, bundled up in coats and hats and five different colors of knitted scarves around their necks. For sure and certain, Anna had knitted every one.

Anna smiled when she saw him, then grimaced and held out her hand as if to keep him from falling. "*Ach*, Felty, you shouldn't be up."

Mamm's eyebrows traveled up her forehead. "That's what I said."

"I wanted to see you." He glanced at Mamm. "And I'm not too tired for visitors."

Mamm had the good sense to look sheepish. She didn't like Anna, plain and simple, and now she knew that Felty knew. He would have to do something about Mamm's dislike of Anna, but first he needed to convince Anna to fall in love with him. There would be plenty of time to work on his *mamm*.

He looked at the plate of small brown pinwheels in Mamm's hand and grinned at Anna. "You brought me cinnamon rolls."

Isaac made a face. "I told her not to add the Red Hots, but she didn't listen to me."

Elmer nudged Isaac with his elbow. Isaac poked him right back.

"Well," Anna said, "they're cinnamon rolls. Cinnamon candies seemed like the perfect addition." She glanced at the plate. "I probably didn't let them rise long enough, but I was in a hurry to get over here and see you. I was almost too worried to bake."

"You look like you need to lie down," Elmer said, his keen gaze probing Felty's face.

"*Ach*, *vell*, I probably do." Felty snatched a roll from the plate and took a bite. Crunchy and compact, just how he liked them. And the Red Hots burned his tongue just a little. He loved it when he could actually taste something. "Anna, these are the best cinnamon rolls I ever tasted, and that includes the last batch of yours. The Red Hots are the perfect touch."

Anna's face turned red with delight.

He motioned down the hall toward the living room. "*Cum reu* and stay for a few minutes."

Mamm's lips twitched in an attempt at a friendly smile. "It's so nice of you to visit, but Felty really has had a hard day."

Felty took the plate from Mamm and ducked into the living room. "It won't hurt for a few minutes."

Anna and the boys followed him. He eased himself painfully into his chair. Anna, Elmer, and Uriah sat on the sofa, and the other two boys sat on the floor. Felty gasped involuntarily when his knee brushed against the edge of the chair.

Anna came out of her seat as quickly as she had sat down. "Are you okay? What can I do to help? Do you need a pillow? An aspirin?"

Felty did his best to give her a reassuring smile. "All I need is this plate of delicious cinnamon rolls, and I'll be right as rain."

Anna blushed. "Don't tease me. I'm worried about

you." She pulled a blanket from the basket next to his chair and put it over his legs. "Is that okay?"

"*Denki.* I haven't stopped feeling cold since this morning. And my whole body hurts."

Owen leaned forward with wide eyes. "Did the car run over your legs?"

Isaac smacked Owen on the shoulder. "The car didn't run over any part of him."

"But Elmer said he got hit by a car."

Felty chuckled but soon stopped himself. His shoulder burned something wonderful, and his whole body ached whenever he moved. Laughing felt like it might kill him. "I fell on the ice and hurt my knee, then the car's side mirror clipped my shoulder as it passed."

Elmer scrunched his lips together. "I don't think it was the side mirror. I think it was the bumper."

"Something *gute* came out of it. I found New Hampshire."

"Was it lost?" Isaac asked.

"It was the car that hit me."

Worry lined Anna's face. "I guess that's something. But it doesn't make up for what happened. I hope this isn't rude to say, but I thought you were going to die, and I screamed until my throat hurt. I'm *froh* you didn't die and *froh* the car didn't run over you."

"So am I," Felty said. He'd almost died four times in Korea. He didn't want to think about death ever again. He tapped his palms on the armrests and gave them his biggest smile. "You're acting like it's my funeral, and I'm not ready to attend my own funeral. If I had died, I wouldn't have been able to eat one of Anna's famous cinnamon rolls. I have a lot to live for, and I plan on living a very long time."

Anna sighed in relief. "That is good to know. I won't worry so much."

"Did you break any bones?" Owen asked.

Felty flexed his left hand. "None that I know of. I just got banged up a bit. Nothing a little rest won't cure."

Owen had obviously come for some entertainment. "Do you have a bruise on your shoulder? Can we see your knee?"

Isaac shoved his *bruder* again. "Stop asking stupid questions. It's not polite."

Felty wasn't about to show them the bruise, because they'd also see the scar on his chest. But Owen would probably be satisfied with the knee, which looked quite gruesome. He raised his hand. "*Nae.* I don't mind." He slowly, gingerly rolled up his pant leg past his knee. He'd put on his baggiest pair of pants after the accident. "Mamm has it wrapped up wonderful *gute*, but she was going to change the bandage, so I don't wonder that she'll be fine if I take it off."

The room fell silent, and his five companions leaned forward ever so slightly as he unwrapped his knee. The brownish-red patch of blood on the gauze got bigger with each peeled-away layer. Uriah started breathing loudly as if trying not to hyperventilate, and Owen's face turned ashy white.

Felty paused and eyed Owen doubtfully. "Are you going to faint? You don't have to look."

Owen sat up straighter. "I'm not going to faint. That's *dumm*."

Felty's knee and leg did indeed look terrible. The

surrounding skin was bruised a reddish purple, and there was a deep hole in his skin where he had fallen on a piece of ice, or maybe a rock embedded in the pavement.

"Does it hurt?" Owen asked.

Isaac shoved him again. "Of course it hurts."

Felty let them all look for a minute, then wrapped his knee back up. "At least I can walk. It won't take too long to heal."

Elmer draped his arm around Felty. "How's your shoulder?"

"It hurts worse than the knee, but I can move it okay, and I think I can still help with the milking. Dat said he'd give me the easy jobs." He picked up another cinnamon roll and took a hearty bite. "Anna, these are *appeditlich*."

Anna grinned. "I'm *froh* you like them. After how brave you were today, I had to bake you something. I'm so happy you didn't die."

"I'm happy I didn't die too." He winked at Anna. "Especially since I haven't received my ASPCA membership card yet. But it wasn't particularly brave. Elmer was looking for candy, or he would have done the very same thing. I was just the one there to see it." Soldiers were trained not to hesitate.

"Of course it was brave," Anna said. "Everybody is talking about it. Even Rosie Herschberger admitted she's been wrong about you."

Felty winced. "Anything to help Rosie Herschberger feel better about herself."

Anna flinched as if she'd been pinched. "*Ach*, I almost forgot. I brought you another gift." She pulled a bright red scarf from her pocket. "You need a scarf to keep your neck warm."

She handed it to Felty, who squeezed it and smoothed it in his hand. "Oh, Anna. This is so nice. I love it. It looks just like the one you let me borrow the other day when we hiked up the hill."

Anna's face got red. "*Ach*, it *is* the one I let you borrow. I hope you don't mind a used scarf, but there wasn't time to knit you a new one."

Felty pressed the scarf to his face, wishing he still had his sense of smell. He imagined the scarf would smell like Anna Yoder. Probably the best smell in the whole world. "*Denki*, Anna. This is truly *wunderbarr*. I love this scarf."

Anna seemed pleased that he liked it. "I can't stand the thought of anybody having a cold neck. It's just not right."

Felty grinned. "I'll wear it every day."

"Even in the summer?" Uriah said.

"Maybe," Felty said, gazing at Anna. "So I'll have a piece of Anna with me all the time." Another knock at the door. Felty heard Mamm go down the hall and open it. He smiled apologetically. "We've had more visitors today than at Christmas."

"Everybody's very grateful. Don't forget that."

By the sound of it, Mamm was overjoyed by whoever had come to the door. Hopefully, Anna wouldn't recognize what a cold reception she'd gotten from Mamm. Felty frowned. There would be time. Mamm would come around to his way of thinking.

"*Cum reu. Cum reu,*" Mamm said brightly. "He's right in here."

Mamm came partway into the living room, with Rosie Herschberger close behind. Felty almost choked on the cinnamon roll in his mouth. "Look who came to see how you're doing?" Mamm gushed, backing out of the room. "And she brought her famous cinnamon rolls. Don't they look *wunderbarr*?"

Rosie walked into the living room as if she owned all the furniture and held her plate of cinnamon rolls like a trophy she was about to award Felty. *Ach*, *vell*, Rosie's cinnamon rolls were famously *gute*. She probably couldn't help being arrogant about them. "*Hallo*, Felty. I hope these will cheer you up. I whipped up a batch the minute I got home from town." She eyed the plate of Anna's cinnamon rolls sitting in Felty's lap. "*Ach*, Anna brought some too. How nice for you. Double the treats." She glanced triumphantly at Anna, no doubt fully confident that Felty would like her cinnamon rolls better.

Anna's shoulders drooped, and the light disappeared from her eyes. Felty longed to tell her what was in his heart, that Rosie Herschberger would never hold a candle to Anna or her cinnamon rolls. There was absolutely no reason for her to be disheartened. "*Denki*, Rosie," Felty said. "Do you mind if I save them for later? I'm afraid I've stuffed myself on Anna's cinnamon rolls already."

"Can I have one?" Isaac said, reaching out for Rosie's plate.

Elmer stretched out his foot and kicked his *bruder*.

Rosie laughed as if she was slightly amused and slightly annoyed. "*Nae*, Isaac. I made them specially for Felty. I said to Lizzy, 'Felty saved Marvin. He needs a sweet roll,' and she said, 'Don't worry about the laundry or dinner. You just go right ahead and mix up a batch and take them to him right quick.' Mamm wanted me to be sure to tell you how grateful she is that you saved

Marvin's life. We're all so grateful, especially me. I'm the one who let go of Marvin's hand when I should have been watching out for him." She turned slightly red, probably remembering that she'd been giving Felty a lecture when Marvin had run off.

"How is Marvin?" Felty asked, with one eye on Anna, who had gone completely silent.

Rosie batted her eyelashes. "*Ach*, he's fine, thanks to you. He has a little scrape on his hand from falling on the ice, but it could have been so much worse. Our family owes you everything, Felty. I'm so sorry we misjudged you. How could anyone doubt that you are truly one of us?"

How indeed?

Rosie droned on and on about how grateful her whole family was and how *wunderbarr* and brave and handsome Felty was and how she didn't care that he'd been a soldier. And that everyone should treat him with Christian charity instead of how they'd been treating him. Rosie pretended she wasn't one of those who had all but ignored Felty, and it didn't really matter. Felty knew the truth, but he was supposed to forgive all the same.

He wasn't one to soak up praise, and he had never cared what Rosie had to say about anything. What he *did* care about was the fact that Anna became increasingly agitated with every word out of Rosie's mouth.

He stared at her, willing her to look at him, wanting to show her the truth in his eyes—the truth that Rosie and her sweet rolls meant nothing to him. But would it do any *gute*? Anna thought herself inferior to Rosie in every way. What could Felty do to convince her otherwise?

Anna suddenly stood up as if she'd been pinched. "We should go."

"But I want a cinnamon roll," Isaac moaned.

Elmer kicked him again. "You're not getting one, and we're going."

"But you just got here," Felty said, his heart sinking.

"We wanted to make sure you are okay and to drop off some treats. Now I need to get dinner on."

Felty made to push himself from the chair, but Anna shook her head. "Don't get up. It hurts too much."

"I want to see you out."

Anna's smile didn't reach her eyes. "We know the way."

Felty grasped at anything that might coax Anna out of her melancholy. "*Denki* for the cinnamon rolls and the ASPCA and your help the other night. I'm so grateful."

Anna wouldn't meet his eyes. "You're welcome. I hope you feel better soon."

He hated to see her leave like this. She was so obviously troubled, and he felt powerless in the face of so much unhappiness. "All I need is a *gute* night's sleep. *Denki* again for the visit and the eats. For sure and certain, cooks all over the country will start putting Red Hots in their cinnamon rolls. They're that good."

Anna's lips curled slightly, but she didn't say another word. Felty didn't take his eyes from her until she ducked into the hall, and even then, he listened carefully for her footsteps among the other four pairs of feet as they left the house. Just the thought of Anna so close was a comfort.

He drew no such comfort from smiling, cloying Rosie Herschberger.

Rosie gazed silently at him until they heard the front door close. Anna and her *bruderen* were gone, and Mamm seemed to have completely vanished—no doubt eager to give Felty and Rosie some privacy. Felty sighed inwardly. Dear Mamm, trying to give Felty a gift he didn't want.

Rosie sat in the exact spot where Anna had been sitting, as if trying to replace her. "Anna is such a sweet girl. I admire how she's gotten along so well without a mother to teach her how to do the wifely things. I'm afraid she's never really learned how to cook or sew with any real skill."

Felty picked up another one of Anna's cinnamon rolls and took a huge bite. He had to chew for a few seconds before replying. "I think Anna is a fine cook. And did you see the scarves they were wearing? She made all of them."

Rosie's lips twitched as if she didn't quite know what to do with Felty's praise. "*Jah*, Anna knits up a storm. Last year she knitted a bright pink sweater for herself. My *dat* had to tell her that she wasn't allowed to wear it. Too fancy. Anna doesn't seem to have a sense about what is proper and what's not. It's a deficiency for sure and certain. But I don't wonder that it comes from not having a *mamm* to guide her through the hard patches."

"I don't think Anna has any deficiencies." Felty glanced at the clock. Rosie had worn out her welcome.

Rosie set her plate on the sofa next to her and coughed daintily into her hand. "*Ach*, *vell*, I didn't come to talk about Anna."

Even though she was the one who'd started criticizing Anna the minute she left.

"I came to see if you would be up to a hayride and caroling on Thursday night. All *die youngie* will be there. We're caroling to some of the shut-ins with hot chocolate and doughnuts at my house after."

"All of *die youngie* will be there?" Felty's heart raced. He'd have a chance to see Anna and make her smile.

Rosie leaned forward and clasped her hands together. "*Jah.* I hope you'll feel well enough to come."

"I suppose I will."

She sensed his hesitation. "I need to apologize, Felty. I'm sorry for disliking you so much before."

What did she want him to say to that?

Apparently nothing. She wrung her hands. "It's just that the ministers and my *dat* preached so much against you and the war, and we all thought you were the most wicked boy in the world. Abe Kiem said you would lead us all into temptation and out of the community and down to hell."

"That's a lot of places for one boy to take everybody."

Rosie grimaced around her smile. "How were we to know what kind of boy you would be when you came back? Violence is against Gotte's law. I don't wonder but killing people changes the people who do the killing."

That was quite a mouthful, and Felty had to admit that killing had changed him. But maybe not in the way Rosie thought.

"You'd always been so handsome and fascinating. My *dat* warned that you might try to lure me and all of *die youngie* to the ways of the world."

"I don't want to lure anybody anywhere. I just want to get baptized and live a quiet life the rest of my days." And marry Anna.

Rosie nodded enthusiastically, sat up straight, and smiled agreeably, as if all that unpleasantness was immediately forgotten. "Of course you do. I knew it the minute you jumped in front of that car to save Marvin's life. I'm sorry I doubted. But all is forgiven. Everyone is dying to make friends with you."

Felty pressed his lips together. What a difference a day made. He was suddenly the most interesting, talked-about boy in Bonduel. Would his popularity be temporary or permanent? If they accepted him, that might make him good enough for Anna, or at least Anna's *dat* and *mammi*. That was who he really needed to impress to have a chance with Anna. "Okay," Felty said. "It sounds like fun."

Rosie clapped her hands in delight. "*Wunderbarr!* We're meeting at my house at six on Thursday. I should go and let you get rested for the hayride." She stood, picked up her plate of cinnamon rolls, and set it directly on top of Anna's rolls that were in Felty's lap. Fortunately, Anna's rolls were sturdy enough that Rosie's plate didn't smash them. "Eat one of my cinnamon rolls. Dat says they're like medicine."

Felty gave her a smile, even though he thought the cinnamon roll trick wasn't very nice. "I don't wonder that they are."

The real medicine would be at the hayride. If he had anything to say about it, he'd sit by Anna the whole time and secretly hold her hand if she'd let him. The best way to drive away the cold was to warm up from the inside out, and his love for Anna was a raging fire.

Chapter 10

Anna threw a flour-sack dish towel over her basket and skipped out the door. It had been two days since the accident, and Anna was very eager to tell Mrs. Vandegrift all about how Felty had almost been run over by a car and saved Marvin's life. It was the kind of story Mrs. Vandegrift would find just terrifying enough to be interesting.

The story was exciting, but Anna didn't take any pleasure in the memory of watching Felty almost die. She couldn't begin to explain how relieved she was that Felty had not been injured worse. She was even more relieved that Gotte hadn't needed another angel in heaven that day. She'd gone straight home and said a prayer of thanks while baking cinnamon rolls. And a prayer of thanks after the cinnamon rolls were done. And two prayers of thanks before bed that night.

Felty was coming to be more and more important to her all the time, and it was very nice of Gotte to spare his life. Even though Gotte probably hadn't done it as a favor to Anna, she was *froh* all the same.

Mrs. Vandegrift lived across the street and down a quarter mile from Anna's house, and she loved visitors, Amish and *Englisch* alike. Mrs. Vandegrift was a ninety-year-old *Englisch* widow who lived alone in a tiny house that she used to share with her husband and five children. Her children were all married with families of their own. Two of them lived nearby, and they took very *gute* care of her, but she refused to move out of her house. She clung fiercely to her independence, even though she was hard of hearing and had never learned to drive. She tended her garden in the spring and summer and watched her television programs all winter long when it was too cold to go out. One of her daughters brought in lunch every day, and Anna took in dinner once a week. Mrs. Vandegrift seemed to enjoy Anna's cooking, but sometimes Anna suspected she didn't enjoy the food as much as the conversation. Not many people enjoyed Anna's food, including most of her *bruderen*.

Anna stifled a yawn. It had been a very late night last night. She'd have to get to bed earlier if she didn't want to catch a Christmas cold.

Anna knocked loudly on Mrs. Vandegrift's door, because Mrs. Vandegrift didn't hear visitors otherwise. Anna heard some shuffling inside, and then Mrs. Vandegrift opened the door. The blare of music from the television attacked Anna like a punch in the face. If Mrs. Vandegrift hadn't been nearly deaf already, listening to the television at that level would have made her lose her hearing right quick.

"Oh, Anna, I'm so glad you're here. My television antenna has gone all skewampus, and I'm missing my show. Would you be so kind?" Mrs. Vandegrift pointed to her television set, where there looked to be a snowstorm going on inside someone's house. "You brought treats. How very kind." She took Anna's basket and shooed Anna to move behind the television. It sat precariously atop a rickety metal TV tray, the kind *Englischers* used to put their food on so they could eat while watching shows. "You're not all that tall, but I think you'll do just fine. Move the antennas around until the picture gets better."

"But I can't see whether the picture is getting better or not."

"That's why I'm so glad you came knocking. It really is a two-person job. Okay, dear, push the one on the right up about half an inch. No, my right, dear." Anna did as she was told. "Now move the left one down an inch." Anna flinched when Mrs. Vandegrift yelled, "Stop! That is perfect."

"Can I come out from behind the television now?"

Mrs. Vandegrift nodded. But when Anna took her hands off the antennas, Mrs. Vandegrift's shoulders slumped. "Oh, dear. It's back to static again. I was afraid of that. This television is very persnickety." She clasped her hands together. "I suppose I can't ask you to stay back there for another fifteen minutes, can I? I just hate missing *Arthur Godfrey and His Friends*, and since you're not supposed to watch television anyway, you might as well make yourself useful."

Anna smiled and wrapped her fingers around the antennas again. Mrs. Vandegrift found a great deal of pleasure in her television shows. "I don't mind," Anna said, pitching her voice so she could be heard over the television. She was practically yelling. "What is the show about?"

Mrs. Vandegrift settled into the green sofa that sat

opposite the television set. She waved her hand again, dismissing any interruptions. "I can't talk and listen at the same time. Give me fifteen minutes, and I'll tell you all about it." She smiled at Anna. "And thank you. You're a very sweet girl."

Anna stood there for fifteen minutes and only moved her hand twice, when she absolutely, positively had to scratch her nose. Mrs. Vandegrift made a face both times it happened, as if a little impatient with Anna, but she also seemed to be enjoying her program so much that she didn't mention it. Anna loved watching Mrs. Vandegrift watch her show. She laughed and smiled and seemed ten years younger.

When the show was over, Mrs. Vandegrift sighed loudly and turned off the television. "You can let go now, Anna. You did a fine job, even with your height deficiency. I'm either going to have to hire you as my permanent antenna holder or get a new television. This one has been acting up for three weeks." She seemed to remember that Anna had brought her some goodies. "What's in the basket?"

"I brought you some licorice-drop snickerdoodles. It's a new recipe I've been experimenting with. I hope you like licorice."

Mrs. Vandegrift gasped as if licorice-drop snickerdoodles were the best cookies she had ever heard of. "I love licorice. And it's very good for my indigestion. You're always so thoughtful, Anna." She pulled a cookie from the basket and took a bite. She chewed for a few seconds and raised her eyebrows. "Delicious. And very licorice-y. Like a good stiff mouthful of fennel."

Anna tried not to let the praise go to her head. "I put a little drop of fennel oil in for good measure."

"I can tell. Very delicious." She sat down on her sofa and patted the seat next to her. "Now, come and tell me all the news in the outside world. Did your aunt have to get gallbladder surgery?"

"Oh, yes, and then she was in the hospital for three days."

Mrs. Vandegrift nodded. "Not too bad for major surgery."

"That's what we all said. We thank the good Lord it wasn't longer."

"I've never had to get gallbladder surgery, or any other kind of surgery, thank goodness. I've never been a patient in a hospital. I don't think I'd like it. No privacy and strong smells." Mrs. Vandegrift took another small bite of cookie. "And what about the young Amish man who went off to war? You told me he came home. How is he settling in?"

Anna's heart raced at the very mention of "the young Amish man."

"It's been hard. The community has had a hard time accepting him."

"That's a shame. I would think they'd be grateful to him for his service to our country. I certainly am. It was brave of him to volunteer. He didn't have to go."

Anna drew her brows together. She had always considered Felty's going to war a sin. The bishop and preachers talked about it that way. Two years ago, she had concluded that Felty was just a rebellious youth who wanted a bit of adventure before he settled down, but she knew better now. He wasn't the rebellious type.

Felty had gone against the wishes of his community

and his faith, knowing that he might very well be killed or have to kill someone else. She'd seen the scar on his face and heard him talk about Korea. It couldn't have been any sort of exciting adventure—more like stepping into a nightmare and being lucky enough to come back. Of course, the Amish didn't believe in luck. Felty's return was Gotte's doing, for sure and certain. Maybe it wasn't a sin. Maybe it was just like Mrs. Vandegrift said. Felty's voluntary service had taken a great deal of courage.

"It . . . it was very brave of him," Anna stuttered, even though she had just now realized it. "And there's something else. Two days ago he saved a child from being run over by a car."

Mrs. Vandegrift's eyes got big. "He saved someone's life?"

Anna nodded vigorously. "We were standing just inside the grocery store, and it was snowing something wonderful. A little boy ran out into the road and fell on the ice. A car was coming, but it couldn't stop because the roads were so icy. Felty bolted out of that store and scooped Marvin up before the car hit him."

Mrs. Vandegrift covered her mouth with her hand. "Oh, dear. Were either of them hurt?"

"We think the side mirror hit Felty's shoulder. He's in a lot of pain, but I didn't think it was polite to ask him to show us the bruise. He *did* show us the cut on his knee. There was a lot of blood." Anna frowned. "He probably needs stitches." She would have to take her needle and thread over there today. That wound wouldn't heal properly if it wasn't sewn up. "He curled his arms tight around Marvin and held him against his chest. The mirror banged against Felty's shoulder as it passed, and Felty fell to the pavement and rolled like a ball with Marvin tucked safely in his arms." Anna's heart did a somersault. "It was really quite spectacular."

Mrs. Vandegrift nodded as if she knew. "See what I mean? Bravery. That boy has bravery in spades. The community doesn't know what a treasure he is."

"Well, he seems to be very popular since the accident. Everybody came to visit. People brought cards and food." Rosie had brought her *appeditlich* cinnamon rolls and a very sweet apology.

Anna's face got warm. Rosie was everything Anna wasn't, and Anna felt completely eclipsed when Rosie was in the room. She'd keenly observed the difference between them at Felty's house. Felty's *mamm* saw how superior Rosie was in every way. No doubt Felty had seen it too. It made Anna quite sad, though she couldn't exactly say why. She had never expected anything different. Anna had resigned herself to the fact that she was mediocre, she would always be mediocre, and there was no use getting upset about it.

"I'm glad to hear it. Soldiers should always be treated with respect."

"You're right, Mrs. Vandegrift. I'm glad the community is warming to him." Felty was kind and cheerful, like bright sunshine on a spring day. He didn't deserve anyone's dislike.

Someone knocked on the door, and Anna could hear the beginning strains of "O Come, All Ye Faithful" coming from outside. Carolers! Anna loved carolers and caroling. *Die youngie* usually went several times in December, but somebody had beaten them to it this year. She turned to Mrs. Vandegrift. "It sounds like carolers."

"Does it? I can't hear a thing."

Anna stepped farther back into the living room. The carolers were for Mrs. Vandegrift. Anna didn't need to be lurking around the front door stealing Mrs. Vandegrift's singing time. Mrs. Vandegrift opened the door, and enthusiastic voices filled the entryway even before the carolers came into the house.

Mrs. Vandegrift clapped her hands, and it did Anna's heart *gute* to see the delight on her face. "Come in, come in," she said. "It must be twenty degrees out there."

Anna glanced out the front window, and her stomach dropped to the floor. There looked to be a dozen carolers standing on Mrs. Vandegrift's porch, all Amish. All from Anna's district. All young people. Had they gone caroling without her? A hay wagon was parked on the side of the road in front of Mrs. Vandegrift's house. Whatever they were doing, Anna had definitely not been invited. She pressed her lips together and swallowed past the lump in her throat. Her eyes stung, and only by blinking very fast could she keep the tears from sliding down her face. She quickly backed up and plastered herself in the corner behind the television. Maybe no one would see her. Maybe they could sing their songs and leave without even noticing that Anna was standing in the corner disintegrating into a pile of dust.

It seemed to work. Singing merrily, *die youngie* filed into the living room, their backs to Anna, their faces turned toward Mrs. Vandegrift and her brilliantly happy features. Mark Hostetler, Andy Mast, and Joseph Lambright were there, as well as Mary Zook and Lily Mishler. Surely Rosie Herschberger was among them. Lily never went anywhere without Rosie.

Anna gasped. Rosie strolled into the room with someone unusually tall by her side. Anna nearly choked on her own spit, and she pressed her hand to her mouth to keep from coughing. Not only had they gone caroling without her, they'd invited Felty. Felty, the boy who until two days ago hadn't had a friend but Anna. How long had he been in on the plan to leave Anna out?

Anna might have squeaked her distress, but they were singing so loudly, not even she could hear herself. She tried to make herself smaller by wedging tightly into the corner. *Ach*, she would have given every raisin in Wisconsin to be anywhere but here. If she tried hard enough, perhaps she could push herself through the wall and into the kitchen.

Felty had a deep, booming voice that stood out from the others. He seemed so happy, so comfortable, so uncaring about Anna's feelings. But then again, how could he care about her feelings when he didn't even know she was in the room? But didn't he feel the least bit guilty for not inviting her?

They finished "O Come, All Ye Faithful," and Mrs. Vandegrift clapped again. Anna tried not to feel offended. Mrs. Vandegrift had never shown that much enthusiasm for Anna's cooking, or even Anna's antenna skills. "That was beautiful. Nobody sings like the Amish," she said. Anna couldn't see Mrs. Vandegrift around the sea of straw hats and bonnets in front of her, but she could hear her just fine. "Who is this tall young man? I don't believe we've met."

Felty stood up front, but Anna could see the back of

his head from her vantage point. "I'm Felty Helmuth. I've been away for two years."

"Pleased to meet you."

"He saved my nephew's life," Rosie gushed. "Threw himself in front of a car."

"Oh, yes," Mrs. Vandegrift said, sounding doubly excited to meet him. "The hometown hero. Thank you for your service to our country."

"You're welcome, ma'am."

"Are you two a couple?"

Anna didn't know to whom Mrs. Vandegrift had directed the question, but Rosie giggled with delight. "No. We're just getting to know each other."

"We're not a couple." That was Felty.

"Too bad," Mrs. Vandegrift said. "You look very handsome together." A short pause. "Anna Yoder was just telling me about you. Do you know Anna?"

Felty nodded as if he wasn't ashamed to admit it. "For sure and certain. She makes the most delicious cinnamon rolls."

It was a nice thing to say, but the praise did little to ease Anna's aching heart.

"She's such a dear girl," Mrs. Vandegrift said.

Felty nodded again. "She couldn't come tonight."

Anna's indignation flared hotter than a cookstove. Couldn't come? It wasn't like Felty to bear false witness. Her heart drummed a wild beat inside her chest. She had to escape. Her humiliation was already choking her. She wouldn't be able to bear it if anyone saw her. She quietly got down on her hands and knees and started crawling toward the kitchen. It was only five feet away. Surely she could make it without being caught.

Mrs. Vandegrift raised her voice as if she thought no one could hear her. "Now where could she have got to?"

"Who?"

"Anna, of course. She was right here."

Anna's heart lurched, and in her haste to get out of the room, she accidentally knocked her foot against the leg of the TV tray where Mrs. Vandegrift's television sat. The tray wobbled dangerously. Anna jumped up, the need to save Mrs. Vandegrift's television greater than her need to not be humiliated. She wrapped her arms around the television, keeping it from falling to the floor, but unfortunately, her shuffle to save the TV and the scraping of the tray's feet against Mrs. Vandegrift's wood floor were loud enough to draw attention. Everyone in the room turned around to stare at her.

"There she is," Mrs. Vandegrift said. "She's done me a great service tonight, holding my antennas so I could watch my program."

Some of *die youngie* laughed at the sight of Anna clutching the television in her arms. Others were probably annoyed to see her, as if she'd planned to interfere with their caroling party all along.

Felty's face lit up like a kerosene lantern, and he nudged the other young people aside to get to her. "Anna," he said, acting as if he was overjoyed to see her. "*Vie gehts?*" He immediately knelt down on his good knee and straightened the legs of the TV tray so it was more stable, and Anna felt better about letting go of the TV. "You run into the nicest surprises while caroling."

Anna smoothed her hands down her bertha, though she didn't really care what Felty or anybody else thought about her appearance. But she was quite particular about always looking clean and comely, as a demure and sweet Amish girl should. It didn't have anything to do with Felty at all, especially since he hadn't bothered to mention that *die youngie* were going caroling tonight. "It looks like you're having fun," she said, the words almost strangling her. She was determined not to be petty or resentful, even though her heart ached with the pain of rejection.

Felty grinned and shrugged. "It would be more fun with you, but I understand why you weren't able to come tonight. You're such a kind neighbor."

"How is your shoulder?"

Felty ran his hand down his left arm. "*Ach.* It still hurts, but I don't think I'll be crippled. I can do the easy jobs when we're milking."

Rosie rushed to Felty's side, as if she were his babysitter and didn't want to lose sight of him. "*Hallo*, Anna. I didn't know you'd be here."

Of course she didn't. Or they probably would have skipped Mrs. Vandegrift's house altogether. "I'm sorry." Anna didn't know why she was apologizing. She hadn't done anything wrong, except for maybe ruin Rosie's perfectly *wunderbarr* hayride. "I was just leaving."

Felty raised his eyebrows in delight. "Why don't you come with us? We've got three more houses, and then we're going back to Rosie's for hot chocolate and cookies."

Rosie attempted a smile. It looked desperate and unnatural on her face. "*Ach*, I don't know that we'll have enough cookies for everybody."

No doubt they would be boring sugar cookies without a bit of licorice.

Felty didn't seem to take the hint that Rosie didn't want Anna to join their hayride. "That's okay. I won't eat any, so there will be enough for Anna."

The color traveled up Rosie's face like the mercury in a thermometer on a blistering-hot day. "*Ach*, *vell*, I guess that would be okay, then."

Anna wasn't about to go somewhere she wasn't welcome. "*Nae, denki.* I've got to get home and do some Christmas knitting."

"Christmas knitting?" Felty said, as if Christmas knitting was as exciting as three buggy races. "What are you making?"

Anna took a deep breath to ease the weight pressing into her chest. It was kind of Felty to try to make her feel included, but he didn't need to pretend for her sake. She would be just fine. She had been left out before. She shook her head. "Uh-uh. Can't tell. I'm making some surprises."

He nodded. "Whatever they are, I know they'll be beautiful."

Rosie was able to look sufficiently disappointed. "I'm sorry you can't come with us, Anna, but Lord willing, you'll be able to come the next time we go caroling."

Mark Hostetler grunted in amusement. "You'll want to hear Felty sing. He doesn't know the words to anything, so he just makes them up."

Felty laughed. "I get them right most of the time."

Joseph laughed. "You do not."

Anna's throat tightened. Felty was already part of the group. Anna never would be.

Rosie gave Felty a beautiful smile. "It's time to go. We don't want to be out too late."

Felty looked at Anna with something like regret shining in his eyes. "I wish we didn't have to go. I'm just . . . I'm just so glad we ran into you."

"You've only sung one song for me," Mrs. Vandegrift said. "I think I'm entitled to at least one more."

Rosie looked slightly put out, but she was always accommodating with the shut-ins. "Shall we sing 'O Little Town of Bethlehem'?"

"Oh, yes. I love that one."

Felty actually put his arm around Anna and steered her closer to the group. "Sing with us, Anna. Just the one song."

One of the boys acted as the *Vorsinger* and started everybody out with a note and the first few words of the song. Anna moved her lips, but she didn't have the heart to sing.

Mark hadn't been kidding about Felty making up words. "O little town of Bethlehem, how quietly you sigh. Above your huts and cabins too, the silent stars go by. Yet in the dark roads shining the everlasting sight. The hopes and fears of all the deers are met in thee tonight."

Anna smiled to herself. What Felty lacked in memory skills, he made up for in enthusiasm. She'd never heard a more rousing rendition of "O Little Town of Bethlehem." It made her all the sadder.

When they finished the song, *die youngie* filed out of Mrs. Vandegrift's house, with Felty lagging behind. He took Anna's hand as if he were going to shake it, but squeezed it firmly instead. "Will I see you at the gathering on Sunday?"

"Probably." A *gute* Amish girl was expected to go to all the gatherings, even if no one wanted her there.

"*Gute.* Just remember the number five."

Anna drew her brows together. What was he talking about? Before she could ask him, he slipped out of the room and through the open door. *Just remember the number five.*

Her heart raced out of control. It felt as if he shared something important just between the two of them, a special secret just for her. No matter what, she wouldn't forget their special number. It was her very *gute* fortune that she had five fingers on each hand. Her cousin's baby had six.

Anna went to the window and watched as Felty jumped into the wagon and sat next to Rosie on a hay bale. He smiled at Rosie as if he was having a *wunderbarr* time. Did he and Rosie have a special number? Anna's mouth went dry. Of course they did. Rosie was irresistible. Rosie was beautiful. Rosie was the most sought-after girl in the *gmayna*. What boy in his right mind would ever pass up a chance to date Rosie Herschberger?

Anna certainly couldn't and wouldn't compete with Rosie. Felty deserved the very best sort of girl. And that girl wasn't Anna, no matter how badly she wanted it to be. Felty and Rosie probably had a hundred secret numbers they shared with each other. The secret number idea made no sense, but thinking that Felty and Rosie had hundreds of secret numbers made Anna feel small and unhappy just the same.

Mrs. Vandegrift joined Anna at the window. "I like that

Felty Helmuth. He's cheerful and humble, and not too hard on the eyes either."

"And Rosie is so pretty. You were right. They make a handsome couple."

Mrs. Vandegrift waved her hand in the air. "Oh, I was obviously wrong about that, dear. That brave soldier boy only has eyes for you."

Chapter 11

Anna loved *singeons* at Christmastime. Christmas songs were her favorite, and they only sang them in December.

Ach, *vell*, she didn't *love* singings ever, but they were bearable at Christmas, especially since Elmer came to singings now. Elmer watched out for her, and she didn't feel so alone, even though it wasn't all that fun spending the time with Elmer's friends. They were nice to her, but they were stupid boys all the same.

Felty was now the most popular boy in the *gmayna*, so Anna didn't need to protect him from embarrassment anymore. There would be girls flirting with him all night long. If they played Please or Displease, there wouldn't be one girl who would refuse to go into the closet with Felty Helmuth, the boy who had saved Marvin King's life. His days in the army had been completely forgotten. Anna was glad that *die youngie* had accepted Felty, but she felt quite sad when she thought about him. She liked Felty very much, but so did Rosie. It made Anna want to cry, and she had only herself to blame for her melancholy. She had been foolish to let herself have feelings for Felty Helmuth. Better to accept her lot in life. No one would ever fall in love with her, and she certainly wasn't going to settle for just anybody. She could take care of Dat until he passed on, and then for sure and certain, Elmer would let her live with him and his family and knit scarves for everybody.

The Mishlers' house was decorated beautifully. Pine boughs hung over every door, trimmed with Christmas-red ribbons at the corners. Bright kerosene lanterns sat on every table, and the smell of hot wassail floated in the air. Anna loved the smells of Christmas, especially the smells of Christmas baking.

Felty was already there, standing on the other side of the room talking to Mark Hostetler. It looked as if they were engaged in a very serious conversation. Felty looked up at her with a blinding smile and immediately left his important conversation with Mark to come to her. Anna wasn't sure what was so urgent, but surely it didn't justify abandoning Mark like that. Maybe it had something to do with the secret number.

"*Hallo*, Anna." Felty studied her face. "Is everything okay? You look as if you don't want to be here."

"*Ach*, *vell*, you know I don't like *singeons*." *And I was thinking of you and how we won't be able to go trap tripping when you marry.*

"I didn't used to like *singeons* either, until I realized I would get to see you." His smile was warm, sincere. "*Ach*, I have missed you. I am slow at the dairy, but I still have to finish my chores every day, and Mamm says she can't spare me for a minute or I would have come to visit you."

"Visit me? I should be the one visiting you, with your sore shoulder and all." Anna felt a twinge of guilt mixed with pain. She had neglected Felty all week because she hadn't wanted to relive her embarrassment at Mrs. Vandegrift's. She felt guilt for not going once to check on Felty since Thursday and pain at knowing he didn't really care if she checked on him or not. Rosie had probably been over there every day. He'd much rather see Rosie. He'd much rather eat Rosie's cinnamon rolls.

Felty winked. "The boy should be the one to visit the girl, but I would never say no to a visit from Anna Yoder."

Anna studied her hands and willed herself to breathe normally. Felty was nice even when he didn't have to be. "I suppose I could come this week, just to check on you."

"I would like that more than you could ever know."

How did Rosie Herschberger just appear like that, as if she'd twinkled down to earth from a cloud? "Felty, I'm *froh* you're here. You need to come and taste the cream puffs I brought. I want to know if I added too much sugar."

Anna wanted to roll her eyes. It was just a trick to get Felty to herself, because Rosie never added too much of anything to her baked goods, and if she did, she would never admit it.

Felty didn't seem inclined to go anywhere. "I'm sure they're *appeditlich*."

"But, Felty, yours is the only opinion I trust. You've been to California and Korea and lots of exciting places. I'm sure you've eaten all sorts of wonderful *gute* food. I want to know how my cream puffs compare to other things you've eaten."

"Most of the food I ate was cooked by the army, and none of the soldiers liked it."

Rosie stuck out her bottom lip. "Now, Felty, come and try my cream puffs or I'll take it personally and worry you don't like my cooking."

"That's impossible," Anna said. "Everything you make is delicious. Everything."

Rosie acted as if Anna had completely surprised her. "Why, *denki*, Anna. You're always so kind, but Felty really needs to try them."

Felty frowned, and his gaze flicked from Anna to Rosie and back again. "Okay. I'll be right back, Anna."

It was doubtful that Felty would be right back. Rosie always got her way where boys were concerned, and it was plain she wanted Felty to herself. Felty wasn't likely to resist all that attention from the prettiest girl in the district.

Felty was back before Anna had time to find a corner to retreat to. In fact, he came from behind so swiftly, he startled Anna, and she flinched and squeaked as if she'd been pinched. Felty's eyes danced. "*Ach*, Anna, I'm sorry. Did I scare you? I didn't mean to scare you."

"*Jah*, you scared me. I thought Rosie would make you inspect every cream puff." She clapped her hand over her mouth. "That didn't come out right. Rosie is very concerned about her cream puffs. I would have asked you to inspect all of them if I were in her shoes."

"She gave me one to taste, and I told her it was *appeditlich*, and that was all. I told you I'd be right back."

Anna felt quite wicked for not believing him. "I'm sorry. I shouldn't have doubted. I should always think the best of people."

Felty winked and grinned. "There's nothing to apologize for. I swallowed that cream puff in one bite. I was in a hurry."

"In a hurry for what?"

"To get back here closer to your pretty face."

Anna felt as if she might be floating just a few inches off the floor, but then her common sense returned. What was Felty talking about? Rosie was the one with the pretty face. Anna was simply mediocre.

The minister got everyone's attention, and Felty gave her a regretful look as the boys and girls went to separate sides of the room and sat down for the singing. The other girls had made it clear that they didn't like to sit next to Anna. She couldn't carry a tune in a bucket, even though she enjoyed singing her favorite Christmas songs. At most singings, she mouthed the words so she wouldn't bother the other singers and then went home and sang into her pillow at the top of her lungs. She loved singing praises to Derr Herr, even though she wasn't so sure her song was pleasing to Him. "'The woods would be very silent if no birds sang there except those that sang best,'" Dat used to say, quoting someone who sounded like he knew what he was talking about.

Maybe it wouldn't hurt to sing tonight, maybe softly so no one would hear her. She did love the Christmas songs.

Joseph was the *Vorsinger*, singing the first few notes of the song before everyone joined in. Felty sat in the front row of the boys, and Anna could hear his strong bass voice even though he wasn't singing to stand out. Rosie just happened to be sitting directly across from Felty, and she was singing a little louder, staring at Felty as if she was singing just for him. Rosie had a beautiful voice, and Anna had always thought that if Rosie hadn't been Amish, she would have been a singing star on the radio.

They sang "Silent Night" and "Joy to the World" and several other Christmas songs. They were all Anna's favorites. Rosie took the lead on some of the songs, and so did Lily. After about an hour, they asked Felty to take the lead. He had truly been accepted into the group.

Anna's heart sank, even though she was very happy for him.

Felty found Anna immediately after the singing. His eyes were bright, and his smile was blinding. "That was wonderful nice," he said. "Singing was one of the things I missed the most in Korea."

Rosie found Felty almost as immediately. "*Ach*, Felty, you sing so *gute*."

Felty took out his handkerchief and wiped his forehead. "So do you. You can hit all the high notes."

Rosie lowered her eyes. "*Denki.* I try not to sing too loud. I want to be humble, but I do love to sing." She glanced at Anna. "Anna doesn't like to sing."

Felty raised an eyebrow. "You don't?"

Anna felt her face get warm, though she didn't know why it would. Maybe it was just another humiliating reminder of how superior Rosie was at everything. "I like to sing. I'm just not *gute* at it."

"You don't have to be *gute*," Felty said. "I watched your face while you were singing. It is enough to make a joyful noise to the Lord."

Rosie laughed as if the joke was on Anna. "But it is much more pleasant to listen to someone who isn't tone-deaf."

Felty rubbed at the whiskers on his chin. "I don't know. I take great pleasure in anything Anna does."

Randy Mishler called everyone to gather for a game. "We're going to play Love in the Dark," he said, and Anna had to stifle a groan. Love in the Dark was the silliest game of them all. Couples paired up and went somewhere in the house together and sat in the dark for fifteen minutes. The couples who were dating liked the game because they could steal a few minutes alone. Anna didn't like it because nobody wanted to sit in the dark with her, and she felt bad for imposing on reluctant boys. And if she was honest with herself, she had to admit that the rejection stung like an angry wasp. And she really hated to be stung.

Felty smiled as if he couldn't have been more delighted. He leaned close to Anna's ear. "Remember the secret number." He didn't exactly say it softly, but since no one but the two of them knew the actual secret number, Anna couldn't see how it mattered.

Anna's pulse pounded in her ears. The secret number? Was this why he'd given her a secret number?

The boys were herded into the kitchen, where they were supposed to line up. In the front room, the girls also lined up. The first girl in line would be paired with the first boy in line, and none of the girls were supposed to know what order the boys had lined up in. Of course, the boys who were dating someone usually worked out a way to signal their partners where they stood in line. Someone in the kitchen clapped three times, and Mary Zook giggled and crowded into the number three spot in line.

With her heart beating like a snare drum, Anna looked at the number five spot. She'd have to slip between Lily and Suvilla, but she couldn't see that they would mind. Neither of them had boyfriends they were trying to couple up with. Maybe they wouldn't care if Anna wedged herself between them.

Anna didn't realize how close Rosie was until she spoke. "What is the secret number Felty gave you?"

Anna frowned. "What?"

"The secret number Felty gave you. I think it's supposed to be for me."

"Why . . . why would you think that?"

Rosie caught her bottom lip between her teeth. "*Ach*, *vell*, Felty wouldn't just come right out and tell me the secret number. It's too forward, and he knows I'm not a flirt. So it's plain he told you the number so you could tell me."

Anna's heart plummeted to her toes. Is that what had happened? "Um, are you sure?"

Rosie slid her arm around Anna's shoulder. "Oh, Anna, you're so sweet and a little naive, but you can't really believe that Felty would want to couple up with you for Love in the Dark. It's just that, well, you're so short, and my cinnamon rolls are so much better than yours. And I can sing. Felty is a music lover."

But . . . why hadn't Felty just gone ahead and shared the secret number with Rosie? Maybe Rosie was right. Felty didn't want Rosie to think he was a flirt. Hadn't Felty gone caroling with Rosie without telling Anna? Hadn't he been wanting to get in the bishop's good graces ever since he got home? Why would Felty want to spend fifteen minutes in a dark room with Anna when he could spend them with the prettiest girl in the district? And probably the best cook in Wisconsin. And the best singer. And Anna wasn't even going to think about Rosie's tiny quilt stitches.

It made sense, but it didn't make Anna happy. She felt sick to her stomach, like the time she ate two-week-old meatloaf from the icebox and threw up for three days. She tried to hold her head high as she slowly backed away from any thought of getting in line.

Rosie furrowed her brow. "Anna? Did you hear me? What is the number?"

Anna didn't speak for fear of disintegrating into a puddle of tears or stomping her foot in protest and making a complete fool of herself. She held up five fingers. Rosie burst into a smile, turned her back on Anna, and practically shoved herself between Lily and Suvilla. She got her spot, and Anna was heartbroken.

Anna turned and walked out the front door. It was cold, and she'd left her coat inside, but she couldn't bear to watch Rosie and Felty take hands and run giggling up the stairs to find some dark corner to sit in. She couldn't do it. Sitting on the top porch step, she wrapped her arms around herself to ward off the cold, but that didn't keep her teeth from chattering. Would it have killed her to put on her coat before fleeing the house? Nobody had noticed her leave without a coat. They certainly wouldn't have noticed her leaving with a coat. Now she was angry, depressed, *and* cold.

Felty hated to be cold. He very well could have lost his fingers and toes in Korea. She was glad he hadn't, because she would never forget the feel of his fingers entwined in hers that one day when he obviously hadn't been thinking straight. Better to have a painful memory with fingers than to be without them.

She jumped when the front door opened. Randy stuck his head out. "Anna, what are you doing out here? We have one extra boy. We need you to play the game."

Anna didn't want to play Love in the Dark with anyone,

but she knew how much it hurt to be left out. Besides, it really was too cold to be outside, and she was mildly pleased that someone had noticed her leave the house. She sighed. "Okay. I will come. Where do you want us to go?"

Randy held the door open for her. "The only place left is the cellar, but it's warm down there."

Anna walked into the house, immediately grateful for its warmth, even though she wasn't thrilled with the sight of Mark Hostetler standing there as if he hadn't a friend in the world. She stifled a groan. Mark was the last person Anna wanted to see right now—well, that wasn't entirely true. Felty and Rosie were high up on the list. Mark didn't look happy to be coupled with Anna, so they had at least one thing in common. *Ach*, *vell*, they didn't have to talk to each other. She could count jars of bottled fruit on the cellar shelves, and Mark could sit in the corner and pout.

Randy handed her a flashlight. "Take this. It will be too dark to see your way down the stairs without it."

"Okay," Anna said. She lifted her chin and motioned for Mark to follow.

Mark shuffled behind her, his reluctance oozing from every pore. "This isn't how I wanted to spend Love in the Dark."

The feeling was definitely mutual. "Don't be so grumpy about it. You can criticize my cooking and poke fun at my knitting. That will make the time go by faster." Even with the flashlight, Anna had to cling to the railing to keep herself from tripping down the stairs. About halfway down, Mark hissed loudly. She turned her head slightly. "Is everything okay?"

"Oh, *sis yuscht*. I snagged my skin on the railing. Don't people know what sandpaper is?"

"*Cum,*" Anna said, stepping off the bottom step. "Let me have a look." She grabbed Mark's sleeve and pulled him to sit on a plastic barrel against the wall. "Show me."

Mark opened his hand, and she shined the flashlight on it. Sure enough, there was a rather large splinter in the heel of his hand embedded under his skin. A drop of blood marked the spot where the splinter had pierced him. It looked deep and painful. "*Ach*, Mark. That must hurt something wonderful."

He pulled his hand away and eyed her suspiciously. "*Jah*, it does."

She held out her hand. "Come on, then. Let's get it out."

He pulled a face. "I don't know. Will it hurt?"

Will it hurt? What, was he five years old? "It will hurt worse if you leave it in. It could get infected, and then gangrene sets in."

"Gangrene?"

"And then they'd have to cut your hand off."

It was a joke, but Mark seemed to take it seriously. "You don't even have tweezers."

Anna touched her hand to her *kapp* and pulled out one of the pins holding it to her hair. "I'll use a straight pin."

His eyes got bigger. "You're going to poke me with that?"

Anna stifled an exasperated smile. "When a splinter is buried under the skin like that, a pin is the only way to get it out."

"Will I get tetanus?"

She held out her hand again. "I'll be gentle. Give me

your hand." He placed his hand in her palm and leaned closer to watch. "Mark, you've got to back up a little or I won't be able to see a thing. Here, hold the flashlight so I can operate."

He took the flashlight and obediently held it over the surgery site. "You never answered that question about tetanus."

With his injured hand cradled in hers, Anna took the needle and poked gingerly at the skin around the sliver. He let out a squeak and pulled his hand away. "Ouch. That hurts!"

"It's not that bad," Anna said. "You've got to hold still or it will hurt worse. Don't be such a baby."

"I'm not being a baby. I just don't like pain. Or blood. Or needles."

Anna giggled. "Okay, then. Just try to be brave, and I'll find you a lollipop after we're done."

"Ha. Ha."

Anna smiled. "Hold still, and I'll be very careful." She set to work again, and he only flinched once, when she had to stick the pin in deeply enough to go below the splinter. Mark had a reputation for having a sensitive stomach. Anna had just assumed it was his excuse for not trying her food. Maybe he really did have a sickly disposition. "You're being very brave," she said, after a few seconds of silence between them. She glanced at his face. Even in the dimness of the flashlight she could see he had turned pale.

He was so different from Felty, who had gone caroling three days after being hit by a car. Felty had a scar and probably a tattoo from the war. Anna couldn't imagine Felty cowering in the face of any kind of pain.

"I'm just . . . I just don't . . . my *mamm* says I'm frail," Mark said. "My *schwester* says I'm touchy. I don't like either of those descriptions, but can I help it if I get queasy at the sight of blood?"

"No wonder you don't like my cooking. You're afraid of it."

He grimaced when Anna poked the needle too hard, then fell silent for a full minute. "You know I'm just trying to be funny, right? Everybody likes a boy who can make them laugh."

Anna was mad at the whole world, so she wasn't inclined to sugarcoat the truth to spare Mark's feelings. "It's not funny to me."

He looked up and stared at her as if he'd forgotten all about the splinter and his possible need for a tetanus shot. "I was trying to be funny." He frowned. "Joseph laughs at my jokes, and Andy, but nobody else. I just want people to like me, so I say *dumm* things." He pressed his lips together. "Sometimes mean things."

"I don't like you better when you say mean things about my cooking."

"Rosie likes it."

Anna cocked an eyebrow. "Rosie likes it when you insult my cooking?"

He shook his head. "Rosie likes to be the best at everything. If she thinks she's better than someone else, it makes her happy."

It was a petty way to live, having to diminish someone else so you could feel better about yourself. And why did Rosie need that kind of approval? She was the best, most perfect girl in the *gmayna*. Couldn't she be happy when another girl baked a delicious loaf of bread or put tiny stitches in a quilt?

Mark pulled his hand away. "Ouch. That hurt. What are you doing?"

Anna grinned. She pinched the splinter between her thumb and index finger and held it to the light.

A smile spread across Mark's face. "You got it."

"That wasn't too bad, was it?"

"*Ach*, it was terrible. But for sure and certain better than gangrene." He studied his palm. "I'm sorry for teasing you about your cooking, but don't you think I'm funny? Even some of the time?"

Anna shook her head. "It hurts my feelings. Laughter at someone else's expense is the worst kind." It felt *gute* to say it out loud, especially since she was pretty sure Mark wouldn't make fun of her for it. She'd just done him a *gute* service.

He huffed out a breath. "I didn't know, Anna. Truly. I've just been trying to get Rosie's attention for three years. I didn't think about anyone else's feelings. But it's not as if Rosie cares. I could stand on my head at *gmay* and she wouldn't even look up from her hymnbook." He took out his handkerchief and dabbed at the blood on his palm. "But it doesn't matter anymore about Rosie, because she's got Felty now, and she won't even remember my name come New Year's."

Anna's eyelid twitched, but she did her best to remain calm. There was nothing she could do about Rosie and Felty liking each other. Rosie was perfect. Felty was even more perfect. They were perfect for each other. Even if Anna baked a hundred Red Hot cinnamon rolls between now and Groundhog Day, Rosie would just bake a hundred and one. And Rosie's would be prettier and fluffier, and it would be impossible to win Felty's heart. There was no competing against fluffiness.

"I'm sorry about Rosie," Anna said, but not in the way Mark might have guessed.

"And I'm sorry I hurt your feelings."

She shrugged. "It doesn't matter. I forgive you."

"I admire that about you, Anna. You don't just pretend to be a Christian. You really try to live it. I've never heard you say a mean thing about anybody, except maybe when you called us party poopers at the last *singeon*."

Anna curled one side of her mouth. "You were being mean to Felty. You needed to be chastised."

Mark nodded. "I guess we did, but it's not like the ministers encouraged us to welcome Felty back with open arms. They thought he'd corrupt all of us. We had to be cautious."

Anna didn't think that excuse justified unkindness, but it wasn't worth arguing about. "*Ach*, *vell*, everything is as it should be now, I guess. I'm *froh* Felty feels welcome in the community."

Mark laughed, but it wasn't a happy sound. "Welcome? He's everybody's favorite. The bishop loves him. Rosie would marry him tomorrow if she could. He's more welcome than I am."

"Or me," Anna said quietly. She pressed her lips together. No need to bring up her own grievances. It was petty and useless.

Mark scrunched his lips together. "That's not true, Anna, but maybe I've made you feel that way. Maybe a lot of us have made you feel that way without meaning to." He patted her hand. "You're one of us, Anna. Maybe a little too smart, but nice and godly and pretty. You're the steady, faithful influence for all of us. I guess I've overlooked you the way Rosie overlooked me."

Anna raised a skeptical eyebrow. *Pretty?* For sure and certain he didn't mean pretty like Rosie Herschberger was pretty. His recent operation had made him delirious. "Don't tease me."

"I know it's hard for you to believe, especially since all I've done is tease you for ten years, but I'm not teasing." He gazed at her as if he'd never really seen her before. "Do you remember when we kissed at that *singeon*?"

Anna nodded, not sure what that had to do with anything. It had been because of a stupid game of Please and Displease. "It was a long time ago."

"I acted like I didn't care if you agreed to kiss me or said 'displeased,' but I did care. And even though I wasn't very nice to you, you didn't embarrass me in front of everybody. That was wonderful nice of you."

"I don't think anybody should be embarrassed over a silly game."

The look in Mark's eyes got more intense. "Maybe Gotte had a reason for bringing us together tonight."

"Of course He did. He knows I am very *gute* at removing splinters. Once Isaac got an inch-long splinter in his foot working in the haymow. I took it out, but not before he kicked me in the chin. I like to think it was just reflex."

Mark slowly shook his head without taking his eyes from her face. "*Nae.* That's not the reason."

"I don't think Isaac kicked me on purpose."

"*Nae*, Anna," Mark said. "I mean that the splinter is not the reason Gotte brought us together in the cellar."

Anna was dying to know Mark's thoughts on the reason Gotte had put them together in the cellar, but Randy opened the door at the top of the stairs and called down to them, "Love in the Dark is over. Come up and have some wassail."

Anna was relieved and mortified at the same time. Much as she hadn't wanted to go into the cellar with Mark, she was even more reluctant to go back up the stairs and face Rosie and Felty. Anna let her gaze wander around the cellar. There were neat rows of slanted shelves for the canned goods and rows and rows of beautiful bottled fruits and vegetables. She caught her breath. There was another set of stairs on the other side of the cellar. "Where do those steps go?"

"How should I know?" Mark said.

Anna took the flashlight, hurried across the room, and climbed the stairs. She opened the door, and a cold wind blew past her. A way out of the house via the backyard. The cold took Anna's breath away, and she shut the door. She couldn't just leave the house and walk home. It was cold, it was dark, and it was probably six miles. She tapped her foot on the step and chewed her fingernail. She could ask Mark to go up and find her coat, mittens, bonnet, and scarf, bring them to her, and then drive her home—if it wasn't too much trouble. But Mark would never be able to find her things when every Amish coat in Bonduel was black and Elmer's mittens were the same color as hers.

Besides, Mark would wonder why she wanted to sneak

out like that, and he'd get suspicious. No one must ever discover Anna's true feelings for Felty. It would be the biggest humiliation of all, piled on an already tall mountain of humiliation. She was stuck. If Mark hadn't been looking at her, she would have sat down on the step and bawled like a baby.

"Are you okay, Anna?"

"*Nae.* I'm feeling very poorly." That was as true as it could be. "I think I need to go home. Could you fetch Elmer and have him come down here?"

"Okay, but we don't have to bother Elmer. I'm happy to take you home."

"*Ach.* Okay. That would be nice. Would you go tell Elmer I'm riding home with you?"

"Don't you want to come up and tell him yourself? You have to get your coat."

Not if there was a chance of running into Felty. Wouldn't he have a laugh if he knew that Anna had thought the secret number was for her? "I don't want to chance getting anybody sick—if I'm contagious, I mean. Could you bring down my coat, my bonnet, my mittens, and my scarf? Elmer should be able to find them for you. My scarf is blue, and it matches my mittens. And my bonnet has my initials stitched into the seam. They all look the same." She sighed. "Do you think that's prideful, stitching my initials into my bonnet? Lots of girls do it, but I wouldn't want anyone thinking I was proud of my name. I like my name, but it's not any better than anyone else's."

Mark looked a bit confused. "I'll ask Elmer."

He clomped up the opposite stairs, leaving Anna in the

oppressive silence, where there was nothing to keep her company but her flashlight and her unhappy thoughts.

She was tempted to open a bottle of peaches and drown her sorrows in sugary syrup. But it wouldn't make her feel any better. Not even raisins and Red Hots could cheer her up. Something told her she'd never be happy again.

Chapter 12

"Don't touch that!"

Anna drew back her hand as if she'd been slapped. Mammi was especially testy today, and Anna was especially eager to please. "Okay, Mammi. I'm sorry. I just wanted to see what it feels like so I know how to do it when you're not here."

"How many times have I told you, Anna? You don't cook by feel. You strictly follow the recipe, and you strictly follow the rules, and you won't mess up. It's the only way to have any success as a cook."

And that was what Anna wanted, to be a successful cook. At least, that's probably what she wanted, even though baking wheat bread without nuts or cinnamon or even raisins was just plain boring. But it seemed to be what all the boys were looking for in a *gute fraa*, and who was Anna to argue with what all the boys were looking for? She didn't have the energy to fight it anymore, and she certainly didn't have the desire. What did anything matter anymore except taking care of Dat and her *brud-eren* and learning to accept her lot in life? She should at least learn how to make an acceptable loaf of bread. It was only Wednesday, and Anna was already wishing for Monday to come so she could do the laundry and not worry about ruining another meal, another loaf of bread, or another batch of cookies. Dat did the cooking on Mondays, and he almost always made chicken noodle soup and blueberry muffins.

Anna eyed the three perfectly formed loaves on the counter. "Mammi, I don't mean to be contrary, but you just touched all three loaves yourself. So am I supposed to touch them or not?"

Mammi poured some milk into a little cup. "I've baked hundreds of loaves of bread, so I know exactly how to test the dough without making it fall. You must press very gently. If you press too hard, it will fall, and if your bread falls, it will either come out doughy or hard as a rock."

"Will you show me the right way to test it?"

Mammi looked as if she was trying for a smile, but Anna couldn't be sure. "Not today. They're ready to bake, and we don't want to ruin them when we're so very close." She handed Anna a pastry brush. "Dip this into the milk and brush it very carefully over the loaves. It gives them a pleasing shine when they come out of the oven."

Anna stirred the milk with the brush, then dabbed the brush onto the first loaf. Milk trickled down the sides of the loaf and into the loaf pan.

Mammi squeaked her distress, snatched the brush from Anna's hand, and nudged Anna out of the way. "You just want to brush the top, Anna. Not drown the whole loaf in milk." With the skill of many years, Mammi brushed the milk onto the top of each loaf without one trickle of milk escaping down the sides. How did she do that?

When she finished with the milk, Mammi opened the back door, letting in a whole bucket of freezing air. "Elmer," she called. "Hitch up my buggy, would you?" After closing the door, Mammi slipped an oven mitt onto one hand, bent over the cookstove, and opened the oven. She stuck her other hand in and promptly pulled it out. "It's just the right temperature." She glanced at Anna, furrowed her brow, and untied her apron. "I really must go. Your *dawdi* needs his supper, and I can't waste the whole day trying to teach you how to cook." She hung her apron on the hook in the broom closet. "Now, Anna, the rest is really very simple. Put the bread in the oven and be sure to give each loaf at least an inch of space. Then time it for thirty minutes. When the timer rings, tap the bread to make sure it's done. Be sure to remove it from the pans after ten minutes, or the bread will sweat in the pans and get soggy. Do you understand?"

Anna nodded slowly. "I didn't know bread could sweat."

Mammi huffed out a breath. "Maybe I should stay. Your *dawdi* can make himself a sandwich."

Much as Anna loved her *mammi*, she didn't think she could stand another minute of Mammi in her kitchen. "*Nae*, Mammi. I'll be just fine. You've done the hard part. It's easy to set the timer. I'll be fine. The bread will be fine."

Anna could see the battle going on in Mammi's head: the choice between overseeing the baking of a perfect loaf of bread and feeding her husband a *gute* meal. Her wifely side won out. "Okay. Just remember to tap it before you take it out. It's the only way to know if it's done."

"Fine, Mammi," Anna said, grabbing Mammi's coat

from the closet. "I can do it. *Denki* for your help." Anna wasn't about to ask Mammi about the bread tapping. She wasn't supposed to touch the bread before it went into the oven, but she was supposed to tap it to know if it was done? Would she hear a message from the bread when she tapped it? Was it a message to the bread to get ready to be pulled out of the oven? All Anna knew was that if she said anything about the tapping, Mammi would stay.

Anna would figure out the tapping on her own.

Mammi tied her bonnet then wound a scarf around her head to keep her ears warm. Felty had used towels in Korea. Anna felt bad she hadn't been there. She could have knitted scarves for every soldier. None of them would have lost their ears.

Anna pressed her hand to her heart to keep the pain from spreading. Would Rosie like Felty as much if he were missing an ear? Anna would. She would like Felty even if he had no ears.

The trouble with baking was, you had too much time to think about your problems while you stirred and kneaded and frosted things.

Anna donned both oven mitts and carefully slid the bread into the oven. She thought about using a ruler to measure an inch between each pan, but the heat would seep out of the oven if she took too long measuring, so she decided to estimate. She closed the oven, set the timer, and plopped into one of the kitchen chairs. Now all she had to do was sit and wait and try not to think about Felty Helmuth. It was a difficult task, because what girl in the *gmayna* wasn't thinking about Felty Helmuth right now? He was handsome and kind and deeply good, and Anna should never have let herself like him.

Dat came in the back door and stomped his snow-covered boots on the rug. "It smells *gute* in here. Did you and Mammi finish the bread?"

"It's in the oven."

Dat took off his coat and hat and draped them over one of the chairs. "I think Gotte gave us winter so we would give thanks for spring."

"It's wonderful cold out there."

"*Jah.*" Dat pulled one of Anna's licorice cookies from the cookie jar and sat down next to Anna. "Felty Helmuth came over again this morning. Went right out to the barn."

Anna shrugged, even though the ache in her heart was almost unbearable. "I know."

"I told him you were making bread with your *mammi* and couldn't be disturbed."

"*Jah.* He came to the house first. Mammi told him the same thing."

Dat reached out and patted Anna's hand. "You're going to need to talk to him sometime."

"I know."

"He won't stop coming over until you do."

"I know."

The lines around Dat's eyes etched deeper into his face. "Even though I never thought he was good enough for you, I'm sorry he hurt you."

"Me too."

Dat clearly wanted to talk about it. Anna didn't. "Maybe he wants to apologize. Maybe he still wants to be friends."

"Maybe." But Anna could never be friends with Felty again. She wanted his love, even though it was an impossible hope.

"I just don't know what he sees in Rosie," Dat said, his mouth full of cookie.

Anna propped her chin in her hand. "I can't do anything, and Rosie can do everything. She's irresistible."

Concern saturated Dat's features. "Do you remember how your *mammi* used to come over every week and try to teach you all the skills she thought an Amish wife needed to know?"

Anna sighed. "I remember. I should have paid closer attention to her lessons. Maybe I would have learned how to sew and cook and butcher pigs."

"You don't want to know how to butcher a pig. It's wonderful unpleasant. I'd rather buy my ham and bacon already butchered."

That sounded like something Felty would say. Anna curled her lips. "I bet Rosie knows how to butcher a pig."

Dat chuckled. "Good for her." He eyed Anna doubtfully. "Do you remember a few months after your *mater* died, and Mammi came over to teach you how to properly clean the wood floor?"

Anna traced her finger along a crack in the table. "*Jah.* I didn't do it right, and she yelled at me something wonderful."

"And then she spanked you hard with the spatula. Thank Derr Herr, I heard you screaming. Do you remember what I did?"

Anna took a deep breath. She'd never seen her *dat* so angry, before or since. "You grabbed the spatula and broke it in two."

"Then I ordered her out of the house. I didn't allow her across my threshold for a whole year afterward."

Anna's heart swelled with pride and affection even as her chest tightened in mortification. Dat had defended her that day, and she loved him dearly for it, but cutting Mamm's family off like that had surely had terrible consequences. "*Ach*. I didn't know."

"You were nine years old. I couldn't let your *mammi* treat you like that—the way she'd treated your *mater*. I fell in love with your *mater* the first time I saw her. After we married, I spent ten years bringing back the joy that your stern *mammi* had squeezed out of her. We were happy, so happy together. I didn't want your *mammi* to ruin you by turning you into some perfect, cookie-cutter, joyless Amish girl. I didn't want you to have to relearn what it meant to be happy. So I decided whatever we needed to know about running a house, you and I could learn together. And I don't think we did half bad."

Anna smiled. "We didn't do half bad at all. All four boys are still alive, and they all know how to read. Isaac has his flaws, but he's bound to get better." She giggled. "He can't get any worse."

Dat grunted. "*Ach*, *vell*, don't say that too loud."

Anna took Dat's hand. "Even though we lost Mamm, I had a *wunderbarr* childhood. I've always been sure of your love and felt free to find what makes me happy, no matter what Mammi thinks."

"Your *mammi* is a *gute* woman. But the sins of the fathers carry on from generation to generation. Her *fater* was a hard man, and his *fater* before him. Your *mammi* does the best she knows how."

"I know she does," Anna said. Everyone needed Gotte's

grace. Everyone needed mercy. *Blessed are the merciful, for they shall obtain mercy.*

"Her anger is born of love and fear."

Anna scrunched her lips to one side of her face. "She's afraid I won't get married."

Dat nodded. "And she fears you'll be lonely. She fears Gotte will hold her accountable for not teaching you well. She fears she can't control you and that she'll lose the part of your *mater* still in there."

Anna slumped her shoulders. "*Ach*, *vell*, she's probably right that I won't get married. And it never works out well when she tries to control me."

Dat smiled wryly. "I wouldn't want her to. I want my *dochter* to be joyful and brave enough to be herself, no matter how much she thinks she should be like Rosie Herschberger."

Except that if Rosie was the girl Felty preferred, Anna wanted to be just like her.

Dat took a bite of his cookie. "I love these licorice cookies. You made the flavor nice and strong." He chewed thoughtfully for a few minutes. "Did you say Mark Hostetler dropped you off on Sunday night?"

Anna caught her bottom lip between her teeth. "*Jah.*"

"Hasn't he poked fun at your cooking before?"

"He has, but who hasn't made fun of my cooking but you, Elmer, and Felty?" The thought of Felty eating all her asparagus bacon casserole temporarily took her breath away. "Mark says he's sorry for teasing me."

"He hasn't gone out of his way to be nice to you before."

"*Ach*, *vell*, I suppose it was because I removed a splinter from his hand. He felt obligated to be nice to me."

"Driving you home from the *singeon* seems like a little

more than being nice. Mind you, I'm not trying to stick my nose in your business or tell you who you should marry, but it wouldn't hurt to keep an eye out for Mark, even though he's known for being a bit of a scaredy-cat."

Anna rolled her eyes. "He has a weak stomach, Dat. He wouldn't be able to eat my jalapeño onion corn bread. It would never work out."

"If he got the chance to marry you, he would probably be satisfied with hot mush every day."

Anna laughed. "If Mark had to choose between being a bachelor and eating hot mush every day, for sure and certain he'd choose bachelorhood."

The timer rang, and Anna furrowed her brow. "Dat, do you know anything about bread tapping?"

"I've never heard of it before."

"I guess the bread is supposed to make a certain noise when it's done cooking—when you tap on it, I mean."

Dat shrugged. "Maybe you should use a toothpick. That's how they do it with cakes."

Anna pressed her lips together. Mammi would probably be angry if Anna didn't explicitly follow her instructions. "I'm going to try tapping it." She slid on the oven mitts, opened the oven door, and tapped on the middle loaf. It sounded just like she would have expected it to sound. "Hmm. What do you think, Dat?"

With a toothpick pinched between his fingers, Dat nudged her aside and stabbed through the top of the middle loaf. He pulled the toothpick out and studied it. "It's clean. I think it's done."

"Are you sure?"

"*Nae*."

Deciding an undercooked loaf was better than an

overcooked loaf, Anna pulled all three loaves out of the oven and set them on the cooling rack on the counter.

"*Ach*, Anna. They smell *appeditlich*."

Anna tapped on each loaf, hoping to hear whatever message the bread wanted to send her. She took off the oven mitts and tapped again. Then she heard it, a hollow thud that, Lord willing, meant the bread was full of light, airy goodness. She grinned at Dat. "I think I got it right this time."

He grinned back. "I think you did too."

Should she put on her coat and run a loaf over to Felty, just to prove she could do something as well as Rosie could? Her heart grew heavier. One loaf of bread would never change Felty's mind, and it was proud to think she could bake anything as well as Rosie could. For sure and certain, Rosie knew how to tap on her bread. Rosie probably made her bread taste better just by tapping on it. Anna couldn't compete with that.

And why would she even want to?

Chapter 13

For the fifth day this week, Felty walked up Anna's gravel driveway, hoping against hope that he would be able to see her. He probably looked calm enough on the outside, but he was beside himself with worry and fear and heartache on the inside. Something was terribly wrong, and he didn't know what to do about it. All he knew was that Anna was avoiding him and he was going crazy trying to make things better.

He didn't know why Anna was upset, but he couldn't make things right if she refused to talk to him. That night at the *singeon*, no one could have been more shocked than he was when Rosie ended up being number five in line instead of Anna. Anna hadn't been in the line at all, and when he'd asked Randy where she'd gone, Randy said he didn't know. Felty should have flatly refused to go upstairs with Rosie, but he didn't know where Anna was, and he didn't want to hurt Rosie's feelings by rejecting her. No one should get her feelings hurt over a *dumm* game.

Rosie had been more than cheerful as they ran up the stairs and sat against the wall in one of the dark bedrooms.

Another couple sat in the same room against the opposite wall, so they hadn't really been alone. Rosie leaned close to him and whispered about dull things like cinnamon rolls and car accidents and how grateful their family was that he'd saved Marvin's life. He'd heard it all before and wasn't interested in hearing it again.

All he had been able to do was nod occasionally at Rosie and wonder how communication with Anna had gotten mixed up. He'd told her the secret number. She was smart enough to figure out that he wanted her to be fifth in line so they could be coupled up for Love in the Dark. What had happened? Had she taken ill? Had she misinterpreted his message? Had she been shocked at how forward he was? Did she think he was a flirt?

What if she hadn't wanted to be coupled with him for the game? That was the most horrible thought of all. What if Anna wasn't interested in him? What if she liked somebody else? After ten minutes, he had scooted away from Rosie so many times that he'd ended up against the dresser drawers with Rosie snugly wedged next to him.

As soon as the fifteen minutes were up, Felty thanked Rosie for a fun time, then apologized for being in such a hurry to leave. He had torn down the stairs to see if he could find Anna. He needed to understand. He ached to know she hadn't rejected him altogether. He hadn't been able to find her, so he found the next best person. Elmer said she hadn't been feeling well and had gone home early.

With Mark Hostetler.

Mark Hostetler?

It was like a knife to the chest. And he knew how that felt.

Felty hadn't even stayed for wassail. He'd jumped in his buggy and gone straight to Anna's house. His heart sank when he saw another buggy pull away just as Felty pulled up. For sure and certain it was Mark. Smug, weak-stomached Mark Hostetler. Felty couldn't bear it.

Uriah, the youngest brother, answered the door and told Felty that Anna had gone to bed. If that was true, Anna had the fastest bedtime ritual in the history of mankind. But he couldn't very well force his way into the house and demand to see her, even though he was a man violently in love. There were still some unwritten rules of courtship, and storming into a girl's house late in the evening was definitely breaking at least one of them.

After milking on Monday, he had gone back to Anna's, hoping to find her home, healthy, and not getting ready for bed. Owen had answered the door that time and, with a very suspicious look in his eye, had told Felty that Anna was unavailable. Felty wasn't about to confront a twelve-year-old about why he was covering for his sister or why his sister wanted him to cover for her.

His visits were much the same on Tuesday, Wednesday, and Thursday. And here he was again on Friday, not about to leave without seeing Anna. He loved Anna down to his toes, and he refused to give up without a fight. In fact, he refused to give up at all. As a soldier, he had learned that you never gave up unless you were dead. Only Gotte had the power to make you stop.

The only problem was, Felty didn't know who or what he was fighting, and that was the thing that scared him.

If Anna couldn't see it in her heart to love him, the world would stop turning. If, incomprehensibly, she was in love with Mark Hostetler, Felty's heart would stop beating. If he'd done anything to ruin his chances with her, he would never forgive himself.

Before he made it to the porch, Mark Hostetler walked out the front door and bounded down the steps. He wore a green scarf around his neck that could only be one of Anna's creations. Felty stopped breathing as he stared at the scarf. Mark looked up and seemed surprised to see Felty. "*Hallo*, Felty. *Vie gehts?*"

Felty recovered himself enough to speak, and he managed some semblance of calm, to boot, even though his first instinct was to demand to know what Mark was doing here and why he had stolen one of Anna's scarves. "I just came to see how Anna is doing. Randy said she wasn't feeling well the other night."

Mark shrugged. "She seems fine. I don't think she was sick. Like as not, she got woozy from taking out my sliver."

"Your sliver?"

"*Jah.* We went to the cellar to play Love in the Dark, and I got a sliver on the stair railing. Anna used a pin to dig it out, and it made both of us a little queasy. She asked me to take her home."

Mark might as well have punched Felty in the gut. "Anna played Love in the Dark with you?"

"*Jah.* We were the last two left, and Randy put us together. I have to admit I wasn't eager to play with Anna, but we had a wonderful *gute* time, except for the sliver. Anna really is a *wunderbarr* girl. She's short, but she's also sweet and pretty and kind to everyone."

Felty's heart sank. Mark had noticed all that about Anna, but soon enough there would be more and more boys taking notice. Was Felty too late? Mark was certainly a more suitable Amish boy than Felty could ever be.

"I think Gotte put us together that night," Mark said. "I've been hoping for Rosie Herschberger, but now that she's got you, I need to move on. Anna and I have kissed once, you know."

Felty drew his brows together. "Rosie doesn't have me. We're just friends."

Mark raised his eyebrows as if he didn't believe Felty. "If you want to keep it a secret, that's no skin off my teeth. I don't have feelings for Rosie anymore. Anna has been there all along, just waiting for me to notice her. Well, I sure did notice her."

Felty bit his tongue before asking if Anna returned Mark's interest. Not even Mark would be able to tell if she did. Anna was nice to everyone. Maybe she wasn't interested in Mark. Maybe she was just being a *gute* neighbor. She'd removed Mark's sliver, and in his gratitude, he had invented something that wasn't really there.

At least Felty felt better telling himself it was true. But not really, because he didn't feel better at all.

Mark zipped his coat higher around his scarf. "It's too cold to be out jawing. I've got to get home for chores." He grinned and fingered the scarf at his neck. "Anna made this for me. Isn't it nice?"

Lord willing, Mark wouldn't notice the red scarf around Felty's neck. It was a different color, but the pattern in the yarn was similar. He swallowed hard. "*Jah*. Wonderful nice."

"We've already kissed. It's a *gute* head start on the relationship."

If Mark mentioned kissing Anna one more time, Felty might have to throw a snowball at him. It had been two years ago during a game of Please and Displease. No reason to brag about it.

Mark jogged out of the yard to his buggy. Felty watched until Mark's buggy disappeared down the road. Felty had thought Anna had given him the scarf because she felt something for him. Maybe she handed scarves out like licorice-flavored cookies. Maybe she didn't feel much for Felty at all.

In that uncheery frame of mind, he knocked on the door and waited for what seemed like half an hour. Finally the door opened. It was Anna's *dat*, and he didn't look the least bit happy to see Felty. Before her *dat* could give him a weak excuse about Anna being ill or asleep or too busy knitting to come to the door, Felty spoke first. "Please, sir, I need to talk to Anna. It's a matter of life and death."

Anna's *dat* cocked a skeptical eyebrow in Felty's direction. "Life and death? That sounds important."

"Wonderful important."

"I'm afraid I can't let you in, son."

Felty cleared his throat. It was plain enough Mahlon didn't like him. "But you let Mark Hostetler in, sir."

Mahlon's eyebrows creeped higher up his forehead. "Mark Hostetler is none of your business. And don't call me 'sir.' I'm no better than any man."

The *sir* was an old army habit, but Felty wasn't about to remind Mahlon that he'd been a soldier. "I want you to know that I'm planning to be baptized as soon as possible. You will never have to worry about me and my commitment to the church."

"I never worried about you in the first place." Mahlon fingered the beard on his chin. "Except to worry that Anna might break your heart."

"You were worried she'd break my heart?" Mahlon was coming dangerously close to what Felty feared was the truth.

"My Anna is a catch. I don't wonder but every boy in the *gmayna* has been in love with her at one time or another. But I've warned her to be picky and not to settle and to try not to break anybody's heart."

It felt as if a Percheron were standing on Felty's chest. "*Ach.* I see."

Mahlon frowned with his whole face. "I must be honest. I would rather *she* break *your* heart, but be that as it may, it seems you have made her very unhappy."

"She said that?"

"I will try to forgive you, but that doesn't mean I'm going to let you into my house. She doesn't want to talk to you."

Desperation clawed at Felty's chest. "But, sir, that is why I'm here. I'm not sure what I've done, but I will do whatever I must to make it right." He stopped short of telling Mahlon how he truly felt about his *dochter*. He wanted Anna to hear it first.

Mahlon seemed to sense Felty's anguish. He placed a hand on Felty's shoulder. "I will honor my *dochter*'s wishes. She says she doesn't want to see you. She tells me you embarrassed her something wonderful."

He'd embarrassed her? When? How?

"Anna does not show her wounds to the world," Mahlon

said. "So some people think she never gets her feelings hurt. But I know she feels things deeply. She hurts deeply." He pinned Felty with a stern and somber eye. "I don't like it when someone hurts my *dochter*. It feels like my own pain. So you can imagine how I feel toward you right now. If you came to apologize, there is no need. Anna has a very forgiving heart. She will be all right. It might take me a little longer. It is a weakness, but I tend to hold on to my grudges." Mahlon reached for a newspaper on the table that sat in the hall. He opened it up and pointed to an article. "I found this."

Felty's heart skipped a beat as he read the headline: *Local Amish Man Saves Boy's Life*. The article took up half the front page, and there was a photo of Felty in his uniform. He didn't know where the paper had gotten the photo, but it was the one taken before Felty had been shipped overseas. His mouth went dry. "May I?" he said, holding out his hand. Mahlon gave him the paper, and Felty devoured every word. The first part of the article was about the accident. It even had a quote from "an Amish teenager named Elmer" and a girl who said she was Marvin's aunt. That was Rosie, no doubt.

The article was glowing and undeserved, calling Felty a hero and a credit to his Amish community, but he didn't see anything that might have embarrassed Anna. Did she think he was proud? But surely she would know he'd had nothing to do with the article. He hadn't even known that the woman asking him questions that day was a reporter.

Felty's fingers clutched at the edges of the paper as he read the rest of the article. The second half talked about Felty's service in the war—the medals he had won, the times he'd been wounded, the story about Sergeant Reckless—

the horse that had carried supplies for the troops—and the soldier who had died in Felty's arms. How had the reporter found all of this information? He hadn't even told Mamm a tenth of the things that were in here.

He labored to take his next breath, and then his next. Mamm would be completely devastated by this information. What had it done to Anna? Was this why she was embarrassed? Or was she horrified? It was one thing to wonder and guess at what Felty had done in the war; it was quite another to actually know.

Mahlon's voice invaded his thoughts. How long had Felty been standing on the porch? "I was ready to put your past in the past, but this"—he pointed to the newspaper—"this is a lot to take in, even for me."

Felty's throat tightened. "I understand every *fater* wants better for his *dochter*."

"I suppose he does."

"But I can promise you that my days of fighting are over."

Mahlon pointed toward heaven. "Swear not at all, young man. You can't make one hair of your head grow any faster." He slid the paper out of Felty's hand. "Lord willing, we will see you at *gmay*. I wish you all the best."

Felty stood on Anna's porch, stunned into silence. He couldn't move, not even when Mahlon closed the door and it came to a stop six inches from his face. Didn't Mahlon know that he would rather cut off his arm than hurt Anna? He'd rather get stabbed in the heart again than see Anna cry.

He took a deep breath, took off his hat, and scrubbed his fingers through his hair. He had done some terrible things, but being a soldier had taught him at least one very important lesson: never give up on a fight until Gotte or your general orders you to stop. And Gotte would have to be the one to stop Felty from fighting for Anna, because no man could.

He had to talk to her, even if she spit in his face and screamed at him to leave her alone. He had to tell her. Had to apologize and make her understand. He closed his eyes and silently prayed for direction. Felty stepped off the porch and looked up at the windows on the second floor. Which room was Anna's? Was she even up there? With ice flowing in his veins, he found a pebble and tossed it at the east window. Nothing. He tossed two more at that window and then moved to the window on the west. He'd try every window in the house if he had to.

Suddenly, like the light of the sun, Anna appeared at the window. He waved both arms back and forth, just in case she hadn't seen him standing in the snow making a fool of himself. "Please, Anna. I need to talk to you."

Anna stepped away from the window, and Felty's heart fell like a rock tossed from a cliff. Then she was there again. She opened the window and stuck her head out. "*Hallo*, Felty." He'd never heard his name spoken with less grace.

Felty glanced at the front door. He had to say what he had to say, even if Mahlon heard him and chased him away with a shotgun. "Anna, we need to talk. I'm sorry for everything. Please come down."

Anna's face was drawn and pale. "I can't."

"Please, Anna. I need to explain."

Anna wasn't the kind of person to let anyone suffer if she could help it, even if it meant sacrificing her own needs, and right now, she looked positively miserable.

"Felty, please don't feel bad. I don't want you to feel bad on my account. These things happen. But everything is still so fresh, and I just might die of embarrassment if you force me to come down there."

"No one is forcing you to do anything. I would never force you."

"Isaac says I'm wallowing in self-pity, but I need more time."

"Anna, you are one of the most levelheaded girls I know. Don't let Isaac tell you otherwise." He swallowed his deepest desires. "If you need more time, I will give you all the time you need."

She sniffled, and even from his vantage point on the ground, he could see a tear glistening on her cheek. His fingers ached to wipe that tear away.

"Anna, anything you have to say is safe with me. Have you ever seen me get mad? You know I won't get mad."

"Do you promise not to laugh at me?"

"Laugh at you? Of course not."

She hesitated. "It's cold out there."

His heart leaped. "We can sit in the barn."

He turned when he heard a buggy pull up the driveway. *Ach, du lieva.* It was Dat's buggy. Mamm and Dat were sitting in the front seat, and someone Felty couldn't see was sitting in the back. Dat got out and strode across the snow, holding a newspaper in his hand. Felty braced himself against the coming storm.

"Felty," Dat said, distress written all over his features, "your *mater* is very upset. She paced the kitchen for an hour, babbling on about you and the war and that boy you carried out of the battle. I fear her nerves are falling apart. You must come home."

Felty looked up at Anna and felt her slipping out of his reach, even though neither of them had moved. He flinched as Rosie jumped out of the buggy and came running toward him as if she belonged there, as if she were a part of his family misfortune. She glanced up at Anna's open window but acted as if she hadn't seen anything in particular. "*Ach*, Felty, I went to your house for a visit, and I found your *mamm* sitting on the stairs holding the newspaper and crying. You need to come home right now. I'll make us all a cup of *kaffee*, and we can help your *mamm* sort out what has happened." She wrapped her arm around his elbow in a possessive gesture. Felty pulled away from her.

He again looked up. "Anna, I need to go, but I will come back as soon as I can."

Rosie was a little too indignant. "How can you even consider leaving your *mamm*'s side tonight? She's upset. She needs her son's comfort."

Keeping his gaze glued to Anna, Felty didn't even respond to Rosie. Anna's reassurance was all that mattered.

Anna shook her head. "No need to come back tonight. Or ever. There's nothing I have to say to you. Have a blessed life."

She closed the window so softly, Felty didn't hear it. But he felt it. Felt the finality of it all the way to his heart.

Chapter 14

The sun was just beginning to set later that day when Anna tiptoed out of the house with her lantern and headed up Sugg Hill. She was bundled from head to toe in warm wool, determined that no matter how cold it was, she would not freeze to death and not even lose an ear or a pinky finger. Felty's stories of the Korean winter had scared her silly.

She didn't really have to sneak out of the house. Dat knew where she had been going every night since the accident. But she didn't want Elmer or Isaac or one of the little boys to try to tag along. Tonight she wanted to be alone. It was wonderful hard to find time to herself in a house of four boys. During the summer months, she could sneak outside and find a suitable tree to hide in. It was too cold for tree climbing today.

Anna made her way up the hill on the familiar path she and Felty had first taken two weeks ago. After Felty had been hit by that car, she had made it her job to look for traps, since Felty could barely walk and couldn't check the traps himself. Besides, as an official member of the ASPCA, her duty was clear. She wasn't as *gute* at finding traps as Felty was, but she had tripped a few and always felt like she had done the animals and Felty a great service, even if neither of them appreciated it.

Now that Felty was so busy with Rosie Herschberger, Anna felt more urgency than ever to keep a lookout for traps. Felty might never come to the hill again, and someone had to care about the animals.

Anna walked up the easy slope opposite the flow of the stream like she always did. She hadn't seen any traps for the last three nights. Maybe the trappers had decided to take their traps and move somewhere else. That wasn't necessarily *gute* news. Anna would have to work harder to find traps if they weren't in their usual places.

She gasped and stopped abruptly when she saw a lone figure up ahead sitting on a tree stump with his elbows propped on his knees and his face buried in his hands. Her heart galloped when she realized it was Felty. Her chest ached at the very thought of him. Should she turn around and quietly make her way back down the hill?

She studied his posture and the curve of his shoulders in the dimming light. He looked as if he'd lost everything he ever loved in the whole world. She couldn't leave him like this. No matter how embarrassed or hurt she was, she couldn't just walk away. She stepped closer. "Felty?" she said, her voice sounding small and timid on the cold night air.

He lifted his head and looked at her almost as if he didn't see her. "I couldn't save it," he said, his voice cracking like a hammer against glass.

Anna crept closer, not sure what Felty was talking about. Then she saw it. About ten feet from the tree stump was a motionless red fox, its nose crushed and captured in the jaws of a steel trap. Anna sucked in a horrified breath. “Is it dead?” she whispered.

He stood up as an anguished moan parted his lips. “It’s not right. I should have been here.”

Whatever anger or embarrassment or heartache Anna suffered was swallowed up in her concern for Felty Helmuth, the gentle, kind man who loved animals and never asked anything from someone else that he wasn’t willing to give himself. “Oh, Felty.” She ran to him, threw her arms around his waist, and pulled him close like she would one of her *bruderen* who needed her comfort. Of course Felty was significantly taller, so she couldn’t nudge his head onto her shoulder. Instead, she burrowed her face into the front of his coat. Felty’s whole body shook with grief, and some of his tears splashed onto her cheek like rain from a sad heaven.

“I can’t stand to think of how he must have suffered.”

“It’s okay, Felty. It’s over now. No matter the pain, he’s with Gotte now, and all is forgotten.”

His pain became an audible thing, stretching as high as the sky and as deep as a chasm. “I didn’t want to kill anybody,” he sobbed. “I didn’t want to.”

Anna’s throat tightened around his words. “I know you didn’t, Felty. I know.”

“That boy, he was so young. He jumped Tooley with a knife. I had . . . I had to do something. I watched him die. I wanted him to die.”

“He would have killed you, Felty. He would have killed Tooley. You did what you had to do.”

Another sob racked Felty’s body. “He *did* kill Tooley. There was blood everywhere. So much blood. I woke up in the hospital with a five-inch gash in my chest.”

The horrors Felty had witnessed seeped into Anna's skin, and she trembled. "You never have to think about it ever again. It's in the past. You can leave it there forever."

"But I can't. Not if you won't forgive me for what I've done. Not if you can't see it in your heart to put it behind you."

Anna reached up and smoothed a tear from Felty's face. "Forgive you? There is nothing to forgive."

He was inconsolable now. "I was a sharpshooter. I killed a lot of men."

"I know. I read the article." She tugged down on the back of his neck and planted a gentle kiss on his cheek. "Hush now," she said, her voice soft and low. "It will be all right. You're safe."

He pressed his forehead to hers and took a deep, shuddering breath. "I stopped counting kills after the first battle. I just couldn't bear the heaviness of it all, the thought of how many lives I'd taken, the horror of what war did to good men." He squeezed his eyes shut. "I shouldn't have gone. I've lost everything. I shouldn't have gone."

"I don't believe it, Felty. You made the choice to leave, maybe not fully understanding war, but knowing what it would cost you with the church and your family. You didn't go because you thought it would be fun. There was nothing fun about it, and you knew it. So why did you go?" She took his face between her mittened hands. "Tell me again why you went."

He exhaled a long puff of air. "I felt a call from Gotte."

"That's right. A call from Gotte. You can't second-guess a call from Gotte. Look what happened to the prophet Jonah. Gotte knew what you would have to do in

Korea. He called you to make the sacrifice for our country. I believe He called you to make the sacrifice for our community. People in town aren't so angry at the Amish for not fighting in the war because one of our own served in the place of other Amish men. You did the right thing. You are brave and selfless, and I am proud of you, even though it is a sin to be proud."

He wrapped his hands around her arms and nudged her away to look her in the eye. "Do you really mean that, Anna?"

"Of course it's a sin to be proud. Just ask my *mammi*."

"But I thought you were horrified at what I'd done. You read the article."

Anna frowned. "I'm not mad or shocked or whatever else you expect me to be. And I don't believe Gotte is either. He called you to go."

"Your *dat* said it was too much for him. He can't forgive me."

Anna shook her head. "*Ach*, Dat will get over that. The article didn't even shock him. We all had some idea of what you'd done in Korea. No one was that naive." Anna looked down at her hands. "Dat is irritated about something else. He holds no ill will for you as a soldier."

Felty stiffened. "But he does hold ill will for me as a person?"

Anna cleared her throat. "He's just trying to protect me."

"From me?"

"*Jah,*" she whispered.

He took her hand and squeezed it gently. "Why?"

Anna hated that she had a tendency to blush. A bright red face always betrayed her emotions. "I'm embarrassed."

To her surprise, tears leaped to her eyes. She couldn't do enough sniffing to hold them back.

"Anna?" Felty wrapped his arms all the way around her and tugged her close. *Ach*, she wanted to stand like this forever, borrowing his warmth, letting the wool of his coat tickle her nose.

She sneezed. And couldn't say another word.

"Anna, please tell me. Your *dat* said I embarrassed you, and I'll do anything to fix it."

"*Ach*, Dat doesn't know when to leave well enough alone."

"I'm *froh* he told me. Please let me ask for forgiveness."

She nodded into the fold of his coat. "I forgive you."

He growled softly. "That's not *gute* enough. I want to know what happened."

"The secret number," she squeaked, too mortified to say it louder. "And the cinnamon rolls and the caroling. And"—she nearly lost her composure—"Rosie Herschberger." Rosie Hershberger was at the root of all her embarrassment and heartbreak, even though Rosie couldn't help being so *wunderbarr*.

"Wait," he said. "That's four things. Could you explain?"

Unable to look at him, Anna kept her face pressed against his chest. She couldn't face the ridicule or censure or whatever it was she would see in his eyes. "It's too embarrassing," she said. And overwhelmingly sad. But claiming embarrassment instead of heartbreak made her seem less pathetic, didn't it? Or was it the other way around?

"I would never do anything to intentionally embarrass you."

"I embarrassed myself."

He pulled her to sit on the stump and knelt down in the snow beside her. He took her lantern and set it on the ground. "Is this okay? I want to look in your eyes and make you understand how sorry I am for everything and anything I've done to hurt you. Okay?"

Anna sort of wilted. She wasn't going to be able to hide from his piercing blue eyes. "You'll get frostbite on your knees."

"I'll take that chance." He took her hand, and her heart started racing. *Ach*, she wished she weren't so weak, but she just couldn't help loving him. "First, I have to know," he said. "Are you in love with Mark Hostetler?"

She drew back, completely surprised at the question. "Of course not."

"But you made him a scarf and let him drive you home."

"I was embarrassed. He offered his buggy." She furrowed her brow. "I can't stand the thought of anyone having a cold neck. I had to give him a scarf. I just had to."

Felty's mouth relaxed into half a frown instead of the dark expression of a few seconds ago. "Okay, then. Since you don't love Mark Hostetler, let's start with the secret number. You did mention the secret number."

She nodded, and her insides curled around themselves. The most embarrassing experience first.

Felty's gaze penetrated her skull. "I gave you the secret number because I wanted you to be number five in line so you and I could play Love in the Dark together. I obviously messed it up somehow."

Anna's heart knocked against her rib cage. "You wanted to play Love in the Dark with me?"

"*Jah.*"

"Are you sure?"

Felty was taken aback. "What kind of a question is that? Of course I'm sure."

"Are you sure you're sure?"

His lips twitched upward, still doubtful but maybe not quite as wretched. "Anna, when Rosie ended up being my partner instead of you, I just about stomped out of the house and set my buggy on fire."

Anna suddenly felt cautiously giddy. "You wouldn't really set your buggy on fire, would you? It would be such a waste."

"Anna," he growled. "Tell me the whole story. Why did you end up going home with Mark Hostetler, why were you embarrassed, and what should I have done differently?"

"It seems so silly now that I know I wasn't just imagining things. Rosie Herschberger heard you say something about the secret number, and she told me that the number was meant for her, that you would never want to play Love in the Dark with me."

Felty's mouth fell open. "And you believed her?" He looked into the sky as if just barely keeping his patience. "Of course you believed her. You have always underestimated how truly *wunderbarr* you are. It makes me so frustrated."

"I'm sorry."

"I'm not mad at you. I'm annoyed at Rosie Herschberger and Joseph and all the people who have ever made you feel small. You are not small, Anna. You have filled every space in my heart."

Now her stomach was doing somersaults, and her heart was performing backflips. It was a whole circus in there. "But it made sense to me. I understand why you would want to be with Rosie. She's perfect."

"Rosie is not perfect. She's devious and a little too big for her britches. Shame on her for taking advantage of your *gute* heart and talking you into revealing the secret number. It was the longest fifteen minutes of my life." A painful emotion traveled across his face. "*Ach*, *vell*, maybe not the longest, but definitely the most unpleasant experience I've had since coming home. I couldn't find you anywhere, and then when I heard you'd gone home with Mark, I was confused and hurt and very agitated."

"I was embarrassed. Mark helped me sneak away so no one would know how humiliated I was." She shrugged. "I guess Mark knew how humiliated I was, but he didn't say anything to anybody out of gratitude for my removing his splinter."

Felty frowned and rubbed his gloved hand down the side of his face. "Mark knows an opportunity when he sees it. But I'm grateful that he was there for you, even though it should have been me."

"You went caroling without me," she said, the memory still pricking her heart.

The muscles of his jaw twitched. "Rosie assured me everybody would be there. When I got to her house, she told me you weren't coming. I should have known you hadn't been invited."

"And I guess I should have known you wouldn't have purposefully left me out."

Felty shook his head and smiled. "I never would have left you out. The only reason I go to anything, including church, is so I can see you."

Anna laughed. "You're such a tease, Felty Helmuth. It's a wonder I believe anything you say."

He suddenly grew serious, as if someone had blown out the candle behind his eyes. "I'm not teasing, Anna. *Ach*, how I want you to understand." He took off one glove and caressed her cheek. A thread of warm liquid trickled down her spine. "I have loved you ever since I was fourteen years old."

Her heart raced like a freight train. "That was a long time ago. Are you sure?"

"What kind of a question is that? Of course I'm sure."

"Are you sure you're sure?"

Felty chuckled. "You are going to drive me crazy, Anna Yoder. It was at that spelling bee. Some of the older boys were mad that you won, but I was amazed at your smarts. And you were pretty and feisty and so different from all the other girls. I fell in love at first sight. Of course, we were both too young, so I sat back and watched."

"You were wonderful quiet about it."

"I like to think I was patient."

Anna giggled, so happy that she thought she might be able to fly. "I noticed you, of course. In elementary school, Rosie Herschberger called you the prettiest boy in Bonduel, and all the girls agreed. But you were just one of the older boys, so tall that I figured you wouldn't even be able to see me down here."

Felty's deep, throaty laugh was like a balm to Anna's heart. "*Ach*, Anna. I adore you. Through the years you've just gotten prettier and feistier and more lovable." He paused, and his expression seemed to turn to stone. "I want to show you something." He nudged her away from him and unzipped his coat.

"Don't do that. You'll catch your death of cold."

"Just for a second." He unzipped the jacket underneath and unbuttoned the top three buttons of his shirt.

Anna struggled to catch her breath as he pulled back the left side of his shirt and the long johns below. A long, jagged scar zigzagged across his skin right above his heart. It was red and ugly and spoke of the pain Felty had endured during the war. "*Ach*, Felty. I'm so sorry."

"I should have died." He gave her a reassuring smile. "When I left for Korea, I begged Gotte to spare my life so I could see you again and have a chance to win your love. Gotte heard my prayers. Maybe it was wrong to ask, but I couldn't bear the thought of losing you."

"I had no idea."

"I know," he said, rebuttoning his shirt. "It's because you think so little of yourself. You can't imagine anyone could see you differently. Gotte saved my life so I could say these words to you. You are my everything, Anna Yoder. I love you with my whole heart. I want to spend every day with you for the rest of my life. What do you say to that?"

Anna didn't know there was this much happiness in the whole world. "Are you asking me to marry you?"

"*Jah.*"

"Are you sure?"

"Of course I'm sure."

"Are you sure you're sure?"

Growling, Felty pulled her to her feet, lowered his head, and planted a kiss right on her mouth. She wasn't ready for it, and he kissed her teeth. She nearly laughed, but she puckered her lips instead so she'd be ready when he tried again. The second try came immediately after the first. He brought his lips down on hers gently, slowly, and she felt the potent ache of his touch clear to her toes. Speaking of toes, she pushed up onto hers and wrapped her arms all the way around Felty's neck, pulling him closer and adding an exclamation point to their embrace.

Ach, she was pretty sure this was what heaven felt like.

Except that heaven would probably be a lot warmer, and her feet wouldn't be stiff like a pair of icicles. She shivered just thinking about kissing Felty by a nice, warm fire.

Pulling her face a few inches away from his, she whispered, "It's sort of cold out here."

His smile made her heart flutter. "I don't feel it. It's like you lit a fire inside me. I want to stand right here with you in my arms and never move again."

"That's the first sign of hypothermia," Anna said. "Not wanting to move. I read it in *The Call of the Wild*."

He squeezed her tightly to him. "But what a way to go."

"Oh, no you don't, Felty Helmuth. You didn't survive the Korean winter just to die of frostbite in Wisconsin, especially not before we're married."

His eyes lit up with delight. "So are you saying yes?"

"*Jah.* I will marry you."

"Are you sure?"

"Of course I'm sure," Anna said.

"Are you sure you're sure?"

Anna laughed and cuffed him on the shoulder. "You are incorrigible, Felty Helmuth."

"I don't even know what that means, but I bet you know how to spell it." His smile couldn't have gotten any wider. "That was my first kiss ever, and it was definitely the most amazing thing that has ever happened to me."

Anna trembled. "It was the most amazing thing that has happened to me too, and that counts the time a bear passed right under the tree I was sitting in and didn't even eat me."

Felty chuckled. "You've led the most interesting life, Anna."

"It's gotten much more interesting since you came along. My only regret is that we waited this long to kiss. Think of all the excitement we've already missed out on."

Felty leaned over and kissed her again. "We have plenty of years to make up for lost time."

"Thank Derr Herr."

Felty glanced in the direction of the dead fox and lost his smile. "Even though I never want to leave your side again, we should get you home."

"What about the fox?"

"There's nothing we can do. Whoever set those traps will be back for it, and I don't want to be here when he comes. I don't know that I could show him any Christian charity."

Anna took his hand. "Let's go, then."

They walked a few steps before he stopped her. "You've been coming out here, haven't you? Tripping the traps."

"I knew you wouldn't feel up to it after the accident."

He pulled her close again. "*Ach*, Anna, I love you for doing that, but I hate that you put yourself in danger."

"There's no danger, except for maybe frostbite, but I

am determined to marry you with all my fingers and toes." His smile was doubtful, but she didn't want to talk about it and pile any more worry on him than she had to. "How is your *mamm*? Was she wonderful upset?"

He tucked her arm in his and tugged her toward her farm. "I'm afraid so. She wanted to pretend I never went to war, but that newspaper article forced her to face it. She's afraid to let me leave the house. She gets anxious when I sneeze. She can't bear the thought of losing me. Dat told her that my life is in Gotte's hands and that we should trust in Gotte. She doesn't like hearing that. My going to war was very hard on her."

"Mothers control so much of their children's lives when they are little. She had to completely let go and trust Gotte to take care of you. That couldn't have been easy."

"Now that I'm back, she wants to take over for Gotte and be in charge of everything I do. Sometimes she comes out to the dairy to watch me milk. She won't let me leave the table until I've eaten two helpings of everything." He pressed his lips together and glanced at Anna. "She wants me to marry Rosie Herschberger."

"That doesn't surprise me." Anna paused. "And I suppose it makes me unhappy."

He put his arm around her. "You know I love only you, Annie."

Anna's heart jumped a mile. He'd never called her Annie before. She liked it. "I know you love me, but I only learned that very recently. Of course your *mamm* would choose Rosie. Rosie is perfect."

"Rosie is not perfect. She's selfish and has too high an opinion of herself." He tempered his scold with a smile.

"I'm sorry, Anna, but I don't want you to spend one more minute worrying about Rosie Herschberger."

"I'm more worried about your *mamm*."

"Once she gets to know you, she will love you almost as much as I do." He leaned down and kissed her, and all was right with the world.

It was almost full dark, and the temperature was dropping. Felty had picked up the lantern, and he held it high so they could see where they were going.

"Hey, what are you doing out here?"

Anna caught her breath as a dark figure approached them from the east. She couldn't see much else, because he pointed his flashlight directly in Anna's face.

"Please lower your light," Felty said, in a voice of perfect mildness.

The light hopped up to Felty's face and dropped to the level of Felty's boots. Felty tightened his grip around Anna's shoulders, but he needn't have been concerned. Anna wasn't afraid. She was furious. The man approaching them had a shotgun in one hand, a flashlight in the other, and a steel-jawed trap dangling from his shoulder by its chain.

The man came closer, stopped, and looked Anna and Felty up and down. "It's a cold night to be out for a stroll."

"Anna's farm is just down the hill here," Felty said. He sounded calm enough, but Anna could feel his tension coiled like a tight spring. Anna didn't know what he would do, but Felty did not have a violent bone in his body. Though he had done his duty in the army, he wouldn't voluntarily hurt a fly. He didn't have the heart for it.

The man stared for half a minute, then grunted. "I

can't figure out you Amish folks by half, but then again, I suppose you can't figure out us normal folks either, so I guess we're even yet. I'm sorry if I scared you. Somebody's been vandalizing my traps, and I've started carrying a gun just in case I need to scare someone away."

Felty squared his shoulders. "I'm the one whose been messing with your traps, sir, and I ain't ashamed to say it."

The man squinted as if to get a better look at Felty. "You been pulling out my traps?"

Felty nodded. "Those traps you use cause a lot of suffering to the animals. It's wrong. That's why I've been pulling them out."

Surprise and anger flared behind the man's eyes. "You can't do that. Those traps are my personal property. It's against the law for you to pull them out. Besides, a man's got to make a living. They don't pay me dang near enough at the garage."

"I understand that you have to make a living, but do animals have to die for it?" Felty said. "There is another way. Those traps are cruel." Anna had no idea how Felty was able to stay calm and rational. She'd seen the condition of the dead fox.

"Those traps are the most efficient way to catch beavers and such. And I can't see as my quitting would make a hill of beans difference. If I didn't set traps, someone else would, and I deserve the money just as much as the next man."

"It seems to me you're doing all right, owning all this property to hunt on," Felty said, his voice tinged with dislike.

"I don't own the property. I got permission from the

man who does." He stared at Felty, and the wrinkles piled up on his forehead. "I know you. You're that Amish boy from the newspaper."

Felty nodded slowly.

The man took a step back. "Well, for goodness' sake. It won't be said that I'm not one to give a man his due. What you did for that little boy was real good. And the way you served your country, son, well, that would make any man proud yet."

Felty didn't relax, but his voice wasn't so sharp when he replied. "Thank you, sir."

The man nodded. "I'm not going to call the police. You did your duty to your country, and you paid a high price. But I'm warning you not to fiddle with my traps again or I *will* call the police, even though you're a war hero. Do you understand, son?"

Felty frowned. "I wish I could help you see—"

"I've seen enough in my day, son. There isn't anything a young fellow like yourself can teach me, even with your war record. But please don't make me call the police. I have to think of my children." The man dipped his head and walked past them without another word.

Felty turned. "There's a fox in a trap a quarter mile up. He's dead." His voice sounded like thin ice.

The man didn't look as pleased about that news as Anna thought he would be. "Thank you. I appreciate that."

His footfalls, crunching in the snow, soon faded to nothing. Anna slid her arm around Felty's waist and nudged him down the hill. He wrapped one arm around her shoulders and pulled her close as they walked, holding the lantern high so they could see where they were going. She looked up. The lantern light reflected the tears trailing down Felty's cheeks. He didn't look at her, didn't say anything, but she could feel his sadness like a blanket of ice.

There was nothing she could do but hold him close and let him feel it. Like he had said, there was so much sadness in the world. And she could only do so much.

Chapter 15

Felty took off his boots and left them on the porch outside the back door. They were even too dirty to be left in the mudroom, and it seemed a waste of time to clean them yet. It felt like the afternoon milking started the minute they finished the morning milking. Of course, that included all the cleanup of the first milking and then the prep for the second. Felty didn't usually clean his boots in between. Besides, they were just the boots he used to walk out to the pasture and round up the cows into the milking barn. His actual milking boots were in the barn standing next to the door, as clean as they could be.

Felty smiled to himself. He would have just enough time between milkings to eat lunch, walk to Anna's house, and spend an hour with her before he came back to start the milking all over again. Maybe they would be able to do a little kissing. He'd be content to stare into her eyes and whisper sweet words to her just so he could see her blush. He loved her blush more than just about any other expression she wore. Her face had been especially rosy when she had agreed to marry him.

A twinge of pain temporarily marred his perfect happiness. That night had been the best one of his life, even though he hadn't been able to save that fox. It amazed him how Gotte was able to make beauty from ashes.

Felty went into the mudroom and hung up his coat and hat, along with the scarf Anna had knitted him. It had become his most prized possession. He buried his face in the soft ridges of yarn. It was like having a little piece of Anna with him wherever he went. He didn't even care if Mark had one of Anna's scarves too. Felty had Anna's heart, and that was the most important thing.

He heard voices coming from the kitchen. Mamm made lunch for Felty, his two *bruderen*, the nephews, and Dat every day after the milking was done. Sometimes Felty's sisters-in-law would come to help cook, but usually it was just Mamm preparing the food. She made hearty, stick-to-your-ribs meals to give everybody plenty of energy for the afternoon milking. *Yummasetti* was one of the family's favorites, but she also made Yankee bean soup, baked chicken with buttered noodles, and Dat's favorite, chicken potpie. Mamm loved making delicious meals for her family. She was actually a lot like Anna that way. Anna took a great deal of pleasure in cooking for the people she loved. That most of them didn't appreciate her efforts didn't seem to dampen her enthusiasm for it.

Felty cocked his head to the side. Who was in the kitchen with Mamm? Lord willing, he wouldn't have to spend time visiting with one of Mamm's friends. He wanted to eat quickly and get to Anna's house. Mamm wouldn't be happy if she knew where he planned to go, so he wasn't going to tell her. He didn't especially like sneaking around, but Mamm's feelings were a bit fragile, and she'd made it painfully obvious she wasn't enthusiastic about Anna.

For sure and certain, Mamm suspected he had feelings for Anna. It had been impossible to hide his unbounded joy after he'd returned from the hill four nights ago. Mamm wasn't going to be happy about his engagement to Anna. He'd save that information until Mamm got over the story of his two weeks spent in the field hospital.

For now, what Mamm didn't know couldn't hurt her. A little sneaking out, a little kissing was normal and absolutely necessary for a man in love. Anna had said yes. He wouldn't want for another thing in his entire life, except to actually be married to her.

Felty walked down the hall and stopped short in the threshold of the kitchen. Mamm and Rosie Herschberger stood at the table rolling out bread. Mamm chattered happily while Rosie pressed the rolling pin back and forth across the cream-colored dough.

Mamm looked up and exploded into a grin. "Felty! Look who dropped by."

Rosie smiled at Felty and batted her eyelashes, perfectly playing the part of the demure, sweet, exemplary girl. Felty could see the appeal, even though he had no interest in her. She *was* what the elders would consider the ideal Amish girl, a girl any man would be proud to take as a *fraa*. She had mastered all the homemaking arts, she was pretty and dutiful, and everybody liked her, including every Amish *mamm* who wanted the best for her son. To add to her appeal, Rosie was the bishop's daughter. It wasn't surprising that Anna felt so small compared to Rosie.

Of course, Rosie understood perfectly well how desirable she was, but she didn't recognize her sense of superiority as pride. She saw it as the honest truth, the way Gotte had made her. It was why she didn't seem to feel the need to strive for humility.

"*Hallo*, Rosie," Felty said, trying his best to hide his disappointment and irritation at who was standing in the kitchen. "It looks like you're cooking up something *appeditlich*."

Rosie gave him a modest smile. "Your *mamm* is teaching me how to make stollen as a Christmas gift for all my neighbors."

Anna made loaves of stollen every year for the neighbors. Did Rosie know that? Was she trying to outshine Anna? And why would she do such a thing?

Ach.

Felty knew why. It was time to put a stop to anyone putting down his Anna ever again. But he'd have to ease into it. "What's for lunch?"

This question seemed to make Mamm very happy. "*Ach*, Felty. It's *wunderbarr*. Rosie brought each of us a special Christmas lunch in a box."

Rosie beamed. "I brought some for your *mamm* and *dat* and you and your *bruderen* and nephews. I made each of you a Christmas cupcake, a miniature Christmas apple tart, and a Christmas ham and cheese sandwich."

Just how was a Christmas ham and cheese sandwich different from an everyday ham and cheese sandwich?

Mamm giggled in delight. "There's a little Christmas star cut out of the middle of every slice of bread."

Well, there you go. A Christmas ham and cheese sandwich.

Rosie clasped her hands in front of her. "It's the least I could do since you saved my nephew's life."

"*Ach*, *vell*, you don't need to keep thanking me for that."

"*Jah*, I do. Besides, even if the accident had never happened, I should be thanking you just for being the man you are. It was shameful, the way they treated you when you first came home."

Now it was the way *they* had treated him? Rosie was trying to separate herself from her own actions. *Ach*, *vell*, it didn't matter. Nothing she said could make him think better or worse of her. He simply didn't care what she thought.

"Rosie," Felty said, "could I talk to you in the front room?"

Rosie's smile was wider than the Wisconsin River. "I just need to finish this stollen first, then I'd be happy to have a private visit with you."

Ach, it had turned into a *private visit*, when Felty was simply trying to save her from embarrassment by taking her into another room where Mamm couldn't listen in.

"*Nae, nae,*" Mamm said, shooing Rosie away from the dough. "Go with Felty. You two have important things to discuss. I'll finish the stollen."

Felty's heart sank through the floor and all the way to Korea. It was just Mamm's wishful thinking that he and Rosie had important things to discuss. *Ach*, it looked like he was going to need a *private visit* with Mamm too.

Might as well get it over with. He strolled into the front room, and Rosie eagerly followed him. He sat down in Dat's favorite chair, expecting Rosie to sit across from him on the sofa. Instead, she pulled the coffee table closer to his chair and sat down on it, facing him with her knees mere inches from his. Would it be rude to stand up and plaster himself against the far wall?

Probably.

"Your *mamm* is so kind to help me with the stollen. Everybody knows she is the best baker in Bonduel. It wonders me why you're so thin, with all the *gute* food your *mamm* makes. But I suppose it's because you're so tall. There's so much more space to try to fatten up. Your *fraa* will need to be a *gute* cook so you won't blow away in the wind." She smiled shyly. "Not that I think it will be a problem. I like that you're tall. Nobody wants a short husband. Or an ugly one."

"Rosie," he began, folding his arms and pulling his legs back, hopefully giving her the message that he wanted no part of his body to touch hers, "did you know that Anna Yoder makes stollen every year for the neighbors?"

Rosie's eager smile wasn't what he expected. "I knew that."

"The Christmas before I left for Korea, I hear she made thirty loaves of stollen, one for each family in the district."

Rosie grimaced. "We all got one. Some people didn't really consider it a present. I don't mean to speak ill of Anna, but it was dry and gloppy and spicy. She put jalapeños in the dough."

"Are you sure?"

"*Ach*, yes. My dat burned his tongue."

Felty pinned her with a piercing gaze. "What I meant was, are you sure you don't mean to speak ill of Anna?"

Rosie's smile fell. She hemmed and hawed, shifted in her seat, and cleared her throat. "We all know about Anna's cooking, and we all feel wonderful sorry for her, growing up without a *mater* and all."

"So why are you giving out stollen this year when you know that's Anna's annual gift?" He leaned forward. "Truthfully."

Rosie drew her brows together. "I always try to be truthful. You don't have to look at me like that."

Felty sat back, willing his temper to simmer. He couldn't help getting riled up on Anna's account. "I'm sorry. I'm just trying to help you understand."

Rosie sighed and regained her smile. "I have to admit that I'm giving away stollen this year because of Anna. I want everybody to experience the true joy of stollen. People should know how truly *appeditlich* it can taste."

"You want to be certain that people know you are a better cook than Anna."

Again her reaction wasn't what he expected. The smile got wider. "*Ach*, Felty, you don't know how long I have waited for you to say that. I thought you hadn't noticed that I'm the better cook. I mean, on the day of the accident you ate three of her tiny, dry cinnamon rolls and didn't touch mine. Do you know how terrible that made me feel?" She glanced at the threshold as if making sure no one was listening in, then lowered her voice anyway. "I don't mean to be rude, but who in his right mind would choose an Anna Yoder cinnamon roll over mine? And I'm sorry if that sounds proud, but it's the truth."

"It's not a competition."

"I know that. I'm just saying what's obvious to everyone."

He didn't want to hurt her feelings, he truly didn't, but Rosie's smug satisfaction made Anna upset. If he had anything to say about it, no one would upset or disregard Anna ever again. He nodded. "You are a wonderful *gute* cook."

She all but came out of her seat with happiness. "*Denki*, Felty."

"But food is a matter of opinion. I've never enjoyed a cinnamon roll as much as I enjoy Anna's. She's not afraid to try exciting new flavors, and she puts so much of herself into her cooking."

Rosie stiffened. "I put my whole heart and soul into my cinnamon rolls."

"I don't wonder that you do. But trying to outdo Anna doesn't seem very nice. In fact, it seems downright petty yet."

Rosie's bottom lip began to quiver. "I'm not trying to outdo her. I just want people to see the difference. I want *you* to see the difference. I'm obviously better than Anna at everything. I'd make a much better *fraa*."

Felty's heart raced, with both annoyance at Rosie and affection for Anna. "I do see the difference, Rosie, but it's less about what you can do and more about who you are. Anna thinks the best of everyone. She always tries to do the right thing, even when it's hard. She's smart and has the kindest heart I've ever known. And even though she's been through some hard things, she chooses to be happy. She chooses to love life. Anna doesn't scheme or manipulate people to get her way. That night at the *singeon*, you made her feel worthless, as if she were a fool for thinking I would want to spend Love in the Dark with her instead of you."

Rosie looked genuinely confused. "But you did want to play Love in the Dark with me. The secret number was for me."

"Because you think so little of Anna. It wonders me if you think well of anybody but yourself."

Rosie's eyes pooled with tears. "Of course I do. I think well of you and my parents and, really, everybody. I like Anna just fine, but you have to admit that even though she's kind and smart and all those other things, she's never going to get married."

Felty drew in a deep breath. Poor Rosie. She refused to see her own weaknesses. "It doesn't matter. I just think that if you examined your own heart, you would treat people with more kindness, even the people you think are beneath you."

Tears rolled down Rosie's cheeks. Was it a sign that she might be considering what he said? "That makes me sound proud. I'm not proud. I'm not better than anyone else." She sniffed loudly. "Is this what you've been thinking of me this whole time? Because I'm nice. I'm just as nice as Anna. Even your *mamm* said she didn't know what she'd have done if I hadn't been here when she read that newspaper article."

Felty didn't want to make Rosie feel any worse. "*Denki*

for being a comfort to her." He handed her his handkerchief.

"I was happy to do it." She wiped her eyes and balled the handkerchief in her fist. "So is there no hope for me? For us? Am I too wicked and horrible to be anybody's wife?"

"Of course not." It was obvious Rosie had set her sights on him, even if he didn't understand why she thought they would be a *gute* match. But was there any way to let her down kindly? "You'll make a fine *fraa*." He looked at his hands. "Just not mine."

Rosie clapped the handkerchief over her mouth and stood up so swiftly, she knocked both of her knees against his. He flinched at the pain shooting from his sore knee. She stormed out of the room, and he could hear her in the hallway gathering her coat and bonnet and such. Whimpering softly, she opened the door and slammed it shut.

He'd obviously given her an answer she hadn't wanted to hear.

Ach, vell. He'd tried to be nice, but unless he wanted her coming over every day to learn how to bake any number of Mamm's treats, he had needed to put her in her place. Still, he always felt bad when he made someone else feel bad, so he couldn't be completely satisfied.

Mamm came storming into the front room. "Where's Rosie?" She propped her hands on her hips and glared at him. "What did you say to her?"

"Mamm, we need to have a private visit."

Mamm pursed her lips and lifted her chin as if daring him to say what he had to say. "Go on."

"I'm not interested in Rosie."

She blew a puff of air from between her lips. "You've only been back for four weeks. It's too soon to decide anything now."

"She practically shunned me when I came home. She ignored me until the accident."

"It took an accident for her to recognize your worth. It wasn't as if she was the only one. They were all stubborn and blind. Everybody ignored you until the accident."

Felty stood up and took Mamm's hands. "Not Anna."

Mamm shrugged. "I never said Anna wasn't smart, but I knew she wouldn't be the only one to come to accept you in the end."

"But, Mamm, if the accident with Marvin had never happened, Anna and her family would still be the only ones to be kind to me. Anna has a *gute* heart, and I like her very much."

"Son, I understand that she was the first girl to notice you when you came back, but that doesn't mean she's kinder or nicer or sweeter than any other girl in the *gmayna*. It just means she had sense enough from the start to see how truly *wunderbarr* you are. Rosie is just as sweet and pretty, and she is fascinated with everything about you. She knows how to cook and sew and behave like a proper Amish girl. Anna hasn't been raised like most Amish girls. She tends to get herself into trouble or create embarrassing situations for her family."

"Mamm, you just need to get to know her."

"I've known Anna for nineteen years. She's an awkward girl who can't bake a *gute* loaf of bread to save her life. Rosie is the bishop's daughter. Anna can't hold a candle to her, as you are fully aware."

Felty realized that he would have to be more plain-spoken, even though his *mamm* would probably never forgive him for passing up a girl like Rosie Herschberger. His heart sank. His astonishing happiness was going to make Mamm very unhappy. He put his arm around her and tugged her down to sit next to him on the sofa. "I know you don't care for Anna."

"I never said that. I simply like Rosie better."

He pinned her with a stern eye. "Mamm, I know you don't like Anna, and I'm not going to try to talk you out of your opinion. But I like Anna. I love Anna, and I'm going to marry her."

Mamm shook her head adamantly. "That's not true. You deserve so much more, son."

"*Nae*, you have it all wrong. I don't deserve Anna, but she has agreed to marry me anyway. I know a *gute* thing when I see it. We're engaged, thank Derr Herr."

Mamm's eyes flashed with panic. "What have you done?" She grabbed his arm as if she could move him with the force of her will. "It's not too late to take it back. Tell her you were teasing."

"Mamm, I'm going to marry Anna. I love her more than anything in the whole world."

"More than me?" Mamm snapped. "More than your *dat*?"

He nodded slowly and lowered his voice to a whisper. "More than my own life."

Mamm pushed herself off the sofa. "This is a huge mistake, Felty. I can't let you do it. Gotte took you from me once. I won't let Anna take you from me now."

Felty's throat tightened. "You don't believe me, but my going to war was Gotte's will."

She hung her head. "That is the worst of it. How can I believe in a Gotte who would ask such a sacrifice of my son, of our whole family?"

"Gotte moves in mysterious ways."

Mamm's eyes flashed with anger. "That is what your *dat* said, but it's just an excuse for when Gotte does something that is incomprehensible. A loving Gotte would never take my son away from me like that. A loving Gotte would have told you to stay home to take care of your *mater*. Don't you see how I have sacrificed for you? Is this the thanks I get, being forced to watch you throw everything away on Anna Yoder? I have given my life to make you happy. Don't I deserve some happiness? Don't I deserve to see you favorably married?"

Felty swallowed past the lump in his throat. "Anna is the best *fraa*, the only *fraa* I could ever want."

"Anna is an odd girl who knits pot holders and puts jalapeños in her crescent rolls."

"I love her crescent rolls, Mamm. I love everything about her. Just let me bring her over. You'll come to love her as much as I do."

Mamm had practically worked herself into a frenzy. "Bring her over? That girl is not allowed in my house ever again. She's pulled the wool over your eyes, and I'm not going to sanction your decision by welcoming her into my home."

Felty closed his eyes and let the heartache wash over him. He had known Mamm would be upset, but he hadn't known she'd be adamantly against Anna. It was too bad, because Mamm probably didn't realize that if she forced him to choose between Anna and herself, he would choose Anna every time. It was a painful decision, but an easy one, all the same.

He stood up and planted a kiss on Mamm's forehead. "I love you, Mamm. Nothing you can do will ever change that. But I can't stay here if the girl I love isn't allowed in the house."

"Then you should choose another girl to love."

Felty wasn't going to argue with Mamm, and she didn't need to see the sadness or frustration in his eyes. He loved Anna. He was going to marry her. Every other concern seemed trivial in comparison. He refused to let Mamm's distress mar his perfect happiness.

He now had a big problem, because for Anna's sake, he had to move out of the house. If Anna wasn't welcome, then he refused to enter the house either. He'd still come for the milking every day. He needed the money and Dat needed the help, but he couldn't live here with Mamm's dislike of Anna tainting everything in the house.

Tooley used to say that problems pushed people forward. If nobody had any problems, they wouldn't work so hard to find solutions. Tooley said that a problem was a gift.

Mamm's stubborn refusal to accept Anna didn't seem like a gift, but he would trust Gotte to show him the way, as He had so many times before. Felty studied Mamm's face. An unyielding determination hardened her features. He needed to get away from Mamm and the dairy and Rosie Herschberger's Christmas-lunches-in-a-box. "I love you, Mamm."

"And I love you. I only want what's best for you."

He turned around, marched into the mudroom, and put on his jacket, then his coat and all his other winter gear, finishing off with Anna's scarf wrapped tightly around his neck. He walked out to the barn, told his *dat* he wouldn't be helping with the afternoon milking, then hitched the horse to the sleigh and headed down the road.

Before he was halfway to Anna's, Gotte gave him a solution to his problem.

It was too bad that the solution involved some wonderful cold nights. Maybe his *bruder* Zeb would let Felty borrow a sleeping bag.

Chapter 16

"*Hallo*, stranger," Anna called, bounding out to Felty's horse-drawn sleigh as soon as he stopped in front of her house. With her thermos in one hand, she pressed her other hand to the top of her bonnet as a cold wind threatened to blow it off her head. Her heart skipped at the thought of spending an afternoon with her fiancé. *Ach*, she'd missed him.

Felty's smile could have warmed three counties, even though he was shaking like a wagon moving over a bumpy road. "I've never seen a prettier sight in my whole life."

Anna's face warmed at his compliment, and she climbed into the small two-seater sleigh—a convenient but uncomfortable way to travel in the winter. Felty was thick with coats and winter wear, and he had a blanket draped over his legs, but he still looked unbearably cold. She would have given him her scarf, but he already had two wrapped around his neck. "*Ach*, Felty, you look as stiff as an icicle." Thank Derr Herr she'd come prepared. She opened her thermos, poured some steaming hot cocoa into the lid, and handed it to Felty. "Drink this. I added little marshmallows and some cayenne pepper. It'll warm you up and clear out your sinuses at the same time."

Felty closed his eyes and breathed in the steam rising from the cocoa. He took a sip and then another and sighed with pleasure. "*Ach*, Annie. This is just what the doctor ordered. I haven't felt truly warm for almost a week."

Anna slid as close to him as she could get, tugged the blanket over her legs, and wrapped her arm around his shoulders. She rubbed her hand up and down his back. "Friction creates heat," she said. "I use this trick every night in bed when my feet are cold. I rub them against the sheets to warm them up."

His smile was so affectionate, she thought the snow under the buggy might melt. "I look forward to the day when we can warm each other's feet in bed."

"*Ach*, Felty, you shouldn't say such things."

"Maybe not, but for sure and certain I'm thinking them. All day long."

Anna giggled and nudged him with her shoulder. "Dat would never let me ride out with you again if he heard such talk."

Felty made a big show of locking his lips together. "I will be as silent as the grave." He finished off his cocoa and handed her the lid. "*Appeditlich*, Anna. My sinuses are dripping already." He jiggled the reins, and the horse moved forward.

A car passed them, crawling at a snail's pace on the icy road. Felty squinted in the bright sunlight and examined the license plate. "Hmm. Wisconsin. I have a thousand Wisconsins. But I saw a Mississippi in Shawano yesterday. I thought, 'Annie knows how to spell Mississippi.' Everything makes me think of you. It's *wunderbarr*, because I love thinking of you. I haven't stopped thinking of you for eight years."

"You haven't been on my mind as long as all that, but I haven't read one book in the last five weeks, because thoughts of you are better than any book."

Felty seemed to like that. "I'm *froh*. It's everything I prayed for." He pointed to the car now far up the road. "I only need West Virginia to win the game."

"We might have to take a trip to Green Bay. There are lots of cars in Green Bay."

"That's a wonderful *gute* idea, Annie."

Anna hooked her arm around Felty's elbow. "What have you been up to? I haven't seen hide nor hair of you for seven whole days, and I was starting to worry that you might be rethinking that proposal."

"Never." Felty leaned over and kissed her right on the mouth, but she hadn't been expecting it, so he got her teeth. Again. "You said yes, so whether you like it or not, you're stuck with me."

Anna smiled with her lips closed, just in case he tried to kiss her again. "I like it, but I don't like not seeing you."

"Did you get my note?"

"*Jah*, but Elmer had to help me read your handwriting." She squeezed his arm. "Did you solve the problem you were working on? I would have helped."

He frowned. "I should have asked. I just didn't want you to worry. My *mamm* . . ." He gazed at the snow-covered road and huffed out a breath.

"Your *mamm* doesn't like me."

He leaned over and kissed her again. This time she was ready and kissed him back without incident or teeth. Her heart fluttered like a thousand butterflies at his touch.

Ach, she loved him so much. "Mamm doesn't know you. She's going to fall in love with you."

Anna frowned in spite of the butterflies doing somersaults in her stomach. "Maybe she'll never like me."

Felty pulled off the main road onto a side road that sloped gently upward. "You're an acquired taste."

"What does that mean?"

"At chow time in the army, they had a vat of green olives at the end of the line at every meal. At first, Tooley hated green olives, but he took a handful because they were there. After about six months, he started loving green olives."

"So I'm like a green olive?"

"Only to my *mamm*," Felty said, watching her doubtfully.

"So you think your *mamm* will start to like me after six months?"

"It won't take that long," he said, reassuring her with a kiss.

Anna was so happy that Felty loved her, she didn't have a lot of room to worry about his *mamm*. It would certainly be awkward whenever she went over to Felty's house, though. "So what is this problem you've been working on, and have you solved it?"

"I've solved two problems at the same time. I want to show you." Felty's cheeks were bright red, and his breath came out like great puffs of smoke.

"I hope it's not far. We need to get you near a fire."

Felty grinned. "Annie, we're almost there."

The wide trail climbed slowly up the hill, and Anna realized it was Sugg Hill, the hill behind her pasture and farm. They were climbing it from the opposite side. The hill flattened out at the top with at least six acres of level land and a whole forest of maple, beech, and white pine trees. An old shed stood among the trees, not quite big enough to be called a barn, but definitely ample enough to hold a couple of horses and a sleigh. Anna grinned. "I love this spot. I come here when I truly want to be alone, or when my book gets so *gute* I can't put it down. There's a thick pine tree just over there that is big enough to hide in and read in peace. Not even Isaac can find me when I shimmy into that tree."

Felty guided the horse down a path that had obviously been used before. They stopped right in front of the shed. Smiling widely, he jumped out of the sleigh and held out his hand for Anna. "Welcome to my new home." He looked down and cleared his throat. "*Ach*, *vell*, our new home, Lord willing, someday soon."

"Our home?" Anna tried hard to smile. The shed was spacious, but that was its only *gute* quality. The wood walls were rotting and moldy, and the roof looked to be caved in on one end. Someone had draped a tarp over half of the roof, and yellowing newspaper covered the inside of every window. The door hung slightly crooked from its hinges, and there was a hole stuffed with fabric where the doorknob was supposed to be. She didn't want to dampen Felty's enthusiasm, but if he wanted her honest opinion, she was going to have to give it to him. Lying was a sin. So was filthiness.

She must have been doing a wonderful *gute* job of pretending, because Felty's smile stretched wide as he saw her looking at the shed. "*Cum,*" he said, pulling her forward, "I'll show you." He drew the wad of fabric out of the doorknob hole and pulled the door open. It shuddered and shrieked as if several cats were dying at the same time. Anna hesitated only slightly before stepping into the dim space. *Ach, vell*, "stepping" was an exaggeration. She sort of tiptoed into the room. She'd rather not step on any mice. Or gophers. Or spiders. And she'd really rather not run into a badger. Those things were mean.

A wall of lukewarm air met her as Felty shut the door behind them and stuffed the fabric back into the hole. A kerosene lantern hung on a hook by the door. Felty quickly lit it with a match from his pocket and hung it back on the hook. With his eyes twinkling merrily, he gestured around the shed. "What do you think?"

"I think . . ." Anna searched her vocabulary for a word to express her feelings without hurting Felty's. "I think it looks as if you've done a lot of work on this shed."

Felty laughed. "I know. Isn't it *wunderbarr*?"

Anna swallowed hard. The packed dirt floor was dry, but the whole shed smelled damp and moldy. Two sheets were hung across the room widthwise, dividing the shed in half. In the half where they stood, a sleeping bag was spread on the floor in front of an ancient potbellied stove that radiated heat. Anna took off her mittens and reached out to warm her hands at the stove. "It's nice and warm."

"I found it at a junkyard, and they let me have it for five dollars."

That sounded like a bargain, but Anna couldn't be sure. The stove was gray with age and had a dent on the side, but it seemed to put out enough heat to bring a little warmth to the shed, even though the wind whistled through the cracks between the walls. Some of the cracks had been stuffed with newspaper, but there were so many, Anna would have given up before she even started.

Felty knelt down and grabbed a log from the woodpile

by the stove. "It's wonderful efficient too. I don't hardly have to burn any wood to keep it going."

Anna didn't want to ask, because she did not want to hear the answer, but there really was no avoiding it. "Felty, are you living here?"

"*Jah.* Remember I told you I found a solution to two problems? Well, this is it."

A potbellied stove in an old shed didn't seem like the solution to anything, except maybe if your problem was keeping your goats warm. "But Felty, this isn't even your shed. And living here is called squatting. I read about it in *The Grapes of Wrath*. That book was real *gute* until the very end, and then all I can say is that I nearly swallowed my tongue and immediately took it back to the library."

Felty wrapped his hands around Anna's upper arms and gazed at her with bright eyes. "I'm not a squatter, I promise. I own this place."

Anna's mouth fell open. "You bought this shed?"

"For you and me."

Anna was in love, so in love with Felty that she'd live in a cave if she could be with him. She tamped down her misgivings, just relieved that she wasn't engaged to be married to a squatter. She'd never forget that scene in *The Grapes of Wrath*. "*Ach*, *vell*, I suppose it will be all right, but I've never tried to cook on a potbellied stove before."

Felty laughed. He obviously hadn't read *The Grapes of Wrath*. "*Nae*, Annie, my living here is temporary. As soon as spring comes, I'm going to clear some of this land and build you a house and a barn, and I'll plant you as many peach trees and jalapeños and raisins as you want."

Anna thought her heart might leap out of her chest. "Raisins?"

"Whatever you want. I'm buying the whole hill."

Now she felt dizzy. "You . . . buying?"

"I needed a place to live, and I wanted to keep that man from setting traps on the hill, so I went to the owner and made him an offer. There's this thing called the GI Bill. Because I served in the army, I qualify for a low-interest loan to build a home and start a farm. And now I can keep trappers off the hill, because it's mine. The foxes and beavers are safe."

"*Ach*, that is *wunderbarr*." Especially the part about Anna not having to live in a shed. And the beavers. She was very happy about the beavers. To keep from floating off the ground, she wrapped her arms around Felty's elbow. "You're going to build me a house?"

"Of course. I'll start as soon as it's warm enough. And then we can get married."

Anna slumped her shoulders. "Not until September at the earliest. It's tradition."

Felty slid his arm around her shoulders. "We could break with tradition. What's stopping us from getting married as soon as the house is done?"

She grinned. "Nothing, I guess, except maybe the bishop."

"I'll just have to get on the bishop's *gute* side." Felty rubbed his hand down the side of his face. "That won't be as easy as I'd hoped. I'm afraid I made Rosie Herschberger cry."

"You did?"

"I didn't mean to, honest I didn't. But she wouldn't

leave well enough alone, and I finally had to tell her I'm not interested."

Despite the fact that Rosie had stolen the secret number, Anna felt sorry for her. How would Anna feel if Felty weren't interested in her? Pretty rotten, for sure and certain. "It's not your fault for making her cry. You're just too *wunderbarr* to lose."

"I think she cried because I told her I like your cinnamon rolls better."

Anna giggled. "*Ach*, *vell*, Rosie takes great pride in her baked goods. I'm sure she was deeply wounded." Something he'd said several sentences ago surfaced from her memory. "Why do you need a place to live? It's warmer in here than outside, but it still can't be more than fifty degrees. You have a nice warm bed just down the hill."

He grimaced sheepishly. "I moved out of the house."

"But why?"

He pressed his lips together and busied himself rearranging the pile of wood next to the stove. "I bought the place. I should live here."

Anna looked around the shed. It was musty, dirty, and cold. The wind made a terrible noise squeaking and squeezing through the cracks in the wall. Could it have been any worse in Korea? Felty hated to be cold. He wasn't telling her the whole reason. She tried not to get upset until she was sure she had cause to be upset. "Did you tell your *mamm* about us?"

He started stacking the logs into interesting configurations on the floor. "I suppose I did."

Anna didn't know whether to be deeply hurt or wildly indignant. "And she kicked you out of the house?"

"*Nae.* She didn't kick me out."

"Then why are you living here?"

Felty fell silent and rearranged the logs to look like a sunburst. He didn't like to speak ill of anyone, except maybe Rosie Herschberger, but Anna deserved to know why he was sleeping in a shed in the dead of winter, risking frostbite, pneumonia, and the irritation of his fiancée.

"Do I need to have a talk with your *mater*? I don't care what she thinks of me, but her son needs a warm bed, an outhouse, and three square meals a day."

"What does it matter as long as we are happy?"

"Felty Helmuth, that is the dumbest thing I've heard all day. You shouldn't have to choose between warmth and happiness. You can have both."

He stood up and hooked his fingers around the back of his neck. "*Ach*, Anna. Please don't think ill of my *mamm*, but she still favors Rosie Herschberger. She told me you aren't welcome in our home. I can't live in a place where my own fiancée isn't accepted with open arms."

Anna's heart hurt at the slight, but she wouldn't ever show that pain to Felty. She blew a puff of air from between her lips and tossed her head back. "What does that matter? I don't have to come to your house ever. You should spend Christmas with your family in a warm house. That's all there is to it."

Felty took her hand. "*Ach*, Annie, you're sweeter than a whole hive of honey, and I do like being warm, but I will not allow my *mamm* to treat you like this. I will not allow anyone to treat you like this. You are my whole life, my whole world. And I will not keep silent and let my *mamm* think this is fair or right. I will not allow it. I'd rather sleep in this shed the rest of my life."

He snaked his arms around her and pulled her as

close as they could get with two coats and three scarves between them. He brought his lips down on hers, and at the spark of his touch, Anna forgot every insult she'd ever suffered and every sorrow that had ever entered her heart.

She pulled away and breathlessly straightened her bonnet. "I'm very fond of this shed."

He smiled down at her. "So am I."

The wheels in Anna's head started turning. "If you're going to be here for Christmas, we've got to make this the best Christmas ever."

He held her in his arms. "*Ach*, Anna. You have agreed to marry me. It is already the best Christmas ever."

Anna's heart beat double time. "I just realized that this shed is a solution to one of my problems too. Mammi is coming on Christmas to cook us a boring, normal Christmas dinner. I don't wonder that she'll let me do anything but stir the pudding. So I have to take matters into my own hands." She caught her breath, threw her arms around Felty, and kissed him. She felt his heart leap in his chest. "I'm going to make you the best, most delicious Christmas lunch anyone has ever seen and bring it right up here for you to eat."

"I don't want you to go to any trouble on my account."

Anna grinned. "Nothing is too much trouble for Felty Helmuth, the prettiest boy in Bonduel. Rosie Herschberger even said so."

"Well, then, if Rosie said it . . ."

"I might have to forgo the asparagus casserole. It isn't in season, and I used the last of our canned asparagus for the fellowship supper."

Felty bent over and kissed her again. "I'll love it with or without asparagus."

"This is going to be the best Christmas ever," Anna said. "I'm envisioning bacon, raisins, and cinnamon rolls with Red Hots. And Jell-O salad with carrots and hot dogs."

Felty's eyes lit up with anticipation. "Nothing says Christmas like hot dogs and carrots."

"I know, right?"

Chapter 17

Felty opened the door, stepped quickly outside, and shut the door behind him so as not to let the warm air seep out of his shed. The snow fell like a slushy, icy waterfall, so heavy the trees looked like ghostly shadows, even from twenty feet away. He worried the edge of his bright red scarf, staring into the storm as if his vigilance would bring Anna through the snow.

He had half a mind to hike down the trail and wait for Anna on the main road, but he didn't know the path well enough to find his way in the blizzard, and his frozen corpse in the snow would not be what Anna wanted for Christmas. But he was tempted to try the trek. Anna should have been here by now.

Yesterday, he'd borrowed a snow shovel from Zeb and this morning cleared a three-foot-wide path all around the shed and an even wider swath in front of the door. The snow was already up to his elbows.

He had spent all morning preparing the shed for Anna's arrival. A delicious Christmas feast needed stunning Christmas decorations to go with it. He'd found a huge fallen maple tree yesterday and used his crosscut saw to cut it the size of a table so Anna had somewhere to eat. It was two feet in diameter, so only two plates and cups would fit on it, but it would be big enough.

Felty smiled, anticipating the day when it would be just the two of them, here on Sugg Hill, making a life together as husband and wife. It was everything he had ever wanted. Everything he had dreamed of on those long, cold nights in Korea.

As if he'd summoned her from his dreams, Anna's horse and sleigh appeared on the trail, crawling as if they could only see a few feet in front of them. "*Hallo!*" Felty called, waving his arms back and forth. The flailing arms wouldn't really help. For sure and certain, she'd seen the shed by now.

Anna called out to him and waved back, but he couldn't hear what she said over the whistling wind. Soon enough she was at his door, smiling as if she was the happiest girl in the whole world. He hoped with all his heart that was true.

She stood up, and he slid his hands around her waist and lifted her down from the sleigh. "*Ach*, Felty," she said, "what a glorious day! The snow is up to my neck. After supper, we need to come out and make snow angels."

Three picnic baskets sat on the floor of the sleigh, and a large cardboard box sat on the seat. "Did you bring your whole kitchen?"

Anna giggled. "Just about." She picked up one of the baskets. "They're heavy."

Felty took it from her and promptly set it down again. "Let me take care of the horse, then I will take care of you."

Her cheeks turned the same color as her cold nose. "*Ach*, Felty, that's all I want."

Felty unhitched the horse from the sleigh, yanked open the shed door, and walked the horse right through his living area, under the sheet hanging from the ceiling, and into what Felty had turned into a stable of sorts. His own horse was contentedly eating oats, and Anna's horse Skipper joined her.

Anna followed Felty under the sheet. "What is this?" she said, half in amusement, half in shock. "Your horse lives in your house?"

"It's too cold for Georgie outside, and there's plenty of room in here."

Anna pointed to the manure on the floor. "It gets a little smelly."

Felty couldn't smell much of anything, so the odor didn't bother him. "Not too bad."

"*Ach*, Felty, you have a heart as big as the whole outdoors."

He chuckled. "And I can't bring dishonor to the ASPCA."

Anna grew momentarily serious. "Of course. We ASPCA members have certain standards to uphold."

Anna ducked back under the sheet to Felty's living quarters. She caught her breath. "*Ach, du lieva.* You made a table."

"A delicious dinner deserves a fine table."

She clapped her hands. "You have pine boughs."

Felty glanced at the string of pine branches he'd hung over the door and every window, trimmed with pine cones and red yarn. "I wanted it to feel like Christmas for you, Annie."

"I've never seen anything so beautiful."

"You're the most beautiful thing in this room, Anna Yoder, and don't you forget it."

"That's not true, but it's sweet of you to say."

Felty grabbed her around the waist. "It is the absolute truth. You will always be the most beautiful part of my life, and I'm going to tell you every day."

"Aren't you afraid I'll get a big head?"

"I don't think that's possible, knowing how little you value your own worth."

She drew her brows together. "I hope I don't get a big head. I'd have to make bigger *kapps* and bonnets, and you know how I hate to sew."

They stepped outside and carried in the box and baskets. Felty set the last picnic basket on the floor next to the stump where they would eat Christmas lunch. They took off their coats, hats, mittens, and scarves and set them next to the stove. "I can't wait to see what you cooked up for us today."

Anna's eyes flashed with excitement. "*Ach*, Felty, you are in for a treat." She knelt down, opened the first basket, and pulled out a milk-glass bowl. "I made four Jell-O salads."

"I love Jell-O."

"This is lime Jell-O with cottage cheese and carrots. I decided to make the hot dog Jell-O with cucumbers—sort of a savory dish to go with the sweet one."

"That was a very *gute* idea."

She pulled a casserole dish from another basket. The colors inside were stunning. "I also made a layered Jell-O salad with five different flavors of Jell-O, and then my *dat*'s favorite strawberry pineapple banana Jell-O. It's not as exciting as the others, but it's a tried and true recipe that my *mamm* used to make."

"I don't know what I did to have Gotte smile down on me like this."

She leaned over and kissed him on the cheek. "You are just your own *wunderbarr* self." Anna scooted the white wicker picnic basket next to her, looking as if she would burst with joy. "Last night, I sneaked down to the kitchen and brined a turkey." She opened the basket and let him look inside.

There was a slightly burnt, slighty crinkly turkey sitting in the basket. "Oh, my. Just the way I like it."

"I let it roast all morning. I can't wait to taste it."

"I can't wait to taste it either," Felty said.

"And most important of all"—Anna pulled a lattice-topped pie from the box—"I made a huckleberry pie from the huckleberries I picked from this very hill last summer. Mammi helped me can them in August. We got eleven quarts."

Tears blurred Felty's vision. He didn't think he could be any happier or any more content. "It's perfect, Anna. Huckleberry pie from Sugg Hill. Our hill. The hill where we'll make a home together, where we'll raise our children. The hill where we'll grow old together." Anna pressed her lips into a hard line. He'd seen that look before. She wanted to say something that she thought he might not want to hear. "What is it, *heartzley*?"

The words sort of exploded out of her mouth. "*Ach*, Felty, I didn't want to say anything because you were so excited about buying a hill."

He furrowed his brow. "I was, but if you don't like it, we can sell it. I'll do whatever makes you happy."

"Don't get me wrong. It's a beautiful hill, even in a blizzard. I just don't know if I can stand living in a place called Sugg Hill. 'Sugg' sounds like one of those fat, squishy worms you find at the bottom of a well or something you see when you cut open a fish's stomach. Or what a cat kills and leaves on your doorstep."

Felty's concern disintegrated into the air, and he smiled. "I think I agree with you."

"You do?"

"'Sugg Hill' is a disappointing name for such a beautiful place."

With a look of desperation in her eyes, she snatched his hand and squeezed it tightly. "What are we to do?"

"Well, Annie, there's nothing that says we can't change the name."

She frowned. "But isn't it listed on the official county maps? I think it's against the law to change the name if it's on the official maps."

"I can't see that it's illegal. New York City used to be called New Amsterdam. It's our hill now. What do you want to call it?"

Anna tilted her head to one side. "I hadn't thought about what I would rename it. I didn't think I'd get the chance." Anna pulled two plates and two cups from another picnic basket and set them on the table.

Felty set the Jell-O salads in a half circle around the table. "I think we should name it 'Anna's Hill.'"

Anna giggled and shook her head. "People will think I'm trying to puff myself up. A humble and modest Amish girl does not name a hill after herself."

He laughed. She was so endearing. "I suppose you're right."

They said silent prayer, and Felty made sure to thank Gotte for a roof over his head and a fire to keep him warm. But most of all he thanked Derr Herr for the gift of Anna Yoder. He would never want for another blessing.

Anna pulled the basket of turkey closer. "Oh, *sis yuscht*. I forgot a carving knife."

Felty grabbed a drumstick and ripped it off the turkey. "*Ach*, *vell*, we can just use our hands."

They both jumped when there came a loud knock at the door. A bit disconcerted and wildly curious, Felty stood, pried the fabric plug from the doorknob hole, and opened the door. Carrying all sorts of bundles and bags, Mamm and Dat rushed into the room, bringing a flurry of snow with them. Felty couldn't believe his eyes.

Mamm raised her eyebrows in expectation. "Well, don't just stand there gawking, son. Take these packages before I drop them."

"Mamm. I didn't expect to see you."

Anna jumped to her feet, took all of Mamm's packages, then helped both Mamm and Dat off with their coats. "I'm *froh* you got up the hill. I don't wonder but the storm is getting worse."

Mamm propped her hands on her hips and gazed around the room. "It looks as if I got here just in time. LeWayne, hand me the green shoebox." She peeked behind the sheet and clucked her tongue. "Felty, I know you love the animals, but horses are not *gute* company at Christmas dinner. What say we put them outside for an hour or two?"

Felty was still trying to wrap his mind around the fact that Mamm and Dat were standing in his shed with relatively pleasant looks on their faces. "But . . . Mamm, what are you doing here?"

"Don't avoid the question. The sheet is not a *gute* barrier against the smell of manure."

"*Ach*, *vell*, Mamm, it's wonderful cold out there. I can't just kick them out into the snow. It's Christmas."

"The smoke leaking from the stove masks the smell of the manure, Edna," Dat said. "And Felty won't really be able to enjoy dinner if we banish the horses outside."

Mamm's lips curled slightly. "Okay then. I suppose you'll want to bring Snapper in as well."

Felty jumped into action. "Of course." He shrugged on his coat, ran outside, and unhitched Snapper from the sleigh. Snapper was a beautiful bay that had once been a racehorse. Felty opened the door and led Snapper past the food and the boxes and the stump that was no longer going to be a big enough table. He tied Snapper's lead to a lantern hook on the far side of the shed, spread out some hay, and left Snapper a bucket of water. Felty eyed all three horses. It was a little crowded in their makeshift stable, but they seemed happy to eat and ignore one another. He wasn't sure Mamm would be so content. He ducked back under the sheet.

Mamm was directing Dat and Anna to tie bright red bows at the corners of each of his pine boughs. Obviously, his yarn trimming wasn't *gute* enough. Felty wasn't offended in the least. Mamm had a talent for making things beautiful, and if redecorating his shed made her feel the Christmas spirit, he was all for it.

Mamm's cheerful manner made him all the more puzzled. "Mamm, I don't mean to pry, but what exactly are you doing here?" He leaned in and whispered in her ear. "You told me you don't want me to marry Anna and she's not allowed in our house."

Glancing at Anna, Mamm pursed her lips and folded her hands. "Anna invited me. It's all her doing," she said, obviously a bit embarrassed but eagerly apologetic.

Anna heard her name and looked up. "It wasn't me. It was my licorice cookies."

Mamm's smile faltered for a half second. "Those licorice cookies are really something."

Anna tied a bow on the end of one of the pine boughs. "Well, it could have been the bright yellow pot holder. My knitted pot holders are like medicine."

Felty's heart felt as warm as a summer's breeze. "I don't doubt it."

Mamm shook her head. "It wasn't the cookies or the pot holder, though I am wonderful grateful for both. Anna told me about how you got stabbed and almost died and how Gotte protected you. I was so mad at Gotte for taking you to Korea that I didn't even acknowledge Him for bringing you back. As soon as you came home, I thought to snatch you out of Gotte's hands, believing I could do a better job of keeping you safe. But seeing how Gotte has led you, even since you've been back, I realized I could never watch over you the way Gotte does." She cupped her hand over his cheek. "He brought you back to me when He could have let you die. It would have served me right for being so faithless."

"Gotte is not vindictive, Mamm."

"I see how much you love Anna. Where could that love come from but Gotte? A man who only cared about the approval of others or his standing in the community would have chosen Rosie. She's near perfect."

"Mamm, I won't have you putting Anna down."

Mamm gave him the stink eye. "Just listen before you

judge. Rosie is a wonderful *gute* girl, but you deserve a special kind of girl. A girl who isn't like everybody else. A girl who was your friend when no one else would be. A girl who checked traps for you when you were injured."

"She told you about that?"

"You deserve a girl who can keep you on your toes. A girl who adores you. A girl you adore. A girl who is humble enough to believe she doesn't deserve you but in truth is completely deserving." Mamm kissed him on the cheek. "I'm turning you over to Gotte and to Anna. I have no doubt they will take better care of you than I ever could."

Felty couldn't speak for the emotion that filled his chest. He squeezed his *mamm* tight and immersed himself in her love. It truly was going to be a Christmas to remember, the best Christmas he'd ever had.

Mamm cleared her throat and blinked the tears away. "Okay then. Enough with the crying. We've got to make this sorry excuse for a shelter look like Christmas." She handed him another shoebox. "Arrange these candles on your little table and maybe in the corners. But not near the sheets or you'll start a fire." She frowned. "On second thought, Anna, will you arrange these candles? Felty can light them."

Anna took the plates and cups from the table and replaced them with the huckleberry pie, surrounded by a ring of small white candles.

"That looks *appeditlich*," Felty said, striking a match and lighting the first wick.

Mamm and Dat stacked their boxes against the wall and used them as serving tables, setting each of Anna's Jell-O salads on its own box. The turkey, in its basket, went next to the cucumber Jell-O salad. Mamm pulled out a loaf of bread and a jar of raspberry jam and set them next to the turkey. It was indeed a feast.

Felty threw more wood into the stove, and they all sat down on the floor. Dat called for *Gebet vor dem Essen*, and Felty didn't mention that he and Anna had already said one prayer. You could never have too many prayers. Felty guessed that Gotte wanted to hear from His children as often as they wanted to talk to Him. Once they had prayed, Mamm pulled a knife from out of nowhere and sliced the bread.

Felty was just about to dig into the lime Jell-O with cottage cheese and carrots when someone banged on the door. Did this shed always have so many visitors? Because if it did, Felty might have to rethink living here. All he wanted to do was be alone with Anna. At the very least, there just wasn't any more room for another horse.

He stood up, pulled the plug from the doorknob hole, and opened the door. Anna's *dat* and four *bruderen* stood outside, wearing snowshoes and covered head to toe with fat flakes of snow.

Isaac pushed past Felty into the shed. "It's freezing. Dat made us walk."

Felty surrendered to the inevitable and stepped back so the other four Yoders could get past him. They trudged into the shed, snow boots, snow, and all. Anna's *dat* handed Felty a warm pan covered in tinfoil. Felty held onto it until he got further instructions. Anna shooed her *bruderen* to the corner, where she directed them to brush the snow off one another and remove their snow boots.

"Out for a Christmas walk?" Felty asked.

Isaac took off his coat and threw it behind the hanging

sheets. He probably didn't know about the danger of manure. "Anna invited us all for Christmas dinner."

Felty looked at Anna. "I thought your *mammi* was making Christmas dinner."

"Oh, she is," Anna said, as cheerful as a knitter with a pile of yarn.

Elmer gently shook his coat, folded it, and set it on the floor next to his snowshoes. "Mammi is at our house cooking right now. We don't eat until five."

Anna draped her arm around Owen's shoulders. "You don't mind, do you, Felty? I just wanted everyone to share in our joy."

"I brought funeral potatoes," Mahlon said. "I figured we'd need more food with all these people."

Anna's mouth fell open. "Funeral potatoes? Dat, really!"

Mahlon chuckled. "They're called funeral potatoes, but your *mamm* used to make them every Christmas."

"All I think about when I eat them is that someone died," Anna said.

Her *dat* pulled off his coat. "I like to think that we eat them at Christmastime to celebrate the death of bondage, ignorance, and evil—all conquered by a babe born in Bethlehem."

Anna sighed and giggled. "Okay, then, Dat. I'll put funerals right out of my mind."

Seeing Anna so happy, Felty couldn't possibly be grumpy about the cramped and crowded shed, even though he had wanted to spend the whole day alone with Anna. He and Anna would have plenty of time for just the two of them, many seasons of joy, and many Christmases to celebrate. For now, he would be grateful that Mamm was warming to Anna, that he could spend Christmas with so many of the people he loved, and that the Yoders hadn't brought another horse.

Mamm and Dat made room, and the Yoders sat down amid the candles and Jell-O salads. They bowed their head for another silent prayer, and Felty just prayed that nobody else would come for Christmas dinner.

They ate and ate and ate, and Isaac didn't complain once about Anna's cooking. It was probably his Christmas present to his long-suffering sister. After supper, Anna scooted right into Felty's arms, and they sang Christmas carols until their throats were sore.

Anna cut the pie and served each person a piece. It turned out to be a little juicy, so she put each piece into one of the mugs Mamm had brought for hot cocoa. Once the pie was served, Anna reached into one of her baskets and pulled out a thin, rectangular gift wrapped in brown paper and tied with a green ribbon. She knelt beside Felty and smiled expectantly. "I got you a present."

His heart warmed like a potbellied stove. "I got you a present too, but I wanted to give it to you in private." He leaned closer and whispered, "Will you come outside with me so we can be alone?"

Her blush traveled past her cheeks to the top of her forehead. "As long as we protect our ears, I'm willing to go out with you. You might not want to marry me if I have to get my frostbitten ears cut off."

It took every ounce of willpower he had to resist kissing her in front of her *bruderen* and his parents. "*Nae*, Anna. I would marry you no matter how many ears you have."

They excused themselves from the pie eating, put on their coats and hats and gloves, and stepped outside. The

blizzard had stopped, and now the snow fell slowly, like little clumps of cotton. The air hung still and silent, and the trees were dressed in icy lace.

Anna handed him the present. "It's not much, but I hope you like it."

"You didn't have to get me anything. Just having you in my life is a gift."

The light on her face could have warmed him until next Christmas. "Open it."

He carefully tore back the paper and gasped in surprise. It was a West Virginia license plate—the last one he needed to win the license plate game. "Anna, this is *wunderbarr*. Where did you find it?" He furrowed his brows. "You didn't take it off someone's car, did you?"

Her eyes twinkled merrily. "I found it at that junk store in Shawano. I was so excited that I almost jumped up and down and squealed, but I was afraid the owner would know how much I wanted it and make me pay double. I gave him the money and ran out of there so fast, he never would have caught me."

He put his arms around her. "*Denki*, Anna. There's nothing like winning the license plate game to make a man feel like his life is complete."

Anna nestled into his embrace. She fit perfectly there, tucked next to his heart. "I thought of a name for our hill."

"You did?"

"Something like Fox Hill or Beaver Hill is cute, but it might attract more trappers. Korea Hill would remind us how Gotte protected you. But I think that would confuse people who aren't familiar with geography." She got on her tiptoes and kissed him soundly. Felty trembled at her touch. Might it be possible to move the wedding day up

to January? "So I thought about all the days I spent on this hill picking huckleberries until my fingers turned purple. I would fill my apron with huckleberries, and my *mamm* would make huckleberry buckle. Then there were the times when she would tell me to go pick huckleberries when she knew I needed to get away from my *bruderen*. I have very fond memories of huckleberries and my *mamm*. I hope to make many more memories with you and our children. What do you think about 'Huckleberry Hill'? Just saying it makes me feel welcome, like I belong here, like I'm home to stay."

Felty nodded and smiled. "I like it. Huckleberry Hill." He kissed her until he became breathless with joy. "This is our first Christmas on Huckleberry Hill, and, Lord willing, there will be many more to come."

"Lord willing," she said. "And now we should go inside. My nose gets drippy when it gets cold, and nobody likes to kiss a girl with a drippy nose."

Felty pumped his eyebrows up and down. "I do." She turned toward the door, but he pulled her back. "I haven't given you my present yet."

Her smile took over her whole face. "What is it?"

"I will show you." He unzipped his coat.

Anna grabbed his hand. "Felty, this habit of taking off your clothes in the dead of winter has got to stop. You're just asking for a case of frostbite. Or hypothermia."

He intertwined his gloved fingers with hers. "It won't be but a moment. Don't you want to see my tattoo?"

She caught her breath. "That's my Christmas present?"

"Only if you want."

"Of course I want."

He unbuttoned the top of his shirt and unsnapped the

first few buttons of his long johns. He stretched his sleeve down past his shoulder and turned so she could get a *gute* look.

Her eyes got as round as buggy wheels. "*Ach, du lieva,*" she whispered. "My life is complete."

Epilogue

Titus hadn't moved a muscle through the entire story. When he realized Mammi wasn't going to say anything else, he furrowed his brow. "Can I see your tattoo, Dawdi?"

Some of the older great-grandchildren had joined the group and were sitting at Dawdi's feet in rapt attention. Dawdi patted six-year-old Caleb on the head. "I wouldn't advise any of you to get a tattoo. It is a permanent reminder of temporary insanity."

"But can we see it?" Titus asked again.

Dawdi chuckled and shook his head. "Your *mammi* is the only person alive who has seen it." A shadow darkened his features. Was he thinking of Tooley? Other friends he'd lost in the war? "When I die, you can sneak a peek before the funeral. That will give you something to look forward to."

Titus frowned. "I don't want you to die, Dawdi, but I sure want to see that tattoo."

Mammi gave Martha Sue a grandmotherly smile. "You see, dear, you may not know it yet, but you want a husband. Felty and I have shared a beautiful life together. It hasn't always been pies and cakes. Once I made Felty sleep in the barn because I was so mad at him. But it's the bad times and the sad times that bring you closer together. It's the late nights and the early mornings, the children and the work and the hard things that make your love grow and bind you together like no glue ever could."

Martha Sue's heart sank to her toes. "It is a lovely story, Mammi. But I don't think it will work for me the way it worked for you."

Mammi shook her head. "Of course not. It will be your own beautiful love story." Mammi's smile faltered. "The truth is, I've already found you a husband. He's coming after dinner to meet you."

Most of Martha Sue's relatives laughed. Some, like Mandy, looked as if they felt sorry for her. Martha Sue felt sorry for herself.

Someone knocked on the door, and Martha Sue nearly jumped out of her skin.

Mammi drew her brows together. "I don't like tardiness, but I dislike earliness even more."

Martha Sue's cousin Moses grinned at her. "You might as well answer the door. Apparently it's for you."

Martha Sue trudged to the door as if she were going toward her doom. It didn't help that every eye in the room was focused on her. She opened the door and lost the ability to breathe. Yost Beiler stood on Mammi's porch bundled up like a snowman and grinning like a cat with a mouthful of mouse.

"*Hallo*, Martha Sue. *Vie gehts?*"

Yost Beiler? Mammi had brought Martha Sue to Huckleberry Hill to match her up with Yost Beiler from Charm, Ohio?

Mammi stood and clapped her hands, obviously willing

to overlook the transgression of early arrival. “Invite him in, Martha. I’d like everybody to meet him.”

Martha Sue stepped back so Yost could come into the house, but as soon as he crossed the threshold, Mammi’s smile stiffened. “You’re not Vernon Schmucker.”

Puzzled, Yost looked behind him, then turned back to Mammi without ever losing that aggravatingly handsome smile. “Um, *nae*, I’m not. I just came to take Martha Sue back to Charm.”

Martha Sue folded her arms. “You’re not taking me anywhere.”

Yost raised his hands and backed away. “I’m sorry. Poor choice of words.” He smiled at Mammi. “I came to beg Martha Sue to come back.”

“I’m not going back,” Martha Sue said.

“Of course you’re not going back,” Mammi said. “You haven’t met Vernon Schmucker yet.”

Yost’s expression fell. “Who . . . who is Vernon Schmucker?”

“Nobody,” Martha Sue said, because even though she wanted Yost out of her life, she couldn’t bear to hurt his feelings.

Mammi slumped her shoulders, then gave Yost a genuine smile. “This isn’t your fault, young man. How could you have known what I had planned for Martha Sue? We’d love it if you stayed for dinner, but I would be wonderful grateful if you would leave before seven. It would be quite awkward if Vernon showed up and Martha Sue’s boyfriend was here.”

“He’s not my boyfriend,” Martha Sue said, but she said it gently, almost regretfully, because she just couldn’t be harsh with Yost. He’d come all this way.

Mammi seemed unruffled. "*Ach*, Felty, this is more exciting than I could have hoped. It's a love triangle."

Yost glanced at Martha Sue, seeking her approval, which he wasn't going to get. "I'd love to stay for dinner."

Mammi shook Yost's hand. "Well, then, welcome, and *Frehlicher Grischtdaag*."

"Merry Christmas to you too," Yost said.

Mammi took Yost's coat, hat, and scarf and led him to the sofa. "Now Martha Sue will have two men to choose from. This is going to be so exciting." Martha Sue pressed her lips together as Mammi showed Yost her latest knitting project and gave him a pot holder to take home, even though he wasn't Vernon Schmucker. "I love Christmas," Mammi said, showing Yost her favorite knitting magazine. "Many of my best memories are of Christmas. Felty and I fell in love at Christmastime, you know."

"*Nae,*" Yost said. "I didn't know that."

Mammi sat down in her rocker. "Well, then. Let me tell you. It all started when he got off the bus in Bonduel in November of 1952. But don't ask to see his tattoo. You'll have to wait until he's dead."